NOAH'S RAVEN

A Novel of Early 20ᵗʰ Century America

By Robert T. McMaster

UNQUOMONK PRESS
Williamsburg, Massachusetts
U. S. A.

Noah's Raven

www.TrolleyDays.net

ISBN 978-0-9856944-6-3

Published by Unquomonk Press, 50 Briar Hill Road, Williamsburg, Massachusetts 01096 USA

The cover illustration appeared as the frontispiece of Edward Hitchcock's pioneering work on dinosaur tracks, *Ichnology of New England*, published in 1858. The author describes the illustration as "a view of the Moody Footmark Quarry [that] exhibits a row of some ten tracks of the hind foot of *Otozoum*, still remaining there, the property of Gilbert A. Smith, Esq., of South Hadley."

Dedicated to my mother

Ellen Stowers McMaster

who inspired me with stories of her childhood.

DECEMBER, 1917

A chill wind whistled down from a leaden sky, whipping up eddies of snow on the icy surface of Hampton Ponds, then hissed through the towering pines that stood like silent sentinels along the shore. Gaunt-stemmed rushes and grasses, wizened by icy blasts, waved wildly at water's edge. What little daylight remained was fading fast.

The scene was nearly devoid of life – nearly, but not entirely. Atop a low earthen dam where a small stream emptied with a trickle into the pond, a single lonely figure stood, immobile, as if weighing several courses of action.

Only a few weeks shy of her fourteenth birthday, Claire Bernard was angry, confused, and all too aware that she was terribly alone in this seemingly God-forsaken place. On the one hand it was familiar. The pond was barely a mile from her family's farmhouse in Westfield, Massachusetts. She had come here often with her brother Jack to fish – from the shore in spring, summer, or early autumn – through the ice on many a winter's day, an incandescent sun shining down upon them out of a cobalt blue sky.

But no sun warmed her today. Her brother was far away in Worcester where he was attending college. Her father and sister were back home, unaware that she had slipped away when she should be doing her chores in the barn. If they had any inkling of her whereabouts – or her destination – they would have been appalled.

Then there was Fergal, her neighbor and friend – well, former friend, she was thinking – she needed him just now. "Never mind about *him,*" she said aloud, as if in doing so she could martial her own courage. She simply had to proceed without him. She took a deep breath, then drew the woolen scarf up around her face against the biting wind. She turned and followed a wide footpath away from the water's edge. Soon she entered an obscure, little-used trail that led uphill toward a long-abandoned stone quarry.

When she reached the top, she stopped and peered cautiously over the edge lest she be seen from below. But there was no need for concern, she realized – the place was as quiet as, well, a tomb. She felt a shiver travel up her spine at the thought, but she steeled herself, a determined scowl gathering on her normally rosy face, then began her descent of the steep footpath that led to the bottom of the quarry and ended at the rear of a dilapidated storage shed.

She and Fergal had visited this place three times in the last month. They had seen things here that made her uneasy – men, dark, suspicious looking men, men smoking cigars, men talking, cursing, loading and unloading trucks. More recently, when they came with Jack and Tom Wellington, they had a most peculiar encounter with a certain Professor Smith. Each time it was Fergal who understood what it all meant. Okay, so he's smart, she thought, and clever. So, if he's so clever, she asked herself, why had he defied her like that, just when she needed him?

Through a crack in the rear wall she peered into the shed's darkened interior. She saw nothing. She turned and gazed up at the jagged quarry wall. It was steep and gloomy, but still nothing out of the ordinary, really. She had been convinced that there was something going on here, something important, something even the police weren't aware of, but now she was beginning to wonder – was this all a waste of time, a fool's errand? Maybe she'd been wrong. And, yes, she thought, maybe she should have listened to *him*.

Suddenly she heard a dull drone rising from the other side of the quarry, the low side where the narrow lane from Southampton Road entered. At that moment a light flickered through the forest and shone briefly against the looming rock wall. But in seconds the light was extinguished, the drone ceased, and all was quiet once more.

Another chill ran up her spine as she considered what to do. She was a good half mile from the nearest road, from help. Where had that flash of light and that sound originated? She must find out. She stood in the darkness, blowing on her cold hands. She wanted to turn, scramble back up the steep trail to the quarry's rim, then down the other side, and make her way back home. But she was so certain she was right, so assured that she needed to do this, that she resisted the urge to flee. Instead, she made her way around the shed, along the rough road leading out of the quarry, all the time preparing to take cover or retreat should a truck or persons unknown appear.

As she approached the rusted iron gate bearing the hand-painted message, *Keep Out*, a brief thud sounded and another flicker of light shone through the trees. A voice could be heard now, rough and rasping, issuing low, monosyllabic commands. She stepped forward slowly, cautiously, hiding behind a thicket in a dense stand of aspens whose few remaining leaves trembled on slender branches in the chill wind. At last she could make out a truck. It was parked in what appeared to be another entrance to the quarry, one long-abandoned. She remembered that a rough woods road crossed the trolley line just a short distance down the tracks from the Pequot Park stop. Maybe, she reasoned, this way had been used to haul rock directly to the trolley line during construction.

Just then the truck's motor started and two bright headlamps pierced the trees, striking her coat and face, illuminating her from head to toe. Had she remained still she

3

might have gone unnoticed, but her instinct was to turn and run, which she did, and immediately she tripped and tumbled to the ground. She heard men's voices, loud and near. She struggled to her feet and started to run again, but in a matter of seconds she was confronted by a man blocking her escape route back to the quarry.

"What the–" began the man as he grabbed her roughly by the arm. They struggled momentarily until another hand pulled her coat from behind and a muscular arm wrapped tightly around her neck. With that she stopped struggling and stared with wide, frightened eyes into the face of Manfred Becker, a gaunt, cruel face with small, dark eyes and a short, ragged beard.

"Who the hell are you – and what're you doin' out here, kid?" he demanded.

Claire tried to reply but the choke hold cut off her air. All that came out were frantic croaking sounds. The man nodded to his companion who loosened his grip.

"I'm – Cla–" she began before she had to take another breath. She tried again: "I'm – I was just out for a walk, with my friend – Fergal. He's gone for help, his farm's just over there. You betta let me go – the cops'll be–"

"Yeh? Is that so?" interrupted Manfred. He scowled at her angrily, then smiled at his partner. "I don' see no friend nowhere. Know what? I tink you're lyin', that's what I tink."

"No–" she replied loudly, but the chokehold suddenly tightened.

"Whatta we gonna do with 'er?" asked the other man. Claire watched Manfred's face for a hint of his reply, a shiver of terror coursing through her blood. He paused as if weighing her fate. Finally he spoke: "I guess we could let 'er go–" Claire relaxed. Then he smiled, a mean, evil smile. "On second thought, she might jus' come in handy–" He jerked his head toward the truck.

4

Moments later she was on the ground, hands bound behind her, a grimy, dusty cotton rag wrapped around her head and in her mouth as a gag. Her feet were secured as well, but with a length of canvas torn from a tarp, cinched so tight she could no longer feel them. She was trying to call out, but the gag muffled her screams. The larger man lifted her like a sack of potatoes and deposited her roughly in the back of the truck. Immediately two heavy doors slammed shut and she was alone in silent terror. As her eyes adjusted to the darkness, she realized the truck was an old ice wagon with no windows, heavily insulated walls, and doors that latched tightly from the outside. She also recognized to her alarm the crates that surrounded her – they were filled with short lead pipes – cigar bombs, she had heard them called – assembled and ready for use.

Furious with fear and rage, Claire struggled against her bonds, but to no avail. For several minutes she could hear the men talking some distance away from the truck. Soon, however, they returned, climbed into the cab, and began cranking the motor. It growled hoarsely, reluctant to start in the cold air. As the motor churned, one of the rear doors opened briefly and the pile of tarps at her feet rustled momentarily. Then as the truck began to lurch forward, the rear door closed gently once again.

Now the full terror of her situation gripped her. She was frightened, more frightened than she had ever been in her life. But she was also furious at her captors with their mean sneers and offensive body odors as they bound her, then wrestled her into the truck and tossed her like so much refuse into the darkness. She was afraid of their anger, but even more their laughter. In her perilous state she could not even think about where she was headed or what her captors had planned for her. All she knew was that she had never, ever in her life felt so helpless, so terrified, so completely and utterly alone.

~ 1 ~

The first Monday of September dawned clear and bright in Westfield. Seventeen-year-old Marie Bernard was up early, busying herself in the kitchen preparing breakfast for her sister and her father. She was determined to have a special breakfast for Claire who would be attending her first day of school in Holyoke today. Having heard no activity from Claire's bedroom, Marie turned down the flame under the griddle and stepped softly down the back hallway to her sister's door, then tapped twice.

"Claire? Claire? Get up and get yourself dressed, dear. It's nearly six-thirty." Just then her sister appeared at the bedroom door. She was already fully dressed in a neat pinafore, white stockings, and tall shoes of shining black leather. Her flaxen hair that normally cascaded in dozens of tiny ringlets was drawn back into a small bun at the back of her head and secured with two tortoiseshell combs. Her face was round, her skin fair, her eyes intensely blue. She was quick-witted and often prone to chatter, but not today.

"Oh, I – I thought you were still asleep," said Marie.

"Nope," replied Claire unsmiling.

"Well, breakfast is almost ready."

"Fine. I'll be right there." Claire returned to her room and stood before the mirror over her dresser, staring intently at her hair. In another instant she had removed the combs and bun, choosing instead a single white satin bow. Her gaze drifted to a sepia-toned photograph in a gilt frame. It was her mother, Evelyne St. Onge, in her wedding dress, smiling softly,

7

serenely. For a moment Claire's eyes filled, her chin quivered briefly. She raised her hairbrush again to make a few final adjustments to her hair.

Marie had returned to the kitchen, amazed that her younger sister was actually ahead of schedule this morning. In grades six and seven getting Claire up, out of bed, dressed, fed, and out the door had been a daily challenge that sometimes led to heated exchanges between the sisters. But this morning all that had changed.

"I can't believe it," whispered Marie to her father. "She's practically ready to go. What do you suppose has come over her?"

Charles Bernard sat at the table, a gray enamel mug in one hand. He took a long sip of hot coffee, then leaned back with a self-satisfied sigh. "We gotta deal."

"What do you mean, Father? What kind of deal?"

"Your sister and me – about her goin' to 'olyoke."

Claire Bernard, like her sister and brother before her, had attended St. Agnes School in Westfield since first grade. It was a small school, a good school, Charles and Evelyne Bernard were quick to say. Their pride was justified, for the school's very existence was due entirely to the French-Canadian families of Westfield. It was a part of what had come to be known as *La Survivance*, the determined effort of immigrants from Québec to preserve their faith, language, and culture in the overwhelmingly Protestant and English-speaking society of New England.

But the nuns of St. Agnes School had their limitations, bless them, and some parents became convinced that as their children approached high school, they could benefit from the much larger Forestdale Grammar School in Holyoke. The problem was the seven-mile trolley ride from Westfield to Holyoke. Jack, Claire's older brother, had traveled that route his first year with his father when he was still working at Wellington Textiles. A few years later Marie had done the same, accompanied by Jack. But for Claire to attend Forestdale this year, she would have to travel that route alone, and that was not something her father was about to consider – she was just too young, Charles had repeated again and again. He knew the line, he'd ridden it twice a day for fifteen years. The mill workers were on their way by five or five-thirty. The men traveling later, he believed, were not going to any job – they were loafers, drunkards, good-for-nothings.

"Your sister put up such a fuss," explained Charles, "I finally 'lowed how she could go. But before I agreed I laid down some rules. Number one, no lollygaggin' in the morning – out the door sharp at seven every day. That way she can ride with Fergal Dooley."

"Fergal's going to Forestdale this year?"

"That's number two. Fergal walks right by the house on his way to the car stand every morning. That boy's like a human timepiece – keeps time better 'an a fifty dollar gold watch." Charles chuckled and shook his head. "She knows she 'as to be ready when he gets here or else – it's back to St. Agnes. That was our deal and it's workin' like a charm." Charles' eyes gleamed as he took another sip of coffee.

Just then Claire appeared and took her seat at the kitchen table before a plate of griddlecakes and a cruet of maple syrup. She finished them quickly, without a word to either her sister or her father.

The clock on the mantle was just striking seven when several sharp raps sounded on the kitchen door. Charles winked at Marie, then opened the door. It was Fergal Dooley, neatly dressed in a freshly ironed white shirt, a green cravat, and gray wool trousers. He was a slight boy, all skin and bones. His head was narrow and topped with a thatch of brown hair carefully combed and parted down the middle. His eyes were large and green, his face pink and dotted with freckles, his mouth tiny and circular, as if he had just seen a ghost. There was, as Charles had observed, a curious mechanical quality to his movements and words.

"Good morning, Mr. Bernard, sir. Is Claire ready, sir?" asked Fergal. With every word the boy's Adam's apple bobbed like a bouncing ball.

"She is indeed, young man," replied Charles with a smug smile. Claire had disappeared into her room but promptly returned to the kitchen, bookbag in hand.

Marie handed her a tin lunch box with a leather strap handle. "Good luck on your first day, dear," offered Marie as her sister walked past. She wanted to add, "Remember what we talked about," but she thought better of it. Last evening after supper, in the privacy of Claire's bedroom, Marie had counseled her sister on the merits of good grammar, careful enunciation, and proper deportment, advice that was received with something less than gratitude. The phrase *now that you are a young lady* elicited a particularly sardonic response.

Charles added, "Oh, Fergal, be sure you two sit near the front of the car – where the motorman can see you."

"Yes, sir," replied the boy. Charles stood at the kitchen door watching with obvious pleasure as the pair made their way across the yard toward the street.

Ten minutes later Claire and Fergal stood at the trolley stand on Southampton Road. The morning air was chilly, turning their breath to wisps as they waited. The sun was just rising over East Mountain, a few small clouds casting shadows across a pale blue eastern sky. The lowing of cows in the pasture across the road seemed to hang in the air like a bovine chorus.

Fergal nervously jangled a ring of keys, then glanced down at his watch that hung by a leather fob from his belt. "Twelve minutes past the hour," he observed. Claire did not reply. "Should be a car any time now – any time." Claire stood expressionless, gazing across the corn fields, lips tightly closed, jaw set.

Soon the squeal of iron wheels on rails signaled the approach of a Holyoke-bound car. "Seven – fourteen," remarked Fergal, cradling the watch in his right hand. "Two minutes late."

Sparks flew from the wires overhead as the car rolled to a stop. Fergal stood aside and nodded for Claire to go ahead. She passed him without acknowledgment, climbed the wooden steps, presented her pupil pass to the motorman, then proceeded down the aisle. Fergal presented his pass, but stood awaiting the motorman's nod. In the few seconds that elapsed Claire continued down the aisle, passing several shabbily dressed men fast asleep in their seats before taking the last seat at the rear of the car.

"Claire – oh, Claire," called Fergal in a loud whisper from the front. She did not respond to his calls, but turned and gazed out the window as the car began to move. "Claire," called Fergal once again as he made his way down the aisle, stumbling awkwardly when the car lurched. "Claire," he began yet again as he stood before her, "remember what your father said? We're supposed to sit up front near the motorman. Remember?" Claire was still gazing out the window as he spoke, leaning toward her. Finally, after a pause, Claire turned and looked up at Fergal.

"Your father–" he began again.

At that moment Claire reached up, grabbed the young man's cravat, and gave it a short, sharp yank, jerking his head downward until his face nearly touched hers.

"Listen to me, Fer-*gull*," she began, speaking his name derisively with a strong accent on the second syllable. The boy's face was suddenly red as a beet and he tried to pull away, but Claire's grasp was unyielding. "I know what my father said – I was there, remember? And I don't need no one, least of all *you*, following me around. I can take care of myself – understand?"

11

Fergal's complexion almost instantly went from red to a pasty white. "But – but I promised your father – we have a deal."

"Fine. As far as he's concerned, you're doing what he wants, okay? But when we're out of his sight, I don't want to *see* you – I don't want to *hear* you – and I *don't* want you gettin' in my way. Is that clear?"

"But–"

She tightened her grip on the cravat, drawing his face still closer to hers. Her eyes glowed like hot coals as she issued her final warning. "And – if you breathe a word to my father or my sister – well, you'll have me to deal with – got it, Fer-*gull*?" The boy nodded meekly and Claire released her grip on his tie. Shaken, he struggled to straighten the tie, then sat down on the bench next to her, looking like he might be sick. She glared at him and he slid to the far end of the seat, as far away from her as possible.

No further words were exchanged, indeed, none were necessary as they rode the twenty minutes to Sargeant Street in Holyoke, Fergal's keys jangling all the while, his eyes darting down to his watch at regular intervals.

Everything was new for Claire Bernard on her first day at Forestdale Grammar School: new teachers, new subjects, new classmates, new routines. Compared to the intimacy of St. Agnes School, this was a noisy, sometimes confusing world. At lunchtime she found a seat in the corner of the windowless lunchroom in the basement and was relieved to have a familiar face approach her, Julie Trottière, from Westfield. The two friends chattered volubly about St. Agnes School until a third girl approached and seated herself next to Julie. She wore a pretty poplin dress, lavender with many pleats, each carefully pressed so that not a wrinkle could be found. Her brown leather boots shone with fresh polish. Her skin was smooth as silk, her blue eyes sparkled, and her long brown hair fell in smooth waves either side of her face, not a strand out of place. She smiled at Claire and Julie.

"Oh, hello Sarah," began Julie, brightening noticeably. "Sarah, this is Claire, Claire Bernard, from Westfield. Claire, this is Sarah Muller–"

"*Saah*-ra," the girl interrupted, "my name is pronounced *Saah*-ra."

"Oh, *Saah*-ra," repeated Julie carefully.

"And my last name is not *Mull* - er, it's *Mule* - er."

"Oh," replied Julie again, flashing a smile toward Claire. "Mule as in jackass?" Julie and Claire laughed and Sarah's face turned deep scarlet. "I'm sorry, Sarah, I was only teasing." She turned to Claire. "Sarah has attended Forestdale since grade one."

Claire was captivated by Sarah's face and smile. Then a curious expression spread across her face. "Do you have a brother Jake?" asked Claire.

Sarah nodded. "*Gerhardt* – his name is *Gare-hart*. How do you know him?"

"My brother Jack and him were friends. They were in the same class in high school, I think."

"Oh, Jack Bernard, I remember him, sure."

"Jack's in college now – in Worcester. He's gonna be a engineer. What about Jerry – er, *Gare-hart*?" inquired Claire.

"Oh, he's working at Wellington Textiles – in the sorting room. They really like him there – he's so strong and he works very hard."

"Claire, did you hear about the grade eight class play?" interjected Julie. "Miss Sussim says they will be holding auditions soon. We should try out, don't you think?" Then she turned to Sarah. "Claire and I both had parts in the Christmas pageant at St. Agnes every year from grade one."

The conversation went on to other classmates, clothing, and needlework until Miss Sussim called for all grade eight pupils to line up and exit to the schoolyard.

The harsh clangor of the bell marked the end of the school day at three o'clock sharp. Moments later the heavy wooden doors swung open and dozens of pupils emerged in a wave, pouring down the broad front steps, all in a rush to be anywhere but in school on a sunny September afternoon. Claire Bernard strolled along Sargeant Street toward the trolley stand alongside Julie.

"I was so surprised to see you in class this morning, Claire," began Julie. "The last time we spoke you said your father would never permit you to go to Forestdale. What changed his mind?"

"Oh, well, a little whining, a little pouting," replied Claire. The two exchanged knowing nods. Just then Fergal appeared a few steps behind them.

Julie drew close to Claire and whispered. "Who is that ridiculous boy? He was hanging around you in the schoolyard after lunch and there he is again. A friend of yours?"

Claire rolled her eyes. "*No*, he is *not* a friend, Julie. Just a neighbor – Fer-*gull* – Fer-*gull* Dooley."

"He's so strange. Have you noticed how he fidgets all the time? You'd think he had some nervous condition — St. Vitis Dance or something. He sat near me in Latin class and he was acting very oddly. His lips were moving constantly – what is the matter with him?"

Just then a Westfield-bound car approached and the two girls were at the head of the line when it screeched to a halt. They boarded, showed their passes, and took seats together near the front. Following close behind, Fergal took a seat directly across the aisle from Claire.

"That girl Sarah, Sarah Muller – do you like her?" asked Claire.

"Oh, yes, don't you?"

"Sure, sure, but – well, all that business about how to pronounce her name, and her brother's name–"

"Oh, that – she just likes to be a little different, you know? But she's very sweet – and smart, too – she already knows Latin. Her mother taught her when Sarah had the influenza last year and was out of school for months." Claire nodded.

"I can't believe we have homework on the first day of school. It is outrageous, Julie, absolutely outrageous, don't you agree? We never had homework on the first day at St. Agnes."

All the way back to Westfield the pair commiserated over the unfairness of it all – life, school, teachers, parents. As the car approached the stop on Southampton Road nearest her house, Claire rose with a sigh. Fergal stood up as well, but Claire shot him a stern look and he sat down abruptly.

"I'll see you tomorrow," said Julie with a smile.

Claire returned her smile, then turned and made her way quickly to the front of the car, exiting as soon as the door opened. Without looking back she started down the dusty road, knowing that her "shadow" would be close behind.

~ 2 ~

A traveler along the Old Post Road from Worcester to Springfield on a sparkling September day like this one was treated to an ever-changing panorama of New England country life. The mostly gravel thoroughfare wound in long, graceful curves through rolling, sun-soaked farmlands, plunged into cool valleys along shady stream-courses bordered with cottonwood trees, then trundled through the centers of nearly a dozen town centers, their main streets lined with stately elms and maples. The larger towns bustled with industry and commerce, the smaller ones languished peacefully in the warm late-afternoon sun.

The road was alive with activity on this Friday afternoon – motorcars, trucks, wagons laden with goods hauled by teams of horses, small buggies, and gigs. Streetcars ran along tracks in the roadway, bells clanging, wheels clattering, sometimes screeching, on the rails. Except for a few short stretches of cobble and brick in the centers of the larger towns, the way was almost entirely unpaved. Plumes of dust swirled around every vehicle, into the faces, hair, and clothing of drivers, passengers, and pedestrians alike.

Amidst the hubbub on this Friday afternoon sputtered a low-slung two-wheeled vehicle, spewing bluish smoke as it bounced along the rutted roadway. Despite the slow going, the operator, eighteen-year-old Jack Bernard, pushed on toward Holyoke, his thoughts fixed on just one thing, Anne Wellington – his Anne. It had been nearly two weeks since he had seen her, since he had left his family's home in Westfield for college in Worcester. Though the distance was not great, barely fifty miles, it was more than enough to inflict pangs in the heart of this young man.

On one long, straight stretch of road, Jack could see for miles ahead. He imagined he could even view the distant summit of Mt. Tom looming over Holyoke like a watchtower. He brought the machine to a halt by the roadside, pulled off his goggles, and wiped the dust from his face and hair. Then he paused to take in the spectacle before him. Flocks of sheep grazed peacefully in a rocky pasture that sloped away from the road, a freight train moved slowly along the far edge of the pasture, and beyond a broad river flowed idly, its waters glistening in the afternoon sun. A forested ridge rose on the far side of the valley, its slopes cloaked in yellowish-green foliage with only an occasional splash of autumn reds and golds.

High above this bucolic scene loomed a stack of snow-white clouds, looking ever so much like down pillows tossed on a featherbed. Jack knew too well what this meant: an approaching rainstorm. Quickly he replaced his goggles and pulled back onto the gravel road, now occupied by only a few small horse-drawn wagons and the occasional motorcar.

Holyoke was abustle in September, 1917. Since the American entry into the war in Europe barely five months earlier, the city's male workforce had been severely depleted. Nearly every able-bodied young man twenty-one years or older had enlisted or been drafted. Meanwhile the city's many factories were booming, none more so than the several textile mills as they churned out uniforms, blankets, and tents for the nation's military forces and allies.

The Holyoke Women's Home was a busy place as well. The red sandstone building with broad granite steps stood on Maple Street, just a block away from the city's main thoroughfare. Filling the vacancies created in Holyoke's mills nowadays were women, young women, some mere girls really. Many came from farms around New England and further away, knowing no one and nothing about this place except to first visit the Women's Home.

And visit they did by the dozens on this day. Anne Wellington, the young assistant director of the Women's Home, greeted each new arrival with a smile. Anne had fair skin, auburn hair, and bright eyes that sparkled like emeralds as she spoke, explaining in detail the services the Home could offer, then directing each young woman to a seat in the long dark common room to complete a registration form.

"Miss Wellington," asked one new arrival, "do you provide meals?"

"Yes, indeed," Anne responded brightly. "Breakfast and supper." She smiled and gestured down the hallway toward the rear where a recently expanded dining room could accommodate nearly thirty at a seating.

Another young patron, barely sixteen, was looking bewildered. "What's troubling you?" inquired Anne softly.

"How will I ever find work, miss? I ain't got no friends in 'olyoke, nobody t'help me."

"The mills are hiring, dear – there are jobs aplenty. We shall provide you a list to take with you. And I will make sure you have one or two other girls to go along with you so you won't feel alone." The girl smiled weakly and looked gratefully into Anne's eyes.

"Cheer up now, everything will be all right."

"Thank you, Miss Wellington."

"Please, call me Anne. And you are–"

"Annette, miss, Annette Letendre."

"Well, we will surely remember one another's names now, won't we?" replied Anne with a twinkle in her eye. She had been on her feet all day, answering questions, handing out forms, reassuring the lonely and confused, all in a day's work.

She had the ability to smile and greet each new arrival warmly and brightly, hour after hour, even as her energy flagged.

"Anne, it's nearly five-thirty," observed Nina Calavetti, director of the Home. "I'll take care of things here until six. Why don't you be on your way, hmm?"

Anne protested. "Thank you, ma'am, but I wouldn't want to leave you here alone. I am happy to stay."

"Nonsense, be gone with you now. You've been at this desk since before eight this morning and it's time for you to be heading home."

"Well, all right then, thank you."

Nina Calavetti had been one of the founders of the Women's Home nearly fifteen years earlier. She and Helen Wellington, Anne's mother, were devoted to the institution and to the cause of aiding young women just arriving in Holyoke. This was a difficult city for the innocent and naïve, full of hardships, sometimes dangers.

"When do you expect Carolyn?" asked Anne as she gathered her belongings. Nina's daughter, Carolyn Ford, was Anne's best friend. The two had graduated from Holyoke High School in June. Carolyn was attending Massachusetts Agricultural College in Amherst where she stayed in the new ladies' dormitory on weeknights. On Fridays she was expected home by suppertime.

"Maybe by seven if the electrics are running on time," replied Nina, referring to the streetcar line that ran the fifteen miles from Amherst to Holyoke. "It worries me so, her riding all that way alone."

Anne smiled and looked into Nina's eyes reassuringly. "Carolyn will do just fine, I'm sure of it. Well, I'll say good evening."

Even as she descended the front steps of the Home, several residents spoke to Anne and she paused to exchange pleasantries. The weariness she felt in her slender body could not dampen her enthusiasm, excitement really, for the work she was doing. It was a labor of love if ever there was one, the rewards she received for her work going well beyond her fifteen-dollar weekly salary.

Anne's walk home, only seven blocks, took her up Appleton Street and her pace slowed as the grade steepened. The mansard roof of her family's stately home was just coming into view when she heard a familiar sound, the unique combination of sputtering and whining that could mean only one thing. As she turned a billow of blue smoke briefly engulfed her. When it cleared, a young man's face appeared, sitting astride a motorcycle and beaming proudly through leather goggles.

"Jackie," squealed Anne. She stepped off the curb, about to kiss him. For that to happen, however, Jack must first remove his goggles, and that was a slow, awkward task. At last she was seeing his shining face, albeit ringed with a red welt where the goggles had rested against his cheeks. His cotton shirt and woolen trousers were sopping, giving him the appearance of a drowned rat. She kissed him on the cheek. "You look like – well, I don't know *what* you look like. Are you all right?"

"I'm fine, Annie, just fine," he began. He stepped off the machine, rested it on the kickstand, and stretched. "Just a little sore from two hours on the road." Then he looked down at his trousers where a layer of brown dust adhered. "I swear there isn't a mile of macadam between Worcester and Holyoke. Maybe once the war is over they'll get 'round to paving more of those roads."

"Oh, Jackie, it's so good to see you. I know it's only been two weeks since you left for college, but it seems like an eternity."

"Maybe to you, Annie, but to me it went by in a flash. But how about you? How's your job going? The Wednesday evening play group? All that?"

"It's wonderful, Jackie, all of it. I feel like, well, like I'm doing something worthwhile – you know, making a contribution." Jack was looking with great pleasure at Anne's shining face, bright eyes, and red lips. "But Jackie, I am exhausted. I have to get home and off my feet. I've been running around since first thing this morning."

"Here, get on and I'll give you a ride." Anne smiled. She couldn't hurt Jack's feelings, even though a ride on his motorcycle was harrowing. But they were only four blocks from her home, a ride she thought she could endure. So she smiled, clambered on behind Jack, and clung to him for dear life as they careened up Appleton Street. Soon they came to a halt before a wrought iron gate. She stepped off onto the cobbled sidewalk and stood close to Jack.

"Won't you come in for a few minutes? Mother and Father will be so happy to see you."

Jack smiled and shook his head as he brushed the dust from his trousers. "They wouldn't want to see me like this, Annie. I'd better be goin'."

Anne smiled, took his hand, and nodded. "Well, I'll see you tomorrow, then – for supper – like we planned?"

Jack nodded. "And don't forget our outing on Sunday."

Again Anne smiled. "What's this secret destination you wrote about, Jackie? Where are you taking me?"

"I'm not at liberty to divulge, Miss Wellington," joked Jack in reply, "but prepare to be amazed." Anne laughed. "Any news from Tommy?" Jack asked, his eyes suddenly anxious and fixed on hers.

Anne shook her head, her demeanor darkened. "Not yet, really. We got a letter on Tuesday, but – I'll tell you all about it tomorrow, okay?" With that she brightened, lightly kissed his cheek, and waved as the motorcycle sputtered and pulled away, leaving another plume of blue smoke lingering behind.

"So how was the ride, Jacques?" asked Charles Bernard as he and his son stood in the yard of the family's farmhouse in Westfield — his father alone was allowed to call Jack by his French name. "Looks like that storm got you pretty good, eh?"

"Yeh," replied Jack with a shrug. "The skies opened up on the Bondsville road – got soaked to the skin." As he lifted his rucksack from the rack on the rear of the machine, water streamed off it and splattered on the lawn.

Just then Marie stepped from the kitchen door and greeted Jack with a kiss on the cheek. "You are a sight, Brother. Better get cleaned up before supper."

A few minutes later Jack clambered down the stairs from his second floor bedroom looking more presentable, although his hair was still wet and matted. He turned into the back hall and tapped on Claire's door. "Sis?"

"I'll be out in a few minutes," replied a muffled voice.

Jack was disappointed. He and Claire had shared a special bond since their mother passed two years earlier. Marie had adopted the role of stern taskmaster to her younger sister. When Claire felt put-upon by her sister or father, she often turned to her brother for consolation and support. But he'd been gone nearly two weeks and was expecting, well, just a bit of enthusiasm from his little sister upon his return. "Okay," replied Jack through the closed door.

In the kitchen Marie was hard at work on the evening meal, scrubbing potatoes, dicing carrots, and stirring a pot of stew. "Don't take it personally, Jackie. She's been a bit moody lately. You know – new school – new classmates – all that."

"Yeh, I sure do remember what that was like." Jack stepped out into the back yard, his eyes on the gardens beyond. Already he was trying to figure out how he was going to accomplish all he needed to in the next three days – gardening, studying, spending time with Anne.

"Got our work cut out, eh?" observed Charles as he emerged from the barn. "Don't worry, Son, we got Elaine to help us tomorrow. An' Émile's comin' home in the morning, too."

The Bousquets – Felix, Madeleine, Émile, and Elaine – were neighbors and friends of the Bernards. They had arrived in Holyoke from Québec only a few months after the Bernards and Charles and Felix had worked together at Wellington Textiles for several years. The Bernards moved into the farmhouse on Southampton Road in Westfield in 1905; the Bousquets purchased the home next door a year later. Émile was Jack's age and the two had been close friends. He was now attending a new school for the deaf in Northampton. Elaine was a year younger than Claire, but a hard worker. Steven, the Bousquets' eldest son, had returned to Canada and enlisted the previous spring. In late July the family learned that he had been killed on the battlefield in France, at a place called Ypres.

"How they gettin' on, Dad?" inquired Jack, nodding toward the neighbors' house.

Charles sighed, then shook his head. "Just barely, I'd say."

It was after seven when the Bernards finally gathered around the kitchen table. Claire appeared last at the table and nodded to her brother, then took her seat. Charles offered a brief grace and the meal began.

"So, Sis, how's school goin'?" inquired Jack.

"It's fine," replied Claire succinctly. There was a palpable silence.

"That's it? Just *fine*?"

Claire nodded. Again there was silence until Charles stepped into the conversational void. "So, Jack, tell us all about college. Classes started this week, eh?"

"Yeh," replied Jack. "It was a busy week. Lectures, laboratory meetings, recitations, homework by the bushel."

"What's it like, I mean, the studies. Hard?" asked his father.

"Mostly okay – chemistry – rhetoric – shop. But the math – trigonometry–"

"You had that in high school, Jackie, right? Mr. Conlon?" asked Marie.

Jack nodded. "Yeh, yeh, but it's different now – all these guys from the city – I feel like –" Jack paused, shaking his head with doubt.

"You'll do fine, Son, once you get used ta it," offered his father.

"How's your new job goin'?" asked Jack of Marie. It was an awkward subject. Marie was a good student and had completed her third year of high school in June. But with Jack off to college she had left school and was working at the telephone company office in Westfield to help support the family in her brother's absence. They'd never discussed this, but Jack wondered if Marie resented having to forego her education for his.

"It's pretty interesting, actually. I work at the switchboard three afternoons a week. And I'm usually home just about the time Claire and Fergal get here."

"Hey, Claire," asked Jack, turning to his younger sister. "I hear Fergal Dooley is your constant companion these days." Claire's face reddened. "Nice kid, eh?" Claire didn't look up or respond. She seemed to be concentrating on her stew. Charles shot his son a look that told him the subject should be changed.

"So how's business goin', Dad?" asked Jack, referring to a new enterprise, a motorcar repair business, just started by Charles and Felix. *B&B Garage* read the sign hanging over the barn door.

"Well, not so bad for starters. Mostly just friends and neighbors so far, but we're hoping to draw in more trade, you know, word-a-mouth. Lucky fer us those old Tin Lizzies start fallin' apart 'afore folks finish payin' for 'em." Charles and Jack laughed.

24

Marie had baked a peach pie in honor of her brother's return. It was his favorite and she watched with pleasure as he devoured one sizable slice, then helped himself to a second almost as large as the first. Charles and Marie each enjoyed smaller servings, but Claire declined and asked to be excused. When the bedroom door had shut, Jack looked into Marie's eyes.

"What's that all about?"

"She's just in a mood, that's all," replied Marie. "You know how girls can be." She peered into her brother's face glumly. Then her eyes lit up. "Speaking of which, Anne was here for supper last night. I believe things are going well at the Women's Home."

"Yeh, I guess so. I'll know more tomorrow. And we're goin' for a picnic on Sunday, up to Smith's Ferry."

Charles brightened. "Them dinosaur tracks? Oh, she'll be fascinated."

Marie spoke with a hint of sarcasm: "I'm sure all you two have to do is talk about giant beasts of long ago, right Jackie?"

Jack's face reddened, then he nodded. "It is pretty interesting, though. You should see them sometime, Marie."

Later in the evening Jack and his father sat on the porch watching the sky over the Berkshire Hills transform from bright red to deep purple.

"What's all this about a fire at the Arsenal in Springfield?" asked Jack, referring to a story he had read in the *Holyoke Daily Transcript*.

"Well," began Charles, "lot a smoke, flames — in the warehouse. They was lucky, though. Coulda been worse. Lots worse."

"How'd it start?"

"The papers are sayin' it was electrical — bad wiring." Jack nodded. Electrical fires were getting more and more common in shops and factories, it seemed, not just in Massachusetts but across the nation — everyone in a rush to electrify, but all too often doing the work on the cheap. Then Charles lowered his voice. "But Felix's old friend, Leo Latour — works at the Arsenal — he says it was sabotage, pure an' simple — work of the Jerries."

"Really?"

"Well, so 'e says — I'm not sure I believe it."

~ 3 ~

Jack was up and working in the family garden by seven the next morning, harvesting squash, cabbage, turnips, peppers, and melons. This was what he loved, good honest labor, hands, arms, legs, and back, his mind focused on the work. The morning was cool and a heavy dew lay over the grass and the nodding leaves as he toiled.

He worked alone for nearly an hour before Claire appeared, ambling across the yard in his direction. She was wearing a long, plain muslin dress and tattered leather boots several sizes too large for her feet, the laces dragging in the wet grass as she walked.

"Good morning, lazy bones," chided Jack with a smile as he leaned on his hoe.

She stopped, sighed, then stood unsmiling. "Whatta you want me to do?"

Jack looked up at his sister's round face. Her usually bright eyes were dull. "Whatta I want you to do? Sass me, that's what I want. You can do it, I know you can."

Another sigh, then, "I'm too tired, Jackie. Just put me to work, okay?"

Jack nodded towards a long row of onions. Then he offered his sister a bushel basket, but just as she extended her hand he pulled the basket back. "Gee, Sis, I been lookin' forward to you givin' me what-for since the day I left. You gonna let your brother down?"

Again Claire sighed. "Okay, okay. Let's see, uh – well – have they kicked you out of that college yet?"

"There, now, that wasn't so hard was it?"

"I figure it's just a matter of time," she added with a slight smile.

"Well, no, they haven't, not yet, 'though after our first tests we'll just hafta see." He was waiting for a response. After a long pause, Claire turned and looked up and into her brother's eyes. He continued, "But if they do, I'll be happy to come back home so I can be put upon by my little sister."

Claire was now doubled over, pulling absently on the tapered onion leaves which, fortunately for her, offered little resistance. Jack crossed to the other side of the bed and commenced pulling onions directly opposite her. After working together for several minutes without a word, he finally broke the silence.

"I get the feeling you're not too happy to see your brother."

"I'm glad you're home, Jackie, all right?"

"Don't sound too convincing. Something I said?"

"No, it's nothing to do with you."

"What, then?"

Claire pulled half a dozen smaller onions and held them in one hand, their leaves draped before her in a green cascade. "School – and Marie – and Daddy – and, well – everything. You wouldn't understand."

"Listen, I know it's hard when you're the new kid in school. I was the new kid at Forestdale once, you know–"

"Yes, Jackie, I know, but that was different."

"How?"

"You're a boy and I'm a girl."

"So?"

"The other girls treat me like I'm some jamoke just off the farm. And the boys make animal sounds when I walk by."

"Just ignore them, Claire. You know, that's how I first met Tommy. Some guys were givin' me the dickens in the schoolyard – I just let 'em wag their tongues. Finally when I thought it was gonna come to fightin', along comes Tommy and they all turn tail. Not that Tommy was that big, ya know. It was his way, all smiles and sweet-talkin'. Just let 'em know you can't be riled. That's all I'm sayin'."

Claire tossed a bunch of onions into her bushel basket. "And there's Fergal."

"Oh, yeh, Dad told me he was riding with you on the trolley. That's probably a good thing. There are some real derelicts on those cars."

Claire grimaced, then dragged the bushel basket a few feet along the bed and resumed pulling onions.

"Hey, Sis, I got an idea. How about if you come along with Anne and me tomorrow, up to Smith's Ferry?" He was not sure she'd be that interested in dinosaur tracks, but he knew how much she enjoyed Anne's company.

"You mean me, you, and Anne?" Jack nodded and smiled. "You sure you want me–"

Jack smiled. "Sure, that'd be keen."

Claire nodded. "If you're sure," she added, then returned to pulling onions.

Later that afternoon Jack sat on a long, velvet davenport in the Wellingtons' parlor. It was a large room, lavishly decorated and furnished, with a high arched ceiling, fine oil paintings hanging on the walls, its gleaming oak floors covered with Persian carpets. The house, one of Holyoke's largest, perched atop a high hill overlooking the city with the Connecticut River shimmering beyond, its shining white walls in sharp contrast to the dull gray and brown wood-framed tenements below. The broad, manicured lawn in front of the house was punctuated with magnificent trees, mighty copper beeches, butternuts, oaks, and maples. The formal gardens on the west side of the house teemed with roses, delphiniums, and gladiolus, all carefully tended by several gardeners and overseen personally by Mrs. Wellington. An ornate glasshouse on that side of the house opened on the gardens, its beds lush with tropical plants – orchids, bromeliads, palms, ferns, and ancient cycads. A collection of acacias imported from South America was according to Helen the only one of its kind north of New York City and west of Boston.

Jack always felt a little out of place in this magnificent home, but his discomfort was eased by Anne's sweet smile. It was four years, almost five now, since Jack met Tom and gradually insinuated himself, without even realizing it, into the Wellington family. He was only fourteen when he rescued Anne and Carolyn Ford from a pair of street urchins trying to steal their bookbags on Maple Street. He had remained faithful to Tom through some difficult times while Tom was away at boarding school, and Jack's position in the family had been secured for sure when he and Anne had to come to Tom's aid after he was accused of setting a fire that killed a man in Holyoke over a year ago.

Anne was seated next to him holding a letter which she read to him:

Dear Mother, Father, and Annie,

Thank you for your letters and postals. I am sorry for the tardiness of this reply. Our class has a 24-hour liberty, the first since I arrived, and honestly this is the first chance I have had to write.

They are working us very hard day and night. We have at least three hours of physical training every day, usually mornings, then we have school all afternoon. This week we started specialized training another 2 to 4 hours every day. By the time we're dismissed all I can do is eat and fall into bed. I am going to communications school, I guess because I told them I used to fool around with my wireless a lot when I was at Dorchester School. It is all very

30

complicated but interesting – sparks, signals, codes
and all that. Will tell you more in my next letter.

Not sure when we get our assignments but
everything is running at full tilt so the boys are
saying we'll be shipping out in just a few weeks. All
the news we hear from France is good and the talk is
that the whole shooting match may be over pretty
soon. Everyone's excited to be learning our jobs and
getting ready for whatever comes.

Give my love to Uncle Richard and Aunt
Charlotte, also Mildred, Morwenna, Bromley and
the rest of the staff. I promise to write again soon.

Love from your son,
Tommy
U. S. Naval Training Station, Newport, Rhode Island
September 2, 1917

P.S. Got a letter from Uncle Jim this morning.
Seems our base commander, Admiral Hobart, is an
old friend of his. Jim promises to come to Newport
for a visit sometime soon.

Anne looked up from the letter beaming. "Isn't that a good letter, Jackie?"

Jack nodded. "Uh-huh, yup – swell. He sounds – good. They certainly do keep those boys busy."

Anne nodded. "No time for getting into trouble." Their eyes met and Jack smiled.

"Do you know, Jack," began Anne's mother, "the Navy has so many young recruits at Newport they are housing some of them in private homes. But we're pleased that Thomas is in a barracks – more supervision." She exchanged a knowing look with her husband. Then she turned to Jack. "Did Annie tell you the other good news about Tom?"

31

Jack shook his head with surprise. "Good news?" He was still looking at Anne's face. She was smiling but it struck him as forced, studied.

"Yes, wonderful news. My brother James, the one Tom mentioned – I hope you will meet him sometime – he served in the Navy during the war with Spain. He's retired now but still has many friends in the service – and in Washington as well." Anne was looking down at her plate, fumbling with her fork, as her mother continued. "We received a call on the telephone from him yesterday, all the way from New York. He visited Tom in Newport on Monday. And he had lunch with the base commander who is an old friend of his. James got the inside word that Tom's ship, the *USS York*, will be transporting troops from the west coast to Virginia. Isn't that wonderful? He'll be far from the war zone." Helen paused, smiled, then held the linen napkin to her mouth. Her eyes glistened.

Jack returned Mrs. Wellington's smile, then turned to Anne. "Well, that *is* wonderful news, isn't it?" Anne looked up into his eyes, smiled weakly, and nodded.

Helen continued: "And everyone seems to think the whole affair will be over in a few months anyway. Oh, we want so to have him back soon. We are of course very proud of him, but it will be a great, great relief when he is home once again. So tell us, young man, what is college life like? Do you find it suits you?"

Jack was always a little uneasy talking to Anne's mother. "It's okay so far, ma'am – so far."

"It must be exciting to be surrounded by so many bright, ambitious young fellows, hmm?"

"I guess so, ma'am."

"And the studies," interjected Mr. Wellington. "How are you finding them?"

Jack swallowed. "Difficult, sir."

"Well, of course, of course. You know you're in one of the finest schools for engineering in the nation – so it's bound to be rigorous. Several of the engineers in the power plant at the mill attended WPI – top-notch fellows." He was referring to Wellington Textiles, the city's largest woolen mill, which he and his brother Richard started over thirty years ago.

"You'll do just fine, I know you will," added Anne, leaning toward Jack and trying to look into his eyes. He turned and returned her gaze. His face was a mask, expressionless, until their eyes met and he brightened, then smiled. "We're all so proud of you, Jackie."

There followed a long pause. Finally Helen continued. "So, you two are off on some sort of excursion tomorrow, hmm? Where to, Jack? Our daughter is keeping us in the dark."

"Oh, just a picnic lunch on the river up at Smith's Ferry, that's all."

"I'm sorry you will miss the festivities downtown, though," added Mrs. Wellington. "It's a special parade in honor of our soldiers and sailors. There'll be all sorts of floats, marching bands – a very big affair, by all reports."

~ 4 ~

The Bernard family attended Mass in Westfield the next morning. Shortly after their return, Jack and Claire boarded the trolley to Holyoke. When they arrived at the Wellington home Anne was waiting for them under the portico holding a wicker basket over one arm. Jack seldom drove his family's Model-T to Holyoke for his visits with Anne; the old jalopy was an utter embarrassment to him, especially when visiting the Wellington home. Mr. Wellington had offered him the family's Pierce-Arrow, but Jack declined politely, using as an excuse that he was still uneasy about driving such a fine motorcar.

After another trolley ride of barely ten minutes, the trio disembarked at Smith's Ferry, then followed a cobbled way that descended toward the river. In a previous time before the construction of the bridges across the Connecticut River, this had been a busy route to the ferry crossing. Today it was a quiet neighborhood of a few ramshackle houses and shuttered storefronts. Close to water's edge, they turned onto a narrow footpath that skirted the riverbank. The way was little used and overgrown with brambles.

"It's fortunate that I'm wearing slacks, Jackie, isn't it?" Jack smiled at Anne, then took her hand. In four or five minutes they were standing on a ledge that sloped toward the river. Anne gasped. "Oh, Jackie, this is lovely. Is that Mount Holyoke?" she asked, pointing to a mountain that loomed above the river's east bank.

"Yep, and that's Prospect House up there." He was referring to the hotel that stood at the top, glistening in the midday sun like a Roman temple. "Ever been up there?"

Anne shook her head. "Although I have been to the top of Mount Tom on one or two occasions," she replied coyly, gazing sweetly into his eyes, her pink skin taking on a rosy glow. "You know, Claire, your brother, Tommy, Carolyn Ford, and I once rode the cable car to the the summit of Mount Tom together." Claire was interested. Anne chuckled. "That was the first time I tried to talk to your brother, but he was so shy. Getting him to talk – it was like pullin' teeth, as they say." She paused, then gave a slight laugh.

"Well," replied Claire sardonically, "he's got over that now – unfortunately." Claire and Anne exchanged smiles.

Anxious to change the subject, Jack spread the blanket on a patch of grass that afforded a wide view of the river and the mountains beyond. He and Claire sat while Anne knelt before the hinged wicker basket assembling a small picnic lunch before them.

"That was kind of the beginning for Tommy and Carolyn, too, remember?" recalled Jack. "Do you think, when Tommy gets home, that those two will pick up where they left off?"

Anne smiled and shrugged. "Who knows in matters of the heart, right?" If Jack had been more observant he would have glimpsed a hint that Anne knew something, a certain something, about her brother and her best friend that she felt she could not divulge, even to him. But his thoughts were elsewhere.

"So, Anne, what's the news about Tommy? Does he write?" asked Claire. Anne's rosy complexion suddenly paled and the smile disappeared from her delicate lips. She looked away and across the rippling water.

Jack shot his sister a stern look. "Well, Claire," replied Jack. "Mr. and Mrs. Wellington received some good news about Tom this week. Anne's uncle learned from a Navy friend of his that

Tom's ship is gonna be sailing back and forth from the east coast through the Panama Canal to California – so it won't be in the war zone. Isn't that good news?"

Claire nodded and smiled at Anne. "You must be relieved, Anne."

Anne nodded and smiled at Claire, but then looked away.

"Anne? What is it?" asked Jack. She turned again and met Jack's gaze. Her expression was somber. "What's the matter? I'd think you'd be happy – I mean, relieved – at the news that Tom's ship will be staying close to home."

After a long pause, Anne began. "I want to believe it, Jackie, more than anything, I do. But–" Another pause.

"What is it, Annie?"

"I don't like to speak ill of a family member, but Uncle Jim – he's a nice enough fellow and we all love him dearly, but – well, he's a big talker, do you know what I mean? He's always telling stories about exotic places he has been, exciting things he has done, and important people he knows. He once told me he met Teddy Roosevelt when he was still a young man and urged him to run for President. The way he spoke you might think he alone inspired the man to run. Maybe some of it is true, but – I don't know – Jackie, I'm still worried about Tommy."

Anne took several deep breaths in an effort to regain her composure. Then she brightened as she reached into the picnic basket. "Time for lunch. Sausage from Belliveau's Market – Jack's favorite – rye bread and cheddar cheese, and the first cider of the season."

Jack shook his head and smiled. "Aren't you something?"

"Aren't I?" replied Anne with a twinkle in her eye. "Now, eat up."

Jack and Claire turned their attention to the picnic as the three looked out on the river.

"So, Jackie," began Claire a few minutes later. "When are we going to see those famous footprints?"

Jack gestured toward the ledge around them. "Look around you, Claire. See something curious?"

"Well, I see a purplish rock with ripples in it. Is that what you're talking about?"

"Look some more."

"And holes, some small, some big."

"That's it – those holes, depressions –*im*pressions really."

At first Anne seemed flummoxed, but suddenly she brightened. "My goodness, Jackie, are those the footprints you told me about – of ancient creatures?"

"Exactly, Holyoke's famous dinosaur tracks. Come, let me show you."

They stood and walked across the rock surface. When seen from the right angle the rocks revealed a series of tracks, some as large as pie plates, but in very distinct lines and curious patterns.

"See, thousands of years ago, this was the bottom of a big, wide lake – soft sand or mud. Those creatures walked in the shallows, probably hunting for prey, maybe fish, snails, worms, who knows? See, there were big ones and small ones, maybe parents and their young, side by side. And when the water level dropped, the mud dried, preserving the impressions – the tracks."

"That is astonishing, Jackie," replied Anne. "Ancient history right before our eyes – right under our feet."

Just then a series of loud, sharp reports rang out from further along the river bank. It was curious how the quiet had been so suddenly interrupted and the three stood and followed the footpath across the ledge back into the shady forest in the direction of the sound. Finally, they emerged into another clearing, another still larger expanse of bare rock, and discovered the source.

"'Lo," said a gray-haired gentleman in brown overalls holding a wooden-handled sledge. His face was red and dripping with perspiration. He was kneeling, driving a stake into the thin soil at the margins of the rock face. He doffed his cap to the young couple, exposing a broad, balding head. Then he smiled shyly and resumed his work, placing stakes at regular intervals around the rock. After driving several more stakes, he was close to the three young people.

"Pardon," he added as he stepped past them and proceeded to pound another stake into the ground.

Finally Jack spoke. "What's all this about?"

The man leaned on the sledge, drew a kerchief from his breast pocket, then wiped his brow. "Setting up a grid, I am." Then he gestured to indicate parallel lines connecting the stakes.

"Do you know about the tracks, sir?" asked Jack. "They're dinosaurs."

The man smiled and nodded. "Ya, I do."

"I'm Jack, Jack Bernard. This is my friend, Anne Wellington, and my sister, Claire."

Again the man lifted his cap and smiled shyly. "Henry Smith, Professor Henry Smith."

"Are you a scientist? Is that it?" replied Claire.

"Ya, paleontologist."

Jack was embarrassed. "Oh, well, I guess you *do* know about the dinosaur tracks then." The professor smiled and nodded. "Are you from Mount Holyoke?" inquired Jack, referring to the girls' college just across the river in South Hadley.

The man shook his head. "No, actually, the University of Colorado. I'm on sabbatical." The confused expressions on their faces prompted him to explain. "I'm on leave – for a time – at Yale University in Connecticut. I'd always heard about the work of Professor Hitchcock and wanted to see for myself. He was the first to – well, you know."

"The first to study these, right? And the first to recognize them as animal tracks?" asked Jack. "Giant birds, he thought.

Noah's raven was what some called them, the huge bird sent from the Ark to find land."

The professor smiled and looked first at Anne, then at Claire. "This young man seems to know a good deal about such things, does he not?"

Claire returned his smile. "He's in college – maniacal engineering – Worcester Polytechnic Institute."

"Mechanical engineering," Jack corrected.

"Ah, yes," replied the professor, turning and smiling at Jack. "Well, first-rate institution that. Have you studied paleontology yet? An old friend of mine is on the faculty there – Vellman. Have you heard of him?"

"Wellman, yes, yes, I've heard his name, but I'm just a freshman, we only began classes last Monday."

"Well, be sure to enroll in one of his classes some time. Especially if you're interested in paleontology."

With some prodding the soft-spoken professor began to tell Anne, Jack, and Claire about the tracks, about the creatures that made them, and about his research. It was intriguing, beguiling actually, the very idea that so much could be learned from the rocks beneath one's feet. He talked of the formation of the valley long before it was the course of this great river, about the conditions that allowed the tracks to form, about the creatures that must have made them, their size and shape, and the seemingly magical transformation of mud into rock. He spoke of time, great expanses of time, not hundreds or even thousands of years, but millions, tens and hundreds of millions of years – all that from a few rocky ledges by the river at Smith's Ferry, Massachusetts.

The professor's monologue went on for some time as the three listened in rapt silence. Finally, Claire spoke up. "Professor, do you suppose there are more tracks like these around? Is this the only place?"

"Well, no, miss, not at all. There are similar beds in Greenfield, and Granby, in New Jersey, Colorado, western

Canada, Germany. Wherever the conditions were right – and at the right time, of course. These large creatures seem to have disappeared from the face of the earth rather suddenly–"

Claire was filled with more questions. "Gosh, Professor Smith, there's so much to learn, to discover. How do you become a – a pale-oh-whats-it?"

"A paleontologist?" He chuckled. "Well, by reading, and studying – and always asking questions. You seem to have that quality, to your credit. Never stop asking questions." The professor paused, smiled, then continued. "And don't simply accept what others tell you, even the experts. Always ask questions, young lady, and you vill go far."

Claire returned his smile, her eyes wide.

"She's pretty good in that way," interjected Jack with a smile. "She never listens to her brother, her sister – or her father." Claire blushed and everyone laughed. "Well thank you, Professor, it's all very interesting. But we have to be going."

Anne spoke up. "Professor Smith, I am the assistant director of the Women's Home – on Maple Street in Holyoke. Are you familiar with it?" The professor shook his head. "We are beginning a lecture series on Friday evenings – for the residents. I wonder — would you be willing to come and speak sometime?"

The professor hesitated. "Oh, I don't know – do you really think anyone would be interested?"

"I do, indeed, sir, I am certain they would be."

"I don't know – I'm rather –"

"Oh please, Professor Smith, it would be the first on our schedule. Won't you please say yes?" she begged with imploring eyes.

"I am sorry, Miss Wellington, but I – it just would not be possible. Please forgive me."

"Well, if you are certain –"

On the way back to the trolley stop, Anne was talking about the professor and his work. "It's so fascinating, Claire, isn't it? All that history written in stone – and those terrible creatures – reptiles – giant birds – whatever they were. And that man, he is intriguing. I do wish he had agreed to speak at the Home. Don't you think he would be a marvelous guest?" Claire nodded. "So, Claire, have you ever thought of becoming a paleontologist? It sounds like a field that would suit you."

"You really think a girl could be a – one of those?"

"Claire, dear, this is 1917. You know about suffragettes — well there are now farmerettes, lawyerettes – Tommy says they even have yeomanettes in the Navy now. Did you know, in Montana they just elected a woman to Congress? These days, a girl can aspire to anything she wants – anything."

Jack seemed to be weighing something. "Jackie, what's the matter, you do not agree?" asked Anne.

"Oh, sure, I suppose so. But I was thinking about the professor."

"What – you don't think he would make a good speaker? Our girls wouldn't be interested in those amazing tracks?"

"No, Anne, it's not that. It's–"

"What, Jackie?"

"I don't know, there was something about him that struck me a little odd, is all."

"What do you mean?"

"For a man who's spent his whole career as a teacher, a college professor, lecturing to students, he seemed – I don't know – a little uncomfortable, nervous, maybe – talking to us just now, you know?"

"Oh, that was nothing, Jackie. We surprised him – interrupted his work – his mind was on other things, don't you suppose? I bet a lot of brilliant men are like that, a bit reticent – it's a sign of a great mind. You know, like Mister Edison and Doctor Freud – and–"

The trolley from Northampton was approaching and Jack lifted the picnic basket.

"Well, maybe you're right, but there was something about that man that didn't seem quite right is all I'm saying. My professors aren't the least bit, eh, *reticent* – I swear they'd go on all night if we'd let them."

~ 5 ~

Gray clouds were looming over Holyoke as crowds gathered along High Street shortly before noon. Hundreds lined the thoroughfare, all dressed in their Sunday best – women in long dresses, white, cream, or black, men in black topcoats, smartly creased trousers, and black derbies. The children were equally well dressed. All were waving Old Glory, its forty-eight stars and thirteen stripes hanging limply in the still air.

The entry of the nation into the war in Europe had been debated vigorously across America in the three years since its start, and while sharp differences remained, now that Holyoke's finest were headed to war, most of the city's residents were succumbing to patriotic fervor. Tables and exhibits filled the broad plaza in front of City Hall this day: the local Army recruiting team, a committee soliciting contributions for war relief, campaigns collecting candy, cigarettes, gloves, hats, and scarves for the soldiers, and a booth for purchasing Liberty Bonds.

Helen and Thomas Wellington had arrived well ahead of time and were already seated in the reviewing stand for city leaders and prominent citizens erected in front of City Hall. "Oh, Thomas, it's beginning – I do hope Richard and Charlotte will be here soon," said Helen, standing and peering up the street in the direction of the Highlands where her husband's brother and his wife lived. Just then she saw them approaching and waved. "Ah, there they are, thank the Lord."

Helen and Charlotte embraced while the men shook hands. "Well, quite a turnout there is," began Charlotte. "My goodness. But what a shame the weather isn't better. We're fortunate to be under cover here. Looks like it could rain at any minute. Where is Anne?"

"Oh, she and Jack are having a picnic up at Smith's Ferry."

Charlotte pursed her lips. "She's still keeping company with that boy? I thought he was away at college."

"Well, he is, in Worcester. But he came home this weekend for a short visit."

"Tut," replied Charlotte, shaking her head. "It would seem time for her to – raise her sights, don't you think?"

Helen, who had been leaning forward to see down High Street, straightened abruptly and turned toward her sister-in-law. "Raise her sights? What on earth do you mean by that, Charlotte?"

"Well, Helen, there are so many fine young men in Holyoke these days, of the very best families and finest breeding. Such a lovely young lady as our Anne could have the pick of them, don't you agree? That boy, Jack, I mean, really, Helen, isn't his family French? And Catholic?"

"They are indeed, Charlotte, and finer people you could not find in Holyoke or elsewhere."

Charlotte was taken aback. "Dear Helen, I am sorry. I mean no offense. Please understand, I'm just thinking that – well – your daughter is not a girl anymore. At her age she needs to begin thinking about marriage."

"Charlotte, Anne was graduated from high school only three months ago, and you're ready to marry her off?"

Just then the sound of drums echoed far down the street and a murmur of excitement spread through the crowd. Then came the cadence of a thousand feet as a large contingent of soldiers from the Yankee Division at Camp Bartlett in Westfield approached. Suddenly the band struck up *Stars and Stripes Forever*. The parade had begun.

The procession was led by a huge American flag borne on a long pole carried by two smartly dressed soldiers followed by

44

an honor guard with representatives of the services, Army, Navy, Marines, Coast Guard, Reserves, all in full dress uniform. An array of soldiers in fatigues came next, perhaps a dozen rows of twenty or more abreast, all marching in near synchrony. They were followed by a massive artillery gun hauled by a team of Belgian draft horses, all decked out in red, white, and blue. The Holyoke High School Band then appeared, striking the notes of the popular Sousa march brightly and confidently, their instruments festooned with colorful streamers.

Next came the floats, beginning with Parsons Paper Company, the city's largest paper mill, its name emblazoned on a colorful banner carried by four young women. Close behind were similar floats of the city's largest textile mills, Farr-Alpaca, Germania, American Thread, and Wellington Textiles. The Wellington float was by far the most elaborate of the four, depicting the history of the textile industry with three generations of looms, all operated by mill workers. It elicited a hearty cheer from a large contingent of young men and women dressed in working clothes that had gathered at the corner of Suffolk and High, all workers from Wellington Textiles who had been given an extended lunch hour from their regular Sunday shift to attend.

Soon a float drawn by a sleek black limousine rolled by carrying a large banner that read *Holyoke Daily Transcript*. In front of the banner stood a half-dozen newsboys dressed in plus-fours, white linen shirts, and woolen caps, each with a canvas bag slung over one shoulder and holding aloft a copy of the Saturday edition.

Across the street, Paddy's, one of the city's dingier watering holes, had just opened. On the sidewalk in front of the bar stood a slender bearded man evincing no enthusiasm for the spectacle unfolding before him. He wore a dusty gray jacket over a tan work shirt, baggy cotton trousers, and a wool cap atop a head of thinning dark hair. His features were sharp, his eyes black and close-set. Periodically he put a cigarette to his lips, inhaled, then after a pause released a plume of smoke that hung just above his head.

A cheer went up as the Mount Holyoke College Farmerettes marched by, each young woman dressed in overalls and carrying a farming implement, a rake, shovel, hoe, or scythe. A horse-drawn wagon followed piled high with produce from the 10-acre vegetable garden the students were working in South Hadley as part of the war effort. Immediately behind the farmerettes marched the Hibernian Pipers band, strains of a familiar Scottish lament swirling about them.

Just then a portly man with a round, florid face and bald head partly covered by a flattened brown cap approached the bearded man on the sidewalk. Their eyes met and they exchanged a few words before the large man gestured, obviously annoyed at the caterwauling of the bagpipes. The pair retreated to the relative quiet of an alley a few feet away.

"Where ees your flag, Becker?" asked the large man.

"Left it home. Too big to lug down 'ere," replied Manfred Becker. He took one long last pull on his cigarette, then dropped the stub to the ground and scuffed it out with his right foot. "So, what brings you ta 'olyoke, Werner? The Kaiser ask you to give me a medal?"

Werner smiled briefly, then shook his head. "Nope, no medal."

"Gee, I'm disappointed," replied Becker. He paused, looking back toward the street as another noisy band approached. "So what then? Send me back to Berlin, is that it? Where I can't screw up no more?"

"Listen, Becker, what ees past ees past – forgotten." Becker threw the man a skeptical look. "So the Springfield job failed."

"I thought you said those Micks knew what they was doin' – just where and when to plant them crackers. You put me onto them, remember? I figured you were vouchin' for 'em."

Again the man smiled, doffed his cap and scratched his broad, bald scalp. "It ees done, over – forget it."

Becker looked the man squarely in the eyes. "Yeh? So what're you here for then?"

"Vell, I got another job for you."

Becker smiled. "You're jokin', right?"

Werner shook his head. "I am serious, Becker, dead serious. In Jersey. They got big plans down there – big plans."

"What's that gotta do with me? You want me to go to Jersey?"

Werner shook his head.

"So it's gonna be here? In Holyoke?"

"Not exactly. A delivery, from Berlin, via Canada. Supplies – you get my meaning?" Becker nodded. "You gonna need a truck to make the pickup. You got a truck?"

"Yeh, sure. I'll be gettin' a truck soon – real soon. When's this pickup?"

"And a good place to store the goods for a veek or two? Someplace outta sight, tight, safe."

Becker was thinking. "When?"

"And a couple guys to make the pickup?"

"Okay, okay, how soon?"

"A veek, maybe ten days."

"And what then? What's the target this time?"

"Like I said, it's in Jersey – New York harbor."

"Whatta you sayin'?" replied Becker, obviously disappointed. "You mean I been demoted to a lousy delivery boy?"

"Listen, my friend, this ees big, real big. Since the Declaration of War, things have been pretty quiet. Rintelen, von Bernstorff, von der Goltz, all gone – deported – in jail – or dead. The Bureau thinks they cleaned 'em out. But a new team just arrived – through Mexico. They got plans for sometink big, another Black Tom."

Becker nodded. The destruction of the Black Tom Island munitions depot in New York Harbor a year earlier, the work of Captain Franz von Rintelen and his minions, was the biggest single act of sabotage by the Germans in the U.S. yet. Seven workers died in the attack, hundreds of tons of arms and ammunition were destroyed in a matter of minutes, windows were shattered in buildings as far away as twenty-five miles – even the Statue of Liberty, that great American icon, had to be closed to visitors for repairs.

"But New York, Jersey, they're lousy vith Feds and troops these days. So the plan ees to assemble bombs somevere else, then deliver them a few days – maybe a few hours – ahead of time. This ees just the first load, there'll be more, but this must go off vithout a hitch. How 'bout it?"

Becker stood impassively, staring at the bare brick wall. "But puttin' these things together?"

"They'll be sending a guy up from Newark to do the dirty vork. You just gotta provide him a place to work, ees all. He'll do the assembly and take care of the delivery to Jersey." He paused, waiting for a reaction from Becker. When none came, he added, "So, you in?"

"When?" Becker replied at last.

"I let you know."

"How?"

"You still livin' on South Street, near Germania Mills?"

Becker nodded. "Room number 7 – old lady Wertz – she's got a telephone. She'll take a message for me."

Werner shook his head. "Nope. No telephone – too risky. They gotta mail box there?" Becker nodded. "I'll drop off a letter with your name on it. It'll tell you a day and time to meet, right here."

Werner nodded and smiled. The pair shook hands and parted just as another band approached amidst the strains of *America the Beautiful.*

~ 6 ~

Helen Wellington was one of Holyoke's most prominent women. It was true that she was the wife of Thomas P. Wellington, Sr., co-owner of the city's largest textile mill, but her renown had to do not merely with her husband's success. She was a doer, an activist, a believer in justice, equality, and compassion, traits that were not always easy to come by in the city.

Childhood had not been easy for Helen Cooke. Her mother had suffered from poor health and when Helen was only twelve she was already shouldering many of the responsibilities her mother could not handle. Her father was an accountant at American Thread Company, but frugality was necessary in the household and the Cooke children, though they were not poor, learned to get by with few frills. When Helen eventually married one of Holyoke's most successful businessmen and moved into their gracious and imposing home on Beech Street, she refused to turn her back on her roots. She used her newfound wealth on behalf of a number of philanthropic causes, the most important of which to her was the Holyoke Women's Home. But she was also active on many city committees and social organizations where she got to know women and men from all walks of the city's life.

Helen walked briskly down Suffolk Avenue early the next day, passing dozens of shops, storefronts, and offices along the way that gave testimony to the rich diversity of Holyoke: Ducette et Fils Hardware, Israel Levine – Haberdasher, Rodowsky Tailors, Cosimo Barone Imports, Steiger's

Department Store, Gerard Photographic Studio, Epstein Furniture, Potvin Real Estate, Hirsch & Sons Stationers.

She paused at the entrance to Goldstein's Dress Shop, briefly admiring an evening gown in the window. Then she entered. "Good morning, Avi," she called warmly to the elderly proprietor. "And how are you today?" She knew Avi Goldstein to be soft-spoken, a bit shy, so she did not wait for an answer. "You look well."

He looked up from the morning edition of the *Holyoke Daily Transcript,* smiled, and nodded. "Goot, yah, goot," he replied in his strongly accented English.

Just then Helen heard a familiar voice from the back room speaking loudly, angrily into a telephone in Yiddish. Helen and Avi's eyes met. "Something wrong with Meira today?" asked Helen.

The old man chuckled and nodded. "Effry day – effry day," he chuckled with a twinkle in his eye. As he spoke the curtains covering the door to the backroom were brushed brusquely aside and Meira appeared.

"Oy, Avi," she began in disgust, not seeing Helen. Then she spouted several sentences of Yiddish that could only mean she was greatly annoyed with something – or someone. Helen was not sure what the subject of her tirade was until she heard the name Whittemore. Just then Meira saw Helen and her tone changed dramatically.

"Ahhh, Meesis Vellington, dear lady. I deed not see you dere. How are you, ma'am?"

"I am very well, Meira, very well. I'm – I – wondered if that organdy evening dress was ready yet. But – perhaps this is a bad time. Shall I come back another day?"

"Na – na – na," replied Mrs. Goldstein. "I am so veery sorry. Eet ees – dat man Vittemore – you know heem?"

"Lawrence Whittemore – editor of the *Transcript*? Yes, of course, we've met – seems like a nice man. And his wife is a supporter of the Women's Home. Why? Has he done something to upset you?"

Meira rolled her eyes. "Have you seen dis mornin's paper?" she asked.

"No, I have not. Why?"

"Dat man, he has no respect. He writes about patrioteesm, loyalty, like dey were de exclusive possessions of de rich – de old families of 'olyoke – de mill owners." She paused, suddenly realizing to whom she was speaking. "Not dat dey are not fine people, mind you – fine, fine people." She shuddered. "But he writes about how vee must be vigilant, alvays vatching for suspicious actions, listening for seditious words – slackers, socialists, pacifists, enemy aliens. *Enemy aliens?*" she repeated forcefully. "Just because someone was born in Chermany, or Czechoslovakia, or Hungary, he is not to be trusted? Is dat what he tinks?"

Helen tried to calm her. "Well, dear, I am certain that he does not mean that."

"Den read it for yourself, ma'am," shouted Meira, grabbing the paper from her husband's hands. She continued but in a more restrained tone. "Maybe I ham crazy, okay, maybe I ham. But leesten to dis–" She folded the paper over, adjusted her spectacles, and tried to read. Only then did she realize that she was holding the paper upside down. She reversed it, red-faced, and read.

Our enemies, the Central Powers, have agents and saboteurs throughout America, and it is the job - nay, the duty - of every patriotic citizen to be on the alert. We are all soldiers in this war and the battlefield is all around us - in our factories, in our shops, on our streetcars, even in our homes. We must be ever vigilant for enemies of this nation who would sow distrust and promulgate treason and sedition. Who are these enemies? The socialists, the radicals, the

51

slackers, the IWWs, and any of the myriad "hyphenated Americans" Mr. Roosevelt has warned us about: German-Americans, Polish-Americans, Jewish-Americans, even Irish-Americans. They are not to be trusted.

Helen listened in disbelief. She understood why the editorial had touched a nerve. It could only be interpreted as a direct challenge, practically an accusation of disloyalty, toward people like the Goldsteins. They had emigrated from Russia nearly fifty years earlier. They were well known in the business community of Holyoke, active in the synagogue, and universally liked and respected. Furthermore, they had been residents of Holyoke for decades longer than Lawrence Whittemore.

"You are entitled to be outraged, Mrs. Goldstein. Anyone should be appalled at what that man has written."

Meira disappeared into the back room and soon emerged with the organdy dress in hand. Helen admired it and arranged for delivery later in the day.

"Thank you, thank you, both of you." She paused, looking first at Meira, then at Avi. "Marjorie Reed is a dear friend. We have served on several committees together. She and her husband own the *Transcript*. I think she and I need to have a few words about this Mr. Whittemore and his editorials."

Meira smiled and thanked Helen repeatedly. Avi smiled as well, but sat silently, puffing on his pipe.

~ 7 ~

A few days later Claire, Julie, and Sarah were seated together in the school lunchroom as Sarah tried to reassure her friends about Latin. Of all the girls in Miss Sussim's eighth grade, Sarah Muller stood out. She was bright, well-spoken, and friendly to all, even the boys. The girls particularly admired her sweet disposition, which, combined with her rosy complexion, blond tresses, and immaculate dresses, allowed her to command their rapt attention whenever she spoke.

"Cases? Oh, they're easy," she began, referring to the morning's Latin lesson. "There are really just five cases in Latin – the nominative, accusative, genitive, dative, and ablative. N – A – G – D – A. No Amiable Girl Deserves Acrimony. See? That's how my mother taught me to remember them. Try it."

Julie and Claire tried the trick together. "No Amiable Girl Deserves Acrimony – nomative, accusative, genitive, dedative, and the ab-bla-bla-blative." They all laughed.

Sarah continued. "There are two more, the vocative and the locative. They're not even mentioned in our primer. So I don't suppose we need know them."

"Good," declared Claire triumphantly, "then they're my favorites." Again they laughed together.

Sarah continued. "Every noun has a different ending depending on its case – how it's used. The subject of a sentence, like a person, or a thing, is in the nominative case. An object, that's the accusative. If it's something that belongs to someone, it's the genitive. An indirect object is the dative. And a prepositional phrase, the ablative."

Claire and Julie exchanged glances and rolled their eyes.

"Let's take a noun like table," continued Sarah. "It starts with *mens*, *m – e – n – s*, but the ending changes depending on its case. If it's the subject, it ends in *a – mensa*. If it's the object it ends in *am – mensam*. *Mensa, mensam, mensae, mensae, mensa*. See? It's simple."

"So that's all you have to know, eh? That's not too bad," offered Claire.

"Yes, well, that's just for nouns in the first declension. There are four more declensions, each with different endings."

Again Claire and Julie exchanged glances. Claire spoke. "Say something to us in Latin, Sarah, like you were just talking to us."

"Um, well – *Gallia est omnis divisa in partes tres.*"

"What does that mean?" asked Julie.

"All Gaul is divided into three parts."

"Huh?"

"Julius Caesar said that to – I forget who. Oh, and *Veni, vidi, vici* – I came, I saw, I conquered."

"Let me guess, that Caesar guy again?" replied Claire.

Sarah smiled and nodded. "Don't worry, it's fun. We'll do it together."

"Thanks, Sarah," replied Claire. "I never thought I would say this, but I think I'm gonna like Latin."

A few minutes later the three were standing among many dozens of children in the dusty schoolyard. "Claire, do you know who else likes Latin?" asked Sarah. "That boy, that friend of yours. What is his name, again?" She nodded toward a figure standing alone by the fence.

Claire rolled her eyes. "That's Fergal Dooley, Sarah. And he is *not* a friend of mine. He lives near me and he rides the electric from Westfield with me. That's all."

"He's very strange," added Julie.

Sarah smiled as she stole another glance. "Really? Hmm, I think he's rather adorable, in a way."

"Yes, in a strange way," replied Claire, "a very strange way." She and Julie laughed together.

Across the yard, a group of children had formed a ring around several grade eight boys who were making a commotion. Hearing shouting and banging of a drum, the three girls approached the group and watched.

Four boys were standing in a line. One was striking a snare drum, another blowing into a pennywhistle, a third carrying an American flag. The fourth, who appeared to be the leader, held a stick as if it were a baton and began to direct the group. The pennywhistler was trying to play a patriotic tune as the boys marched in place, then the quartet circled around several times in procession, finally coming to a halt about where they had begun. By now practically the entire eighth grade was watching the performance.

The drum continued as the leader began to speak, reading from a paper. "We hereby declare that Forestdale Grammar School is a member in good standing of the American Protective League. We pledge our support for our men in uniform against the Kaiser and his Huns."

Shouts of support and some applause arose from the pupils who were watching the spectacle.

"We furthermore pledge to resist those foreign aliens in our midst whose one desire is the victory of Germany in the Great War. We will rout out those dangerous demons and destroy them." Again a few shouts of encouragement rose from the pupils watching while many others stood confused or only vaguely interested in what was going on.

At that moment a fifth boy appeared wearing a paper hat and vest painted to resemble Uncle Sam and a white beard made of lamb's wool. The boy had a malevolent leer in his eye as he circulated among the crowd holding something inside his vest. Suddenly he withdrew his hands, producing a can of poster paint from the art room and a long narrow brush. He dipped the brush into the paint, raised it threateningly above his head, and began to circulate among the onlookers. Pupils backed away from him causing him to run still faster. Then he brought the brush down with a sharp motion and gobs of red paint flew, spattering over the hair, face, and clothing of two pupils, one of whom was Sarah Muller.

Sarah stood shocked, wiping paint from her face, hair, and dress. There were shouts of dismay and screams from several girls as they formed a circle around her and tried to assist her. The other target of the paint smearing was a tall boy with wavy brown hair, now streaked with red. He pushed the paint splatterer and the two got into a shoving match that quickly expanded into a general melee.

Claire and Julie, who had been watching aghast, also tried to come to Sarah's rescue. But she refused all help and ran toward the school entrance while several teachers looked on in surprise.

"Come on," called Julie to Claire, "we have to go help Sarah."

"You go, Julie, I'll be there in a minute," replied Claire. The shoving match appeared to have ended and the boy who had been splattered was standing alone wiping paint from his hair and clothing as Claire approached.

"Thank you for putting that wretched creature in his place. I'm sorry about all this. Why'd they pick on you and Sarah?" Claire asked.

The boy looked up. His eyes were green, his features soft and delicate. "Because they're jackasses, that's why."

"Well, thank you anyway." She smiled at him and his grimace softened, then he smiled.

"What's your name?" asked Claire.

"Albert, Albert Albrecht."

Claire turned and walked toward the school with Fergal close behind. He said something to Claire. "What?" she barked.

"Germans," replied Fergal.

"What are you mumbling about, Fergal?"

He spoke softly, slowly. "Sarah, Albert – their families are from Germany. Albert's father and Sarah's brother, Jake — some say they are German sympathizers. That's why those boys did that."

Claire looked at Fergal, thinking, trying to make sense of what he was saying. After several seconds, she finally replied: "I gotta go help Sarah."

"It simply cannot be tolerated, Miss Bernard. It is most unladylike, I trust you will agree," declared the principal sternly. It was the day following the paint incident.

"Yes, Mr. Patton, of course," replied Marie. "I am terribly sorry for my sister's deportment and can assure you that it will not happen again." She shot an angry look at Claire who stood in sullen silence beside her in the principal's office. "Good day, sir." She exited quickly, ushering her sister ahead of her into the corridor and then out onto Sargeant Street where she had parked the Model-T and where Fergal stood looking nervously, first at Claire, then at Marie.

"Would you like a ride home, Fergal?" offered Claire politely in what appeared to be a sudden and uncharacteristic outburst of kindness toward the boy. In truth it was a strategy calculated to delay the reprimand she knew would be coming as soon as she and her sister were alone.

Sure enough, the moment Fergal climbed out of the car in front of the Dooleys' farmhouse on Southampton Road, the scolding commenced. "I am very angry with you, Claire Bernard," began Marie. Claire sat motionless in the car that had now come to a halt in the Bernard's yard, her eyes averted.

"And when Father gets home, well, I cannot imagine that he will feel differently."

Mention of her father finally loosened Claire's tongue. "Please, Marie, don't tell him."

"Don't tell him? That you were fighting in the schoolyard? That you struck a boy? And made him cry? That when your teacher asked you to apologize to the child you refused? You expect me not to tell Father?"

"Arnold Wilmot is hardly a child, Marie. He's practically six feet tall. And that crying was just an act. He knows why I hit him – he knows, the teacher knows, I'll bet even Mr. Patton knows. Arnold and his friends have been cruel and heartless to Sarah – they call her names in the lunchroom, in the schoolyard – they spattered her and another pupil, Albert, with red paint. And the teachers just look the other way, or laugh. It's so unfair. I just – had to put him in his place, that's all."

"Claire, I feel certain that there is more to this than you know. Perhaps – perhaps Sarah and that Albert boy were somehow provoking him?"

Claire turned and gazed on her older sister with disbelief. "Sarah Muller is the sweetest, most harmless girl in the world, Marie. And Albert is very quiet as well. It's just because–" She paused.

"What, Claire, what are you saying?"

"It's because they're German."

"What?"

"They call Sarah and Albert names – Krauts – Huns. In the schoolyard they salute them like German soldiers when they walk by."

"Well, people are alarmed, you know, about the war and the horrible things those German soldiers have done in Belgium – and those dreadful U-boats."

"But that has nothing to do with Sarah – or Albert. They are just as loyal to America as anyone else. Sarah said Albert's older brother is planning to enlist in the Army at the end of this term."

"Well, maybe you are right, Claire, and if that's true then they are being very cruel. But that doesn't give you the right to go around picking fights, does it?"

"Please don't tell Daddy, please."

Charles and Felix returned from Springfield shortly before suppertime, a broken-down Chevrolet sedan in tow behind their truck. Claire was on her best behavior and especially solicitous of her father during the meal. Afterwards when he was seated by the fireplace reading the newspaper, Marie spoke to him about Claire's pugilistic excesses while Claire insisted on doing the dishes.

"Well, I suppose she's standing up for her friend, and that's not such a bad thing," offered Charles philosophically. When Claire had finished in the kitchen, he called her into the parlor.

"Marie tells me you had a bit of a – er – dust-up?" Charles was stern-faced and Claire feared the worst. "Why do you feel so hell-bent to defend that girl? Can't she fend for 'erself?"

"She's – she just lets them taunt her. And I can't stand it, Daddy. It's unfair, and the teachers just look the other way."

"Well, bully for you for standing up for her, Claire. But in the future I hope you will limit your defense to a few choice words, hmm? Can you promise me you'll do that?"

"Yes, Daddy, I promise I will. Thank you, Daddy." She put on her most angelic face for his benefit and retreated to her bedroom feeling victorious. Already she was considering her next move.

~ 8 ~

It was Friday afternoon and Anne was busy in the office at the Women's Home conversing with a representative of one of the city's mills. As they spoke a figure appeared in the front entryway, his back to Anne as he peered tentatively into the lounge.

"Excuse me just a moment," said Anne to the mill representative. Then she approached the man who had just entered. "Sir? May I help you?" The man turned and she recognized him immediately. "Why, Professor Smith, it is very nice to see you. Welcome to the Women's Home. What brings you here? Are you perhaps reconsidering my invitation to speak at one of our Friday night lectures?"

"I'm considering it, Miss Wellington, just – considering. I thought I'd see what the Home is all about."

Anne's eyes shone as she sensed an opportunity. "I'm in the middle of something in the office at the moment, Professor, but why don't you wait here and as soon as I'm free I'll take you for a tour."

The professor nodded, then seated himself on a settee in front of one of the windows that looked out on Maple Street. He picked up a copy of the *Daily Transcript* and began reading. A few minutes later Anne reappeared and showed him around the Home, the lounge, the dining hall, the library, and the office.

"We have rooms on the upper floors and can provide temporary housing for twelve. We serve breakfast and supper for them as well. In addition to assistance with finding work, we also offer aid in locating permanent lodging, in boarding houses or in private homes."

"Very impressive, Miss Wellington, very impressive. What brought you to this place?"

"My mother, Helen Wellington. She was one of the founders, nearly fifteen years ago – she, Nina Calavetti, and several others. I worked here as a volunteer starting when I was twelve and, well, when I completed my education I was offered the position of assistant director. One of my projects is to provide educational opportunities for our girls. We have a needlework group that meets almost every evening in the lounge, a play-reading group on Wednesday nights, and, as you know, we begin our Friday evening lecture series next week." She paused, hoping that Professor Smith would reply. But he stood nodding and fingering his cap nervously. "Professor Smith, won't you please reconsider?"

Again there was a pause. "Well, Miss Wellington, if you are certain it is a subject the young ladies would find of interest–"

"Oh, I have no doubt of it, Professor, no doubt whatsoever."

"Well, then–" He paused, then looked up slowly into Anne's eyes. "I suppose I could."

Anne beamed. "Oh, that is wonderful, Professor Smith, just wonderful." They spent several minutes discussing the arrangements for the lecture, timing, seating, and so forth. Finally, when the professor had received answers to all his questions, he stood as if to leave.

"Professor Smith, before you go, I wonder if you could tell me a little bit more about yourself. I will of course be introducing you that evening." The man nodded. "You told me you were on the faculty at the University of Colorado. How long have you been there?"

"Oh, nearly twenty years. I was hired there shortly after receiving my degree."

"And where did you receive your degree?"

"The University of Edinburgh – in Scotland."

"Oh, Professor Smith, I've always wanted to travel to Scotland. They say it is very beautiful."

The professor nodded and smiled. "Beautiful, ya." Anne was hoping to hear more about Scotland but he paused, then stood once again. "I'm afraid I must be going now."

"Do you have a family back in Colorado?"

A wistful expression spread like a shadow across his face. "Ya, uh-huh. I have two children – well, they are no longer children – a son and a daughter."

"And your wife?"

"She passed a few years back – she had been ill."

"I'm so very sorry – I did not mean to pry."

The professor shook his head. "My son is in France – he enlisted last spring, right after the Declaration of War. And my son-in-law has just been called up, too." He looked glum. "We are very worried for them both."

Anne's smile vanished and she spoke softly, her eyes glistening. "My brother enlisted in the Navy – he'll be shipping out soon."

"Well, you must be very proud, as am I," replied the professor. Anne nodded. "Well, Miss Wellington—"

"Please, Professor, call me Anne."

"All right, then, Miss Anne, I'll see you next Friday evening at six o'clock sharp."

Anne arrived home that evening exhausted but exhilarated; her dream of kicking off the new lecture series was soon to be realized.

"I have the best news," she began when her mother greeted her in the foyer. Do you remember that professor I told you about, the one who studies the tracks of dinosaurs?" Helen nodded. "He has consented to speak at the Home next Friday evening. Isn't that wonderful, Mother?"

Helen smiled at her daughter, pleased to see her so utterly absorbed by her work. "That is wonderful news, Anne. I wonder, though, if such a subject will prove of interest to the residents."

"Oh, I am certain of it, Mother, yes. In fact, I told several of the girls about it already and they were very enthusiastic. But I also plan to publicize it around town. Wouldn't it be exciting to have others attend? What wonderful exposure that would be for the Home. We may attract all sorts of interested individuals. We might recruit a few volunteers, maybe even receive some donations from a few well-heeled citizens." She could see that her mother was distracted. "Surely you don't doubt that this will be a good thing for the Home?"

"Oh, no, not for a moment. It will be wonderful, dear – wonderful." Only then did Anne notice that her mother was holding an envelope. "Anne, a letter arrived in the afternoon post – from your brother."

Anne's ebullient spirits subsided noticeably. "Oh, Tommy? Well, what does he have to say? May I read it?" Helen smiled and handed the envelope to her daughter. Anne quickly shrugged off her winter coat and handed it to the maid along with her hat, gloves, and scarf. She followed her mother into the parlor, took a seat by the fire, and read.

Newport, Rhode Island
Sep 14, 1917

Dear Mother and Father,

Many thanks to you all for your cards and letters. The package arrived in good condition last week. Please tell Mildred that her cookies and fudge were devoured in no time!

You probably have heard from Uncle Jim that my ship, the destroyer USS York, will soon set sail.

We are not allowed to reveal our mission. Our letters are read by censors and any sensitive information extracted.

All the boys are excited to be putting to sea, myself included. I've learned a lot about communications and am glad to be doing such important work. Just hoping I'll have a chance to put all my new knowledge and skills to use, though the way everyone is talking the whole thing may be over before we've had a chance to do our jobs.

Keep writing me at the Newport address and your letters will reach me wherever we sail.

My love to you both, to Anne, and everyone.
Thomas

After she had finished reading the letter to herself, Anne sat looking at it, at the envelope, at the familiar hand. For a moment she felt as though her brother were standing next to her, the old, familiar Tom, smiling, self-assured. Then suddenly she was back in the present.

"Well, my goodness, things are moving quickly, aren't they?" As she spoke she looked up and into her mother's eyes that were glistening in the firelight. "Has father seen it?" Her mother nodded. "Well, that's Thomas, now, isn't it? Raring to go. No moss grows under that boy." She smiled and laughed, a laugh meant to lighten the moment. But Helen knew her daughter and could tell that it was a laugh for show. "I – I will write him, this very evening," promised Anne. With that both mother and daughter turned and stared into the crackling fire.

The following morning Helen sat in the breakfast room sipping her tea and gazing absently at the stained glass image of an exotic bird that hung in the window. The sun's rays scattered as they struck the glass, casting a rainbow across the floor. Just then the maid entered with Helen's morning tea.

"Good morning, Ma'am."

"Good morning," replied Helen. "Morwenna, have you seen Anne this morning?"

"Yes, Ma'am, she arose very early, Ma'am. Rushed through her breakfast, she did. Said she had to be off to the Home."

"On a Saturday?"

"Yes, Ma'am. She said she had a good deal o' work to do today."

"I see," replied Helen. "Yes, of course."

~ 9 ~

Claire was walking up Sargeant Street after school a few days later. Fergal followed close on her heels, looking perplexed. "C-C-Claire – where are you going?"

"I've got an errand to do Fergal, over on Chestnut Street." She was about to add a rude comment that would dissuade him from following, but she thought better of it. "If you want to come along you can. Just don't dawdle."

She quickened her pace and Fergal had to run to catch up with her. "But – but – your father said–"

She stopped, turned, and glowered at Fergal. "My father asked you to accompany me, right? Well, then, you're accompanying me. Okay?"

"But – where?"

Now they were walking side by side and she spoke in a low voice. "I'm goin' to find Jake Muller, Sarah's brother. She said he's boardin' with a Mrs. Collins on Chestnut. If he's still workin' the night shift maybe he'll be in his room."

"But why?"

"I just need to do a little investigating, that's all – find out if what they say 'bout him is true. When he hears what those boys did to Sarah, maybe he'll set 'em straight."

Fergal asked no further questions but grasped his book bag firmly to his chest as the two walked briskly up Sargeant to Chestnut. Shortly they were standing in front of a shabby-looking wood-frame house that might once have been a farmhouse. A hand-painted sign hanging in a front window read *M. Collins - Boarders Taken*.

Claire gazed on the unattractive structure before them. "You wait here, Fergal."

66

The boy stood looking nervously about him as Claire climbed the steps to the front door and rang the bell. Soon a gray-haired woman opened the door, frowning. She had a gruff, wizened face and a small, crooked mouth that revealed several large gaps in her teeth.

"Whatever you're sellin', girl, I ain't buyin'. Now git."

"No, ma'am, I'm not sellin' nothin'. I'm lookin' for Jake Muller, one a your boarders. Is he in?"

"Nope, he's out. Probably at the mill. You his sister? He owes me two weeks' rent so maybe you want to settle up before I throws 'im out."

"No, ma'am, I'm not his sister, just a family friend."

"Well, like I says, he's out." She began to close the door. But Claire was not about to give up that easily.

"I–" began Claire, thinking quickly, "I was hopin' you might 'ave a room? I – I just come ta 'olyoke and I got a job at the mill and I need a room."

The woman looked her over suspiciously. "You look kinda young to be workin', child. Shouldn' you be in school?"

"Oh, no ma'am, I'm sixteen – I'm finished with school. I gotta job–"

The lady still looked dubious but she didn't want to miss a chance at filling a vacant bed. "Well, I s'pose – got a week's rent? Two dollars and fifty cents – in advance."

That was more than Claire's entire life savings at the moment, much more. Nevertheless, she looked squarely into the woman's eyes as she spoke. "Oh, yes, yes ma'am, that sounds fine. But I wonder, could I see the room first?"

The woman sighed. "C'mon." Claire turned and beckoned to Fergal who was now standing at the foot of the steps looking uneasy.

"Ma'am, this 'ere's my brother Ferrr – erguson. He – he needs a room, too."

Again the woman sighed, nodded, and turned. It took several more sharp gestures from Claire before the boy ascended the steps and entered. Then they followed her up the stairs to the second floor where several doors opened off a narrow, dimly lit hallway.

"Your room'd be down 'ere," the woman explained to Claire. "Fellas bunk together in the attic." She pointed up a steep stairway and turned to Fergal. "You c'n have a look yerself."

Claire pointed up the stairs. "Come on, Ferguson, let's have a look-see."

"Nay, boys only up 'theya. Too steep for girls. 'Sides, might be some fellas sleepin'."

Claire took Fergal's sleeve. "Okay, you go up, Ferguson, have a look around – a *good* look." Meanwhile Claire followed the lady to the end of the hall and peered very briefly into the shabby looking room that would be hers.

"It looks fine, ma'am. Just fine. So, how long has Jake Muller been boardin' here?"

"Long enough to owe me," replied the lady impatiently. "Listen, you gonna take the room or just jibber-jabber?" she asked as they retraced their steps along the hallway.

"Well, it's really up to Fer – erguson," replied Claire, peering up the stairs. "I wouldn't–"

Before she could finish the sentence the lady had climbed the stairs, Claire following close behind. Fergal was standing by a dresser next to one of the beds beneath the sloping attic roof. He was holding an envelope and looking intently at it, unaware of the woman's approach.

"What the 'ell you doin there, kid? Stealin'?"

"No, ma'am – I was jus' – jus' lookin'." He placed the envelope back on the dresser.

"So that's what this is all about, eh? What else d'you cabbage?"

"Nothing, ma'am, I –"

She reached out and grabbed the boy's earlobe. "I oughta call the cops." And she hustled Fergal down the steep stairway, still grasping his ear, Claire nearly tripping in her haste to follow and try to separate the two. At the front door the woman yanked hard on Fergal's ear and sent him flying onto the porch where he scrambled down the front steps. Then he took off running down Chestnut Street, bookbag in one hand, his other hand clasping his ear, Claire following close behind.

Back on Sargeant Street they boarded the first Westfield-bound trolley. Fergal sat without a word and Claire knew that he was upset. She tried her best to make conversation with him but to no avail. But as the car passed through pastureland and forest, she could see his lips moving. He was counting, counting something, but exactly what she couldn't tell. Finally she spoke to him sharply. "Fergal, what in the dickens are you counting? You do that all the time, do you know that?"

"Poles – electric poles."

"You're counting the electric poles? Why? What possible reason would there be?"

Fergal shrugged and looked down at his feet.

"Claire Evelyne Bernard," called Charles loudly from the kitchen shortly after she returned home. "Come out here this minute." Charles Bernard was not a man readily inclined to anger, so on the rare occasion when he spoke sternly to his children they knew enough to respond and quickly. Claire stepped through the kitchen door onto the back walk. Her father stood glaring at her.

"Fergal here has something to say to you." He turned but the boy was nowhere to be found. "What – now where did he go? You wait here young lady – you got some explainin' to do." He walked around the front of the house only to see Fergal running down Southampton Road as fast as his skinny legs could carry him. Exasperated, Charles returned to his daughter.

"Claire Bernard, that boy—" He paused, shaking his head. "— is terrified."

"Terrified? Of what, Daddy?" she replied, a look of utter innocence on her face.

"Of *you*, for Pete's sake, he's terrified of *you*. He was in tears – sayin' you tease him and call him names and – and *threaten* him – and he no longer wishes to accompany you to school each day. What do you have to say to that?"

Claire looked stunned. She wasn't certain how much Fergal had divulged of the day's adventures and so thought it best to say nothing.

"Well, you know what this means, I imagine."

Claire nodded, her head hanging down pathetically. "I should apologize to him." She paused, then looked up hopefully into her father's eyes. Charles shook his head. "Extra chores for a week?" Again her father shook his head. "Two weeks?" she pleaded.

"What it means, young lady, is Monday morning – it's back to St. Agnes for you."

Claire was stunned. "But Daddy, you can't – I have – assignments – and the Latin Club fundraiser – and the class play, Miss Sussim wants me to be in the play."

"Well that *is* a pity now, isn't it? I'll go with you to St. Agnes on Monday morning and talk to Mother Superior. I know she'll be glad to have you back – and none too surprised I dare say. Now, go to your room while I decide on further punishment. This is a serious matter, Claire Bernard, and I hope you will learn a good lesson from it."

Claire's face reddened and her eyes glistened. Head hung, she turned and began walking toward her bedroom when her father spoke again. "One more thing, young lady. Fergal said something about *investigating*. What, I'd like to know, is he talking about?"

Claire turned back to her father with a carefully crafted look of confusion. "I haven't any idea, Daddy, but if you ask me that boy has an overactive imagination."

Claire was devastated. She lay sobbing on her bed for nearly an hour. Finally having realized the gravity of her situation, she emerged. She knew that extreme measures would be required to extract herself from this predicament, perhaps including a pretense of deep and genuine contrition. It worked with her father who finally agreed that she would not have to return to St. Agnes, but next she must persuade Fergal to change his mind, and that would require all her wiles.

"Hello, ma'am," she said to Fergal's aunt as she stood on the front porch of the neighbors' farmhouse. "May I please speak to Fergal? It's about school."

"'e's out yonder," the woman replied, nodding toward the barn.

She found Fergal leaning into a stall, gently stroking the head of an enormous draft horse.

"Fergal?" she asked softly. He did not respond but continued caressing the animal's nose and murmuring gently to it. She stepped up to the rail, her eyes on the horse. "Hey, boy, how are you? Aren't you a handsome fella, huh? I'm Claire."

Even the mammoth animal seemed uneasy in her presence. Still Fergal would not look at her.

"He's a beauty," she observed. "What's 'is name?"

"Castor," replied the boy, still stroking his head, "like in the myth."

"Where's Pollux?" she asked.

"Dead," answered Fergal without emotion. "Colicked last summer."

Claire's tone was as soft and gentle as she could muster. "Gee, Fergal, I'm – I'm sorry – really, really sorry." She could see tears welling in his eyes and she continued: "Not just about Pollux, you know."

He nodded very slightly.

"I guess I – I been not very nice to you lately, Fergal." Again he nodded. "It's just that you – well – you're different." The boy's chin began to quiver. "But *good* different, I mean. You're – you're smart and – and dependable – *very* dependable–"

"You're just saying that–"

"No, Fergal, that's not true. I really mean it. And I swear to be nice to you, and to not laugh at you, from now on."

"If?" replied Fergal, his eyes still on the horse.

Claire shook her head. "No — no *if*. Whatever you decide, I promise to be nice to you. But please, Fergal, please say you will accompany me to 'olyoke. If you don't, my father will send me back to St. Agnes on Monday. I like Forestdale and I like my new teachers and friends and – and I – I like *you*."

Finally the boy turned toward her, his watery eyes meeting hers, as she continued: "And I promise to sit where you want me to on the cars – and —"

"And no more *investigating*?"

"And no more investigating, Fergal, I swear – on a stack of bibles."

~ *10* ~

On a cool, crisp Saturday afternoon hundreds gathered for the last day of the season for the Holyoke Papermakers, the city's semi-professional baseball team. This year's team was the strongest in years, clinching the league championship several weeks earlier. Today was a special day for fans of the Papermakers, but also for many citizens of Holyoke and the surrounding towns. A pre-game ceremony was planned to honor the nearly three hundred fifty local men who had entered the military service since the declaration of war in April. It would be a particularly poignant occasion, as the roster of casualties would be read including a number of men from Massachusetts who had already given their lives fighting the German war machine in Europe. Among those to be honored would be Stephen Bousquet.

Stephen's decision to return to Québec to enlist in the Canadian Expeditionary Force the previous autumn had taken his family by surprise. The Dominion of Canada was a member of the British Empire, so when Britain went to war in 1914, Canada, too, took up arms against Germany and Austria-Hungary. It was a sunny afternoon in July when Charles and Felix were working on several motorcars that an official automobile pulled into the Bousquets' yard. Charles Bernard was no stranger to family tragedy, but witnessing the shattering of the lives of dear friends at the news that their eldest son had been killed in the trenches of Belgium would haunt him forever.

Charles, Marie, and Claire Bernard accompanied Felix, Madeleine, Émile, and Elaine Bousquet on this day, trying their best to support them through the somber event. Three flags – American, Canadian, and Massachusetts – cracked like whips in the brisk breeze that blew across Elmwood Park as the official city band played *O Beautiful for Spacious Skies*. A procession led by the mayors of Holyoke and surrounding towns, local legislators, and clergymen then entered, the dignitaries taking seats on a platform erected on the gravel infield just for the event.

After brief words from the mayor, Father Lajoie of Blessed Sacrament Church stood and spoke, offering a prayer for the dead, for their families, and for those brave Americans living amidst the horror of war. Finally, he asked that the audience stand for a minute of silence. A hush fell over the crowd.

Claire was standing next to her sister on the top tier of bleachers, eyes closed, listening to the wind whistle through the pine trees that lined Beech Street, thinking about her friend Elaine, about Stephen, about her own brother, and about Tom Wellington. Just then she realized she was hearing voices, muffled voices, not far away. Where she was standing she may have been the only person in the bleachers who was privy to the commotion in the midst of the solemnity of the occasion, and it surprised her and shocked her. She turned slowly and peered through the boughs that hung below her, and there, just behind the next tier of bleachers, stood a group of boys and young men, smoking and laughing, engaging in light-hearted horseplay despite the request for silence. She spotted a flask hoisted by one of the men and raised toward the flags that flew not far from where they stood. Then she recognized one of the younger members of the group; it was Jake Muller, Sarah's older brother.

That night Claire sat at the small desk in her bedroom, quill pen in hand, writing a letter to Jack. She brought him up to date on the events of the week since he had returned to Worcester including their Thursday supper with Anne. She finished by recounting the commemoration at Elmwood Park, the solemnity of the affair, and the pain she knew the Bousquets – and all those present – must be feeling. Then she described what she had witnessed just out of sight of the rest of the audience, the callous indifference of the young men behind the stands. She was shocked at what she had seen, unable to make sense of it. And she was confused – angry, really – to see the older brother of one of her classmates apparently making light of the solemn occasion. "How *could* he?" she asked her brother. Her thoughts returned to her neighbors and their grief and she finished, "Please take care of yourself, Jackie. We all miss you." She signed the letter simply, *Sis*.

~ *11* ~

One day during the following week Claire stood on the street in front of her school, waiting and watching for her friend, Julie Trottière, with whom she rode home whenever possible. Soon Julie appeared, stepping through the heavy wooden doors. Claire greeted her with a smile and invited her to walk the few blocks to the Women's Home on Maple Street. The two turned and started down Sargeant Street, bubbling with stories of their school day. Fergal followed several steps behind.

Anne was busy in her office when the girls entered the front door, but she heard a familiar voice and emerged smiling. "Hello, Claire, how are you?" Anne asked brightly.

"Anne, this is my friend, Julie Trottière. She went to St. Agnes School with me and now–" Claire turned and smiled at Julie "– she's in my class at Forestdale."

"Well, that's wonderful, Julie. I believe I know your brother Jim."

At that moment the door opened once again and Fergal entered. Claire turned and looked, then turned back to Anne. "I was hoping you could help me, Anne, to think of a present for Marie. Her birthday is next week. I'm knitting her a scarf but I wanted to – I don't know – find something a little more exciting for her. I thought perhaps you would have a suggestion. I've got some money and–"

Anne interrupted. "Of course, Claire – but would you excuse me for a moment?" She approached the boy who now stood before a bulletin board in the hallway examining the notices for residents, his woolen cap in his hands. He was looking very carefully at the announcement of the lecture by Professor Smith displayed prominently beside a striking lithograph of a dinosaur.

"May I help you, young man?" Fergal did not reply.

Claire spoke up disdainfully. "Oh, that's just Fergal – Fergal Dooley. He's – with us–" She paused and glanced at Julie, then added, "in a way."

"Ah, I see. How do you do, Fergal? I'm Anne Wellington." The boy looked up, smiled nervously, but did not speak. Then he looked down at his cap. Anne turned back to Claire and Julie.

"Well then, about Marie – she has such lovely hair – perhaps a comb. Or think about what she wears to work – maybe a brooch or small lapel pin. You should try Besse Mills on Suffolk Street," added Anne, referring to the largest women's clothier in Holyoke. "They have a wonderful selection of ladies' fineries and accessories. I'm certain you will find something there."

Claire and Julie thanked Anne and were about to leave when Anne spoke up again. "Oh, Claire, don't forget that lecture on the dinosaur tracks. It is this Friday evening. Jack will be there. Maybe you and Julie could come." Claire smiled and nodded, then Anne added, "You're welcome to come as well, young man – I bet you'd find it fascinating." Again Fergal looked up at Anne briefly, his face reddened, then he nodded once.

~ 12 ~

*Z*wei Bier bitte," called Hank Köhler to the bartender as he and Jake Muller slid onto narrow wooden stools in *Das Bierhaus*, a dark, dingy saloon several steps down from the sidewalk on Jackson Street, in the heart of Holyoke's German neighborhood. Only a block away from the massive Germania Mills, it was a popular gathering spot for workers before or after their shifts at the mill, although on this rainy evening the two friends had the place nearly to themselves. On a high shelf above the bar stood a collection of dozens of antique German beer steins. The walls were adorned with fading prints meant to trigger nostalgia for the customers' homeland – a Berlin street scene, a sweeping view of the Bavarian Alps, a barge plying the waters of the Rhine.

At nineteen, Jake Muller was already a veteran mill-worker. His parents, having emigrated from Germany three decades earlier, lived in a tenement owned by the mill on Park Street. Their children were christened at the German Evangelical Lutheran Church down the street and attended the church's grammar school. During summers while he was still in school, Jake hefted bales of wool in the sorting house at Wellington Textiles alongside Jack Bernard, then left school to work full-time. He was dark-haired, short and muscular, a smiling, willing worker capable of the most physically demanding tasks the mill could require of him. Just a few months earlier he had moved out of his parent's apartment and found a room in Mrs. Collins' boarding house on Chestnut Street. Unfortunately, his meagre paycheck barely covered room and board, and his rent was now in arrears, a situation he knew must soon be rectified.

Hank Köhler was several years older than Jake. Born in the German industrial city of Essen, he came to Holyoke with his family when he was ten and had been working at Germania Mills since he was fourteen. His mother's death and his father's drunken rages made life in the Köhler household unbearable and Hank eventually moved out. He was now renting a room in a shabby boarding house near the mill. His face was narrow, his features sharp, his mouth formed into a permanent sneer. These days when he and Jake talked, he spoke of little but his hatred of the mill, the city, and the life he had been dragged into when his parents emigrated.

The pair sat in brooding silence until tall steins of Holsten Pilsener were placed before them.

"I gotta find another job – soon," began Jake after taking a first, long sip of his beer. "Any openings at Germania you know about?"

Hank shook his head and grunted in disgust. "You sure you wanna work in that dump?"

"Well, yeh," replied Jake enthusiastically. "I don't care what the work's like, I jus' gotta make a few more bucks is all."

"It's a crap-hole, that's what it is. The bosses, they're jackasses – the owners are worse. Wouldn't give a plug nickel for the lot of 'em. I thought you had a good job at Wellington anyway. What happened, they fire you? Catch you stealing?"

"Nah, nothin' like that. What they're payin', it ain't nearly enough. All they care 'bout's the almighty dollar. And they don't mind how they get it. Makin' a mint on the war – uniforms, tents. What a waste, you know?" Jake knew enough about Hank to know how to get him riled up.

"Hmph," replied Hank scornfully. "Our infantry's rollin' now – broke through the Allied defenses in Belgium and northern France. Von Hindenburg, von Kluck, they know what they're doin'. They'll be marchin' into Paris a few weeks from now, and when they do, the French army's gonna collapse like a house a cards. They got nothin'– nothin'."

Jake nodded in agreement. "Them U-boats are everywhere, too. Got the Brits outclassed by a mile. And the Yanks – they don't know the first thing about submarine warfare."

"All this war hoopla," added Hank, shaking his head. "Wait 'til a few of Uncle Sam's troop ships get torpedoed – all of a sudden these people gonna change their tune, just watch 'em."

The banter grew louder and more boisterous as the two young men finished their first tall mugs of ale.

"God, I hate this place," continued Hank. "Soon as the war's over I'm goin' back home. My uncle works in a big factory in Essen. He says he can get me a job there, too. That's where the future is, *Mein Junge*." They clinked their mugs and took deep pulls on their lagers.

The bartender and owner, Bruno Wyss, was always careful not to be drawn into political arguments, knowing too well what they could lead to when mixed with lots of strong lager. He stood drying glasses at the far end of the bar.

"*Auch das Vaterland–*" slurred Hank loudly, "to the Fatherland." Bruno shot Hank a stern look, then went back to drying glassware.

"*– das Vaterland,*" replied Jake, sloshing his beer onto his shirt as he shouted.

Hank turned to see if anyone else in the bar was listening. It was only then that he realized there was but one other customer, an older man seated in the shadows at a small table near the back. The man looked up briefly, acknowledging Hank with a brief wave of his stein.

"Manfred, hey, didn't see you there," shouted Hank. The man kicked two chairs away from his table and waved them over.

"Come on, Jake, I'll introduce ya to a comrade."

A few minutes later the three were seated around the table, their steins refilled. The older man raised his and growled, "*Prost.*"

Hank introduced Jake. "This is Manfred, Manfred Becker – from Germania Mills. Manfred, this here's my chum Jake, Jake Muller."

Manfred shook Jake's hand and smiled briefly. The three sat in silence for a moment, savoring their lagers.

Finally Hank broke the silence. "Jake here's been at Wellington – what, couple a years, Jake?"

"Almost five now. Since I turned fourteen."

"Yeh, well, I worked there, too, once," explained Manfred. "Hated that place. Lousy job, lousy boss, lousy pay. Then they cut our pay – cheap bastards. I told 'em to shove it, walked right out the door."

"Pay's still low," replied Jake.

"So, you plannin' on going back home after the war like your buddy here?" asked Manfred.

"Maybe, maybe so," replied Jake haltingly, masking his surprise. Returning to Germany was something that had never, ever occurred to him before, yet it seemed a sentiment he ought to embrace at the moment. "But I gotta save some money first, I'm outta do-re-mi. You know of any jobs?"

Manfred gazed into Jake's face and smiled briefly. Then he turned and looked at Hank. He saw two strong young men, smart, but not too smart – just the kind he needed. He looked around briefly. Bruno was in the back room now, well out of earshot, so it was just the three of them. He turned back to the pair and leaned toward them.

"I just might have a little extra work for both you boys, I just might – if you're interested." At that moment Bruno reappeared, so the man lowered his voice to a whisper.

"Listen," he continued gravely, "you guys wanna help the cause, right? I mean – *das Vaterland*?" They nodded and leaned in. "Okay, I got a job for ya – the both of ya. But this is strictly confidential, got it? Just between us." The pair nodded eagerly. "I mean it – word gets out, there'll be trouble – for me – for you – big trouble. Get my meaning?" Again the pair nodded.

"Awright, then, listen good. I need you guys to make a pickup for me – up north. You gotta drive my truck to New Hampshire – six, seven hours. Meet some comrades – at night. They'll have some stuff, okay? All yous gotta do is load it in the truck – get it back to 'olyoke before dawn. That's it. Whatta you say?"

"When?" asked Hank.

"Can't say until I get the word – so you gotta be ready on short notice."

"Why at night?" replied Hank.

"Less risk, is all."

"Risk? What's the risk? Stolen goods, you mean?"

"Nah, nah, nothin' like that," responded Manfred. "But the fewer people see you on the road, the better."

"So, we get paid?" asked Hank.

"Yeh, sure, I'll give you fifty bucks – twenty-five each – when you deliver the stuff. But remember – you're doin' it for the cause, not for the money. Right?"

Jake was obviously excited, but Hank was uneasy. "This stuff – what is it, booze or something?"

"Don't you worry 'bout it. Just make the pickup, deliver it. *Alle für Deutschland,* boys, that's all you need to know." He looked at Hank. "We'll meet right here, soon as I get the word, and I'll tell you everything – where, when, how."

Hank nodded. Manfred turned to Jake who was smiling, then reached out, grabbed his coat lapel, and yanked it as he spoke through clenched teeth: "Listen, kid, you spill this to anyone – *anyone* – you'll be pushin' up daisies – or maybe swingin' from a tree with a nice view a dem daisies – am I makin' myself clear?"

Jake nodded, his smile vanished, his face suddenly turned pale.

"And you?" asked Manfred, looking at Hank who nodded. Then Manfred relaxed his grip on Jake's jacket and smiled. "I knew I could count on you guys – real patriots."

~ *13* ~

It was five o'clock Friday afternoon and the usually calm and self-possessed Anne Wellington was a nervous Nellie as the hour of the lecture approached at the Women's Home in Holyoke. In between attending to new arrivals at the office, she had spent an inordinate amount of time arranging and re-arranging the chairs in the lounge, sweeping and dusting the room and then, for extra measure, sweeping and dusting again. At her request several of the residents had fashioned a garland of ferns and autumn leaves to hang over the entrance. Upon the several windowsills she had placed arrangements of chrysanthemums and daisies in milk glass vases, each of which she plucked at again and again in an effort to achieve just the desired effect, all the while in a low voice running through the introduction she had memorized.

She wanted the event to go perfectly, not only because it would draw attention to the lecture series but because of the distinguished speaker and her hopes that his topic would prove popular to the residents and guests. She was also uneasy knowing that several members of the Home's board of directors would be present including her mother. She was naturally looking forward to seeing Jack, but a bit unnerved at the thought of his presence and the additional pressure that would place on her to do her best.

Professor Smith arrived early and began setting up some equipment. He had neglected to tell Anne that he would be bringing a Magic Lantern and she was flustered as he began to move chairs for placement of a small table to support the device, then further shaken as he climbed onto the windowsills to lower the seldom-used shades. In so doing he knocked over one of the vases which shattered sending water, flowers, and bits of glass hurtling across the floor. All was not lost, however, as the debris was quickly cleaned up, a damp spot on the carpet the only evidence remaining from the debacle.

By twenty minutes past six o'clock only three residents had arrived and they sat tentatively in the back row, as if they might leave at any moment. But in the last ten minutes many more residents appeared and a surprising number of outside guests entered, most apparently friends or co-workers of the residents. Also arriving were Charles and Claire Bernard and Fergal Dooley. Marie had sent her regrets as she was working the evening shift at the telephone office. Jack, who would be arriving directly from Worcester on his motorcycle, was nowhere to be found as the clock struck the half hour.

Her stomach in a veritable knot, Anne stepped to the front of the room and smiled at the nearly two dozen in attendance. Slowly she began her introduction of Professor Smith. At first her unease was apparent, but as she spoke her usual air of self-confidence returned, her voice became stronger, her smile more convincing. Just as she finished her introduction, Jack entered at the back of the room. She smiled at him, then at the audience generally.

"Ladies and gentlemen, it is my pleasure to introduce Dr. Henry Smith, Visiting Professor of Paleontology, Yale University, for this evening's lecture, *Evidence for ancient reptilian quadrupeds in the Connecticut River Valley*. Professor Smith."

A ripple of applause greeted the professor as he rose from his chair and faced the audience.

"Thank you, Miss – er – Miss Wellington – for your k–kind words of introduction. I – I am – that is I hope I may–" He stood stone-faced, then turned and looked at Anne who was now seated at the end of the first row of chairs. She smiled brightly and nodded encouragingly. The professor returned her smile, then continued.

"My topic this evening are the – is the very interesting, extraordinary, actually – profusion of evidence laid down in the Triassic strata of this famous valley of the mighty Connecticut River, evidence of the peculiar denizens that wandered this valley long ago." Again he turned his gaze toward Anne who smiled reassuringly.

"First let me say that the study of these w–w–wonders was the work of the late P-P-President Hitchcock of Amherst College. Their elucidation was only one of the many scientific achievements of that distinguished gentleman – in geology, paleontology, botany, physiology, theology – he was truly a genius and I – we all are in his debt for his p–p–pioneering work in many fields."

"This evening I shall endeavor to – to convey to you some of the insights we have gained from those tracks in stone – *footprints on the sands of time,* they have been called. This is by no means a finished study, but rather a work in progress that c–c–continues to this day. I have for you just a few photographs in my Magic Lantern that will I hope aid in visualizing my subjects."

The professor turned to the box of tin and glass on an elevated table at the center of the room. Anne stood and extinguished two gas lamps at the rear. A gray, fuzzy image appeared on the wall. The guests buzzed at the sight. The professor bent over the lantern, fiddling with the knobs and lenses. Gradually the image sharpened, and as it did, gasps arose from the audience.

"Here we have an artist's rendition of the setting at that time. What we today call the Connecticut River Valley was much wider then, a broad lowland bounded on both east and west by elevated terrain. Sediments carried down from those higher regions were regularly deposited in the valley in the form of broad mudflats. Without this source of water and sediment the conditions would not have been suitable for formation of animal tracks."

He removed the image of the artist's sketch and quickly replaced it with a photograph. "Here we see just a small section of the excavation at Smith's Ferry where I have been working for several months. As you can see there are dozens of tracks – impressions in the sandstone. Most of these may be seen to be three-toed, though some are four or five, with digits sometimes appearing webbed much like those of waterfowl."

Again several young ladies in the audience gasped. "From the outset Professor Hitchcock and many of his c–c– contemporaries attributed these marks to avians – birds – or at least bird-like creatures. In this next photograph may be seen a grid of twine laid over the rock at three-foot intervals. As you may observe, the tracks vary in length from eight inches to upwards of two feet."

"Those would have been enormous birds, Professor," commented one young lady, shaking her head in disbelief.

The professor nodded and smiled. "Indeed. Made, no doubt, by creatures that no longer exist anywhere in our world."

"Victims, perhaps, of the Deluge described in Genesis in the Holy Bible," another guest interjected.

Again the professor nodded. "In fact they – the creatures that created these tracks – have been referred to as *Noah's raven*. According to the Bible, when the Ark was adrift on the seas during the Great Flood, Noah dispatched a large bird to fly out across the vast waters in search of land. Hence the name."

"So the biblical legend is proven."

Professor Smith paused, smiled, then nodded. "Perhaps so – perhaps so – although according to Scripture the inundation occurred but a few thousand years ago. The Triassic period of these tracks is – well – considerably before that time."

"Well, how much earlier, Professor?"

"Approximately 200 million years before the present."

A collective gasp rose as the audience contemplated this.

"I realize," continued the professor, "that such an expanse of time contradicts many long-held beliefs about God's creation, but the scientific evidence is really quite consistent and unequivocal."

"Do you mean, Professor Smith – are you suggesting that the Good Book is in error?"

"Ma'am, I have the greatest respect for the Christian faith. I myself was raised within the Lutheran Church and continue to adhere to my faith despite what I know to be scientific fact. After all, who in this day and age takes every word of Scripture literally? Surely we do not advocate stoning as proper punishment for a rebellious child, nor death for an adulterer – or one who does work on the Sabbath." He paused. "The Gospels were not written by scientists and we cannot use the Bible as a basis of our knowledge on such matters. We must rely on factual information whenever possible, on pure and natural science."

There followed a good deal of murmuring among the audience.

"Professor," came a man's voice from the rear. "You advocate strict adherence to the truth, so why then have you deceived your audience?"

"Deceived?" replied the professor.

"Yes, deceived, Herr Schmidt." A heavy, uncomfortable silence fell over the room. "Doktor Heinrich Schmidt, if I am not mistaken? Born in Hamburg, Germany, educated at the University there. Only recently arrived in America, and having returned to the Fatherland on numerous occasions since emigrating. Is that not so?"

The professor's face was suddenly bright red and he was sweating profusely. There was a long silence as the audience awaited his reply.

"It is true, sir, quite true that I am German by birth. I did read geology at Hamburg. And then received my doctor's degree at Edinburgh. From there my wife and I traveled to Colorado where I have been on the faculty in geology for over twenty years. But I am now a naturalized citizen of the United States and proud to be. I have no reason to hide any of this. It has nothing to do with my work."

"Then why present yourself as Professor Henry Smith?"

"When we arrived in America my wife and I decided to anglicize our names. It is a common practice among many immigrants to America. We wish to be regarded like any other American citizens, that is all."

"And as an American citizen, what is your position on the war in Europe? Are you sympathetic with the Kaiser and his military ambitions, Herr Schmidt?"

At that moment Helen Wellington stood up. She had recognized the speaker and her blood was boiling. "Mr. Whittemore, we have gathered here this evening for a discussion of science, not of political philosophy."

"Ma'am, I only wish to inquire of the speaker's loyalties," replied Whittemore.

"Sir," Helen responded, her ire growing with every word, "you have had ample opportunity to express your opinions in the *Transcript*, distasteful though they may be to many of us. I would ask that you spare us all your grandstanding this evening and allow the professor to continue his lecture." With that a ripple of applause rose from a number of members of the audience while others sat in confused silence.

Finally the professor continued, though clearly flustered and upset. After about forty-five minutes, he concluded. "Well, then, if there are no further questions – thank you all for your attention and do f-feel free to come forward if you have additional questions. I have copies of one of my monographs at the rear – p-please take one if you like."

With that the event ended. As the guests rose, several stepped forward to speak to the professor. Among them was Helen Wellington.

"Professor Smith, my name is Helen Wellington. Anne is my daughter. I want to thank you for your fascinating lecture – and apologize for the rudeness of Mr. Whittemore – that man is despicable."

Anne had been shaken by the confrontation and she was standing with Jack at the rear of the room. "He never told me he was German," she was whispering. "Not that it matters, really, but–" She could see that the professor was beginning to pack up his equipment and she spoke to him. "I am so very sorry, Professor Smith."

The professor shook his head. "It is not your fault, Miss Wellington. I suppose it is to be expected. Everyone is on edge these days, understandably. If you are from Germany, or Austria, or anywhere thereabouts, you are distrusted. You see, I thought I would be speaking solely to residents of the Women's Home this evening. I had no idea you were planning to invite the public. If I had known–"

"Again I apologize, Professor Smith, I am really, truly sorry. But I wish people like Mr. Whittemore would take the time to learn the truth. You are as patriotic as the next person. After all, you have a son and a son-in-law fighting for the Allies in Europe."

The professor nodded, then shrugged his shoulders. "It is quite – understandable."

Helen spoke up. "No, Professor, it is inexcusable."

"Pardon me, Professor Smith," said Claire, holding a copy of his monograph. "Would you please sign this for me? I'll put it in my remembrance book."

The professor smiled. "I would be delighted, young lady. I remember you, from Smith's Ferry — a future paleontologist, perhaps?"

Claire returned his smiled. "We'll see." The professor inscribed the document, then handed it back to Claire.

"I know a place near my house where there is lots of ledges kinda like Smith's Ferry, Professor. Do you suppose there could be dinosaur tracks there?"

"Quite likely, miss, possibly – well, you never know. It would bear exploration."

"What's that?" Claire asked, pointing to what looked like hieroglyphics scrawled across the cover page of the monograph. The professor's inscription read, "To Claire Bernard, future paleontologist – ερώτηση πάντα."

"It's Greek, young lady. It's a quote from the famous Greek philosopher Euripides." Then he pronounced the Greek slowly and carefully, syllable by syllable: "Air – oh – tes – ay pahn – da."

"But what does it mean?" asked Claire.

The man looked her squarely in the eyes and spoke softly but emphatically: "Question everything."

"Oh, Jackie, I wish you didn't have to go back to Worcester so soon," complained Anne the next day when he made a brief visit with her in Holyoke. They strolled together through the rose garden, heady fragrances still rising with the warmth of the October sun.

"I have two big tests and a recitation to prepare for next week. I'm sorry." He stopped and turned toward Anne. "On top o' that, I have two football matches this week."

"Football? Since when?"

"Some of the fellows in our house talked me into joinin' the football club." He rolled his eyes. "Just what I need is more to do."

"Well, you could have declined, Jackie, couldn't you? Tell them you're too busy."

Jack grinned. "I don't know, it's fun. They're a good bunch and they keep tellin' me how bad the team needs me. We play our first match against Thompson House tomorrow afternoon."

"What does your father say about that?"

"Dad? Oh, he's keen on it. Says he's gonna come to one of our games someday, him and Felix. They expect to go to Worcester soon to pick up some equipment for the garage – a hydraulic lift, some jacks."

"Well, maybe I could come to a game sometime, too, hmm?" The couple walked through the Wellingtons' rose garden where a few blossoms remained even though a hard frost had laid low most of the other flowers in the gardens.

"So what's new with Carolyn these days? You've hardly mentioned her," Jack asked.

They sat on a granite bench in the sun. "Well, I can't say as I have much to report. All I've heard is what her mother says at work, and, well, you know how she feels. She was dead set against Carolyn going off to college to begin with, and now all she does is worry about her."

"Do you think when the war is over and Tommy comes back, that the two of them will finally – well, get together?"

Anne looked away, fearful of revealing the truth about the couple. She sighed, took a deep breath, then turned to Jack, shaking her head. "I don't know, Jackie – I just don't know." Anxious to change the topic, she reached out and stroked his hair, then kissed him lightly on the cheek. "Speaking of getting together, when am I going to see you again, Jack? Please say it will be next weekend."

Jack smiled, then shook his head. "Two matches, one Friday afternoon, another Sunday."

"So, this is how it's going to be now that my beau is an All-American, hmm?" she asked with a twinkle in her eye.

"It's just intramural sports, Annie, and the football season ends before Thanksgiving."

"Well, you'd better be on your best behavior, Jack Bernard, because one day soon your dear Anne is going to make an appearance at one of your matches, and she'll be mightily aggrieved if the bleachers are filled with other female admirers." She gave him a knowing wink, recalling just such an unfortunate event that had come between them a few years earlier when Jack was on the track team at Holyoke High School.

Jack blushed but smiled. "That's ancient history, Anne, long ago and forgotten."

"Long ago, perhaps, Jack – but *not* forgotten," she replied with a wry smile.

They walked hand-in-hand to the driveway where Jack donned his goggles and prepared for the motorcycle ride back to Worcester.

~ 14 ~

On Tuesday Anne received a long letter from Jack written after Sunday's match recounting the important plays of the game. He made little of his role, although several of his teammates had heaped praise upon him for his defensive performance. Anne laughed as she read his letter. But on Wednesday morning another letter arrived, a letter that changed her mood abruptly. It was from Tom and addressed to her at the Women's Home. As she sat at her desk reading, the color in her cheeks faded:

> *September the 28th*
> *Dear Annie,*
>
> *I have just written to Mother and Father but wanted to say a few things just for your eyes. That is why I am addressing this letter to you at your work rather than at home.*
>
> *I hope you are not worrying. I am doing fine. I do wonder about the future and when I think about it I cannot help but think also of the past. I know I caused you, Mother and Father a lot of heartache and I wish I could go back and change that. Dearest sister, you stood by me through the worst of it for which I will always be grateful. I remember how you tried to help me understand how Matthew's death affected me. I have not gotten over his accident and doubt I ever will no matter how long I live. I know that now.*

Enclosed is a letter in a sealed envelope. It is for Carolyn, but please give this to her only in the event that the worst happens. I beg you not to tell her about it unless it becomes necessary. I cannot say more now.

We are very busy aboard ship these days and have little free time. Which is as well. When I have too much time on my hands I start to think about what may be coming. It is better that I just allow my work to absorb all my attentions.

Annie, please forgive my many trespasses and always think well of me as I surely will of you.

Your loving brother,
Tommy

"Ahem, Mister Bernard, may I have a word?" asked Miss Hulbert, matron of Jack's dormitory, as he returned from his last class. She was tall, stern-faced, and she glowered at him over a pince-nez perched precariously on her nose.

"Yes, ma'am?" replied Jack.

"You had a call – on the telephone – a young lady – a Miss Wilmington."

"Oh?"

"I told her she would have to call back at five," she added curtly.

"Oh, sure, yes ma'am, I'll be here right at five."

"See that you are, then. I can't be chasing around after you. And mind that the office closes sharp at quarter past."

As promised Jack returned at five, excited to speak to Anne but at the same time worried. She had not written him in several days. As he sat on a hard wooden chair in the foyer outside the dormitory office, he tried not to think too much, to worry too much about why Anne would be calling him.

Several minutes went by and Jack watched anxiously as three classmates played backgammon at a table nearby. Other young men came and went noisily, some returning from classes, others heading out for intramural sports.

"Hey, Bernard, we got football practice in ten minutes at Alumni Field. Better get a move on."

Jack nodded. "Okay, yup, I'll be there."

Just then the telephone in the office jangled. He could hear Miss Hulbert's voice. "Yes. One moment." Then she appeared in the office doorway glaring at Jack: "Mr. Bernard? Hurry now." She thrust the handset toward him. Jack rose and stepped through the office door. "Keep it short, young man, this is not a social club."

Jack nodded, grasped the handset, and stood leaning against the wall. "Hello? Annie?"

"Hello, Jackie," she replied. "Can you hear me?"

"Yes, just fine. "

"It's good to hear your voice, Jackie. How are you?"

"I'm fine, Annie, just fine."

"How is the weather in Worcester, Jackie?"

"Oh, it's agreeable, you know, a bit of rain last night. But today it's been sunny and—" His eyes met Miss Hulbert's which were shifting from him to the clock on the wall and back. "Everything all right, Annie?"

"Jackie." Anne's voice suddenly dropped to a whisper. "Jackie, I'm worried."

"Why? What's the matter? What's happened?"

He waited for several seconds. Finally, Anne replied. "Jackie – I – I received a letter from Tommy in the morning post – it frightened me."

"Why? Whatta ya mean?"

"It didn't sound like Tommy at all – he – he seemed – worried – down." She paused. "You know how he is, usually, as though he hasn't a care in the world and everything is just splendid? He seemed different, Jackie – unlike himself. He said he was nervous – about the future. He went on about his regrets, about what he had put me and Mother and Father through, about his troubles – his – habits – and about Matthew."

"Well, I suppose it's to be expected – in wartime."

"But his ship. If it's only escorting troop ships between California and Virginia, why would he be —"

"Well, there's always dangers, you know. And maybe he's just – homesick."

"Jackie." She paused again. "There's one other thing."

Just then Miss Hulbert spoke to Jack. "All right, Mr. Bernard, you'll have to be ending the call. We're closing up now."

Jack nodded and held up one finger. "Just one more minute, ma'am."

"What did you say, Jackie?" replied Anne.

"I'm sorry, Annie. I was speaking to someone in the office. I can't talk much more."

"Jackie – in his letter was a small sealed envelope – for Carolyn."

"Oh?"

"He said—" Again Anne's voice grew thin. "He said to give it to her only if – if the worst happened." Now she was crying and Jack's heart was breaking, he wanted so to hold her and reassure her. Meanwhile Miss Hulbert was approaching, a stern expression on her face.

"Everything is going to be all right, Annie. I know it is. Don't worry. I have to hang up now but I'll write you tonight."

"All right, Jackie. Thank you, Jackie. I love you."

Jack was now eye to eye with Miss Hulbert. "Yeh, me too. Goodbye, Annie." He gently placed the handset on the hook.

"Thank you, ma'am," he said brightly, smiling, then turned and walked briskly out the door and across the green toward Alumni Field.

Late that evening Jack sat at the small desk in his room, pen in hand, looking down at a blank piece of stationery. He wanted to write Anne and reassure her without sounding like a Pollyanna. But he couldn't think of how to begin or what to say. Truthfully, he thought, he was as worried about Tom as she.

Instead he began the letter recounting the football game that he had joined after their telephone conversation. Then he wrote about a hilarious prank perpetrated by several of his dormitory mates late the previous night that involved climbing out on the dormitory roof and hanging a lantern from the outstretched hand of Athena, the Greek goddess, perched high above the greensward. Finally, he paused and reread what he had written. For a moment he sat gazing blankly through the writing paper, thinking – then abruptly crumpled it, tossed it aside, and sat shaking his head. In the end he wrote a short note, trying his best to be optimistic, and urging Anne not to get discouraged. At the bottom of the page he paused again for a long time, then added simply *Yours always, Jack.*

~ 15 ~

It was a blustery Friday afternoon as two football teams faced off at Alumni Field. Jack's team had just scored a touchdown and was running back upfield when Jack heard the team captain call his name from the sideline. He stopped and turned, hands on hips, looking mystified. Standing next to the captain he saw his father waving toward him. Another player ran out to take Jack's place as he walked slowly from the field.

"Dad – hey, Dad – what are you doin' here?"

"Just thought your team needed a little encouragement, 's all."

"Well, thanks. I'm kinda surprised the old Model-T made it."

"Yeh, well, it didn't. I mean, Felix let me borrow his new truck."

Suddenly Jack felt uneasy. "Dad – what is it? Is something wrong?"

Charles winced, his face now pallid. "Son, I got a call on the telephone this morning – from Anne. It's – about Tom."

Jack's blood suddenly went cold.

"His ship – they got a telegram from the Navy late last evenin' – it went down – torpedo hit it – somewhere off France." Jack gasped. His father continued. "They say a few sailors were rescued – but the rest are – well – all they say now is missing – missing in action – that's all they know."

Jack slumped to the ground, his head between his knees, his breathing labored as he struggled to bring his emotions under control. Finally he spoke without looking up: "How's Annie doin', Dad?"

"Well, you know – they're all in a state. She asked me to tell you – she couldn' bring herself to even post a letter this morning – so I decided to come myself. I'm sorry, Son."

"But his ship – they were only goin' to the west coast and back – that's what Anne's uncle said."

"Yeh, well, I guess he got it wrong. Maybe that's what the Navy wanted folks to think. From the sounds of it things have been goin' badly in France and Belgium the last month or so. Mr. Wilson and General Pershing decided everything had to be speeded up, includin' gettin' our boys over there."

"I gotta see Anne, Dad. I gotta– "

"Well, I was tinkin' maybe you could come back home with me now – spend the weekend with her – I bet she'd 'preciate it. We can get you back on Sunday one way or other."

Jack rushed back to his dormitory room and hurriedly stuffed a few essentials in a duffle bag. He paused in front of his dresser, gazing at a photograph of him and Tom swimming in the Westfield River when they were fourteen or so. He swallowed hard and fought back tears. Outside he clambered into the waiting truck and it sputtered away.

Hardly a word passed between father and son until they were well out of the city and moving along more smoothly through the countryside.

"What do I do, Dad? I haven't the first idea what I should say when I see Anne and her parents."

"Son, you won't need to say a word to that girl. Just sit with her – that's enough." He paused. "Ya know – ya might not remember much 'bout when your sister passed, but your mother was – well, she was beyond consolin' – I felt so 'elpless. Just sittin' with 'er, holdin' 'er hand – makin' 'er tea – that was all I could do. An' tellin' 'er it weren't anyone's fault, too. 'Cause she was lookin' to blame 'erself."

Jack nodded. "That's what Annie's gonna say, she should never a let Tommy enlist – I just know it. But jeez, he'd already made his mind up – I mean, he knew weeks before he told them

– even when Congress voted not to draft eighteen-year-olds, that didn't change his mind for a second. He was bound an' determined."

Another long silence fell over the two as the truck chugged through the Brookfields. The skyline was as lovely as always, Jack noted – blue sky streaked with wispy clouds like horsetails, distant hills incandescent in the late day sun. How unfair, he thought, that there should be all this beauty, this tranquility, while soldiers and sailors were fighting – and dying – in Europe.

"They must have rescue boats out there," said Jack at last. "Don't they have boats patrolling, looking for life-rafts – survivors?"

"I bet they do, Son, I'm sure they do. And they're doin' everything they can to save our boys, be sure of that."

Again a pall fell over father and son as the truck made the last ten-mile leg from Palmer to Holyoke. As they approached the bridge that spanned the river between Chicopee and Holyoke, Charles pulled the vehicle to a halt on a grassy shoulder. "How's 'bout if you take the truck and drop me at the trolley stand on High Street? That way you can stay as late as you want with Anne."

Jack agreed. The two swapped positions and Jack dropped his father off in downtown Holyoke, then with a heavy heart made his way up the hill to Anne's house. Normally a visit to that house, seeing Anne, made his heart pound. His heart was pounding today, for sure, but it was all different.

One of the Wellingtons' maids, her eyes moist and red, greeted Jack somberly at the door and ushered him into the parlor. Flames crackled in the fireplace but no one was seated before it. "I'll tell Miss Anne you are here," she added. Several minutes elapsed before he heard soft slippers on the stairs, then

Anne appeared in the doorway. She was calm and composed, but Jack had never seen her look so poorly, so utterly forlorn. Her usually rosy complexion was ashen, her eyes that could shine so brightly now a dull gray.

Jack stepped toward her, wrapping his long arms around her slender frame and holding her as tenderly as he knew how. Her composure almost instantly disintegrated. She cried softly into his shoulder as he stroked her hair. It was matted where she had been lying on it and he gently combed out the tangles with his fingers.

Finally, after what seemed like many minutes, Anne steadied herself, leaned back against Jack's arms, looked into his grayish-blue eyes, and spoke softly. "Thank you, Jackie – for coming. Did you ride your motorcycle?"

Jack smiled, then shook his head. "Nah, it's up on blocks, prob'ly for the winter. Dad come to get me."

She stroked his hair. "Time for Marie to give you a trim." Jack nodded and smiled. He looked squarely into her eyes and her chin began to tremble. "Oh, Jackie, what are we going to do if – if Tommy – what if we've lost him?"

Just then footsteps could be heard in the hallway. Anne separated from Jack and the couple stood awkwardly as Helen Wellington appeared at the door. Her face was puffy and red, although she wore a convincing smile as she always did, and it reminded Jack of the first time he met her, in this very room. She seemed so happy then, the day after Christmas nearly six years ago, but he had felt then that there was something unspoken and painful hiding behind her smile. He was right, it turned out. It was the still fresh ache for her oldest child, Matthew, who had been lost. And now–

"Good gracious, hello young man. How kind of you to come – we've been missing you. I hope you didn't have to miss your classes."

Jack could not bring himself to mention Tom. "No, not at all, ma'am."

Soon Mr. Wellington appeared, walking with a cane in one hand, his nurse on his other arm. He greeted Jack with a smile. "Thank you, my boy, for comin' by. How's college life goin'?"

Jack was relieved to be provided a topic and he started going on about his classes, dormitory meals, and some of the antics of his classmates. Casual conversation continued for some time. It was nearly six o'clock when Jack turned to Anne. "Well, I'd better be gettin' home."

Anne took his hand and spoke softly. "Won't you stay for supper, Jackie? Mildred's expecting you. You can use the telephone to call Marie."

Jack agreed and made the telephone call from the library. Carefully he replaced the handset, then stood, his eye scanning the room, its shelves lined with leather-bound volumes – the complete works of Thackeray, Proust, the poems of the Brownings and Longfellow. There was a large, brightly colored globe mounted on a mahogany stand by the window – he spun it absently. Then his gaze fell on a painting hanging on the wall, a Wellington family portrait – Helen and Thomas Wellington and their three children, Matthew, Anne – and Tom, a young Tom, innocent, smiling. Jack's eyes smarted. Finally he turned and found Anne standing in the doorway. She shut the door behind her, then took his hand and led him to the settee by the window. She clearly could not bring herself to look at the painting.

"Jackie, I'm so scared. I need you to help me be – be brave. Will you help me?"

"Of course, Annie, of course," whispered Jack.

"I want to be brave, Jackie, I do so want to. But what if – I mean what if his ship went right to the bottom – and he and all those men were just—" She shuddered. "It's just too terrible for words, Jackie."

"That ship, Annie – it's over three hundred feet long – that's longer than a football field. A ship like that's not gonna go down in seconds no matter where it's hit. And if he was in the radio room at the time, he probably had a good chance of gettin' to a lifeboat. We know they picked up some of her crew, right? I'm sure they're out there lookin' for more."

Anne nodded, a hopeful look in her eyes. "Jackie, I – I need to tell Carolyn. She should know as soon as possible."

"Why don't you write her tomorrow, first thing. They're good friends, she would want to know."

Anne shook her head. "No, Jackie, a letter will not do. I must talk to her myself. Jackie–" She was obviously struggling with herself.

"What, Annie?"

She breathed deeply, gazing out the window. Then she turned to him. "Jackie, Carolyn and Tommy are *not* just good friends."

"What?"

"Jackie, there is something you should know about Tom and Carolyn. I have wanted to tell you, to confide in you, for the longest time, but I felt I – I–"

"What is it, Annie? Please tell me. What about Tommy and Carolyn?"

Anne took his hand in hers and stroked it softly. Her eyes rose to his as she spoke. "Jackie, my brother and Carolyn – are engaged."

Jack's jaw dropped and his eyes grew large. "What? When did this happen?"

"The day he left for the Navy. You remember – I told you – about the morning that Tommy was leaving for Newport, how he asked us not to accompany him to the station – he said it would be too hard to say goodbye there. Well, I went anyway. It was not my intention, really, but I was walking to work that morning and it was about the time his train was due, and I just – well, I just kept walking, all the way to the depot. There they were, Tommy and Carolyn, together on the platform. Just then they disappeared behind a stack of freight. It was barely a minute but then they reappeared, kissed, and Tommy started to board the train. I stood beside Carolyn. Tommy turned and waved to us from the train just as the door was closing."

"But how do you know they are engaged?"

"Carolyn turned red as a beet, and she was stammering like I've never seen her, Jackie – it was obvious something was going on between them. One day a few weeks later we had lunch together at Hampden Park – Carolyn was still working at Gregoire's Shoe Shop then. We were talking about Tommy and I saw her reach for something on a silver necklace. It was hidden just beneath the collar of her shirtwaist. That's when I really began to suspect that he had given her a ring that she was at pains to keep hidden."

"But are you sure?"

Anne nodded. "Remember that envelope I told you about the other day on the telephone, the one addressed to Carolyn and only to be opened if the worst should happen?" Anne paused, then her eyes fell. "Jackie, I opened it."

Jack stared at Anne, his mouth open, but he did not speak.

"I know, Jackie, that I should not have done that. But I had to know. So I put a kettle on the stove and steamed it open. I only read the first sentence – that was enough to confirm my suspicions. He told her that the memory of her, standing on the platform, accepting that ring, and confirming their troth, that it had helped him through the difficult days and weeks leading up to his ship's departure."

Jack buried his face in his hands.

"Please, Jackie, don't think badly of me. I know it was a violation, but I had to know. I could not imagine delivering that envelope to Carolyn not knowing what it would say, how it might affect her. Now at least I know, it was Tommy at his sweetest, most sincere. It will break her heart, I know, but maybe it will also be of some consolation."

Jack looked up and into Anne's eyes. He hesitated, not sure how to proceed, but he felt he needed to say something, to provide some solace. "Annie, your brother is the strongest, most determined boy I've ever known. He's strong in muscle but even more in heart. What I'm tryin' to say is, if there's a chance, the slightest chance, that he can save himself, he will. That's how he is. If he has to swim across the English Channel, or drift about in a lifeboat for days, he's gonna do it, I just know it. So we gotta believe in him, Annie, we gotta."

"I do Jackie, I do."

"Maybe, just maybe, you'll never have to deliver that letter to Carolyn."

"Oh, Jackie, I dearly hope you are right. But Carolyn is my best, oldest friend, and her fiancé is – missing – at sea. I need to see her, to tell her – in person."

"Of course, yup, uh-huh."

"The problem is that she is staying at school this weekend. Her mother told me – she of course is worried sick every minute about Carolyn. Would you take me, Jackie, tomorrow?"

"Eh, yeh, sure, I can do that."

"We can take Father's motorcar. I – I could ask Bromley to take me and Mother, I thought about that. But I know what she is thinking right now, she wants to be at home in case there is word." Jack nodded. "And Jackie, I need you there. This – this will be the most difficult thing I have ever had to do in my life. I – I just know I'll need you."

The Wellingtons' Pierce-Arrow was parked at the curb in front of the women's dormitory at Massachusetts Agricultural College the following morning. Jack stood leaning against the gleaming dark green fender, looking up at the three-story brick structure. It had been nearly an hour and he was worried about Anne, and about Carolyn. Young women came and went constantly, all beaming and full of energy. Not too different, he thought, from the scene in front of his dormitory in Worcester, except, of course, for the obvious difference in the sex of the students. As he watched them come and go, he could not help but think about Marie and how he wished she could be pursuing her education, were it not for him. And Claire, he wondered – would his younger sister be able to attend college one day?

Finally Anne and Carolyn appeared in the entrance. Jack stood up and took a few steps up the walk, smiling and waving at Carolyn. But her face was flushed, her delicate eyebrows contracted in a grimace. She gestured briefly to Jack but then retreated. Anne descended the steps alone, then turned once to wave to Carolyn, but she had disappeared inside.

"How did it go, Annie?"

Anne's delicate features twisted and her voice cracked. "Take me home, Jackie, okay?"

As soon as they were underway she began to sob. The motorcar labored up through the Notch south of Amherst. At the summit he steered the long car over onto a gravel pull-out where travelers could stop and admire the view toward South Hadley and Holyoke. He shut off the motor. Anne immediately slid over on the broad front seat, buried her head in his shoulder, and sobbed softly. Jack stroked her hair, then drew her to him.

Back in Holyoke he pulled the car up in front of Sacred Heart, the city's largest cathedral. The massive sanctuary was quiet and nearly deserted but for a few individuals seated near the back, heads bent, lips moving, no doubt repeating the prayers they had learned as children, words that promised mercy, forgiveness, and eternal life to those who believed. For Jack there was an intimacy here, a familiarity, that was welcome and badly needed. He hoped it might have a similar effect on Anne, but her family was Episcopalian, and church attendance was rare.

They prayed in silence. Some twenty minutes later they emerged from the deep, somber dark of the sanctuary into a bright midday sun.

"Thank you, Jackie," offered Anne softly as they walked along the sidewalk. She breathed deeply, feeling some relief and solace. But as they drove up Appleton Street and the Wellington home came into view, the massive weight of worry, of fear, of regret once again bore heavily on her shoulders.

~ 16 ~

Later that day Retired Lieutenant James P. Cooke made an unannounced visit to the Wellington household. As they sat in the parlor, he spoke softly to his sister and brother-in-law.

"Helen, Thomas, I've just been back to Newport and came here immediately to tell you what I've learned."

Helen gasped and held her husband's hand. "James, you have news of Tom?"

"Well, no, not exactly. But I can tell you that a number of sailors from the *York* were rescued the day after the ship went down. They were in lifeboats and had drifted southwest, out of the Channel, into the open sea, nearly fifty miles from where the ship sank. No, Tom was not among those rescued," he explained somberly. "Not yet. I am sorry."

Helen dabbed at her eyes with a hankie as her brother continued. "But as a result of those rescues our search boats have been augmented by British naval and civilian vessels including many fishing boats – they call them the Dover Patrol – trawlers, drifters – even some pleasure yachts. They're covering a wider area in hopes of finding more survivors from the *York* and a smaller English naval vessel that went down the same day in the Channel."

"Oh, James, do you suppose – they'll find more survivors?"

"We must not give up, Sister. There is still hope." Then he spoke with emotion about Tom and how impressed he had been with him on his visit at the Newport Naval Training Station just a few weeks earlier.

Anne had been sleeping since her return from Amherst several hours earlier and Helen chose not to wake her during her Uncle James' visit. But shortly after his departure she tapped on Anne's bedroom door. She sensed that Anne did not have great confidence in her uncle's words, especially since he was proven so terribly misinformed about the *York*'s assignment. So she tried not to overstate what he had told her. The search for survivors was continuing and some sailors from the *York* had been recovered. Nothing more.

Anne's letter to Jack that evening made no mention of her uncle's visit. She only stated to him that she had not yet given up hope. She also reported to Jack on a series of dreams she'd been having, dreams in which Tom appeared smiling and healthy, then faded from view. Each night she woke up with a visceral sense of dread. Her vivid descriptions of her dreams sent a tingle up Jack's spine – for he had been having very similar dreams.

~ 17 ~

Back at school in Worcester, Jack was preparing for examinations scheduled for the following week. He wrote to Anne every day, some days twice, carrying the letters across the campus to the mailroom in hopes of speeding their delivery. He wrote little of Tom. After all, what was there to say? He could think of no words that might offer Anne even the tiniest shred of relief for her worries and fears. Rather he confined himself to accounts of his daily endeavors — classes, assignments, labs, football games — and occasional anecdotes about his housemates and their antics. It all seemed so trivial he thought, so meagre and meaningless compared to trench warfare in Europe, poison gas, U-boat attacks.

Several days went by without a letter from Anne. This began to worry Jack and he considered placing a telephone call to her home, although to do so would mean subjecting himself to the reproaches of Miss Hulbert. But on Thursday morning, a letter arrived from Anne. It was brief, a single sheet, but as he opened the letter a small square of newsprint fell out. It was a clipping from the *Daily Transcript* dated the previous Saturday:

MISSING IN ACTION IN EUROPE
Seaman Thomas A. Wellington III, son of Mr. and Mrs. Thomas A. Wellington of Beech Street, Holyoke, has been reported missing in action by the United States Navy. Seaman Wellington's ship, the USS York, was sunk in the English Channel on Wednesday, October 10, by a German U-boat.

As he read the brief news item in the mailroom, Jack could feel the blood drain from his face. He felt faint and sought the nearest chair. He sat there alone in the drab room, staring at the clipping, exhaling audibly. Somehow seeing Tom's name in print along with the spare, cruel facts about the sinking of his ship, gave it a new sense of reality, a palpable, oppressive heaviness. Jack's arms, legs, neck, and head all began to ache with the pain, the worry, that he bore and that he knew was being borne by Anne and her parents.

That evening Jack sought out several of his dormitory mates in hopes that some light-hearted banter about classes, professors, and football would distract him. Apparently another prank had been perpetrated by boys from the residence house across the street: a bust of Plato at the entrance to the college library had been decorated with a lacy brassiere. They all laughed at the image of the revered Greek philosopher thus adorned. It felt good to laugh, thought Jack – it was just what he needed this evening.

Soon, however, the conversation turned to the war. One of the group reported on a student from another house who had learned just that morning that his brother was missing in action in France. Jack knew the young man from trigonometry class and was determined to speak to him the next day, to ask if there was any further news about his brother. The young man was in class, but slipped out before Jack could speak with him. The next time the class met, he was absent. When Jack inquired about him, he learned that the fellow's brother was no longer missing — he had been declared killed in action. The student had gone home and was not expected back. Jack paled at the thought.

That evening Jack was up late trying to study, but his mind kept trailing away to Tom, war, and the cold waters of the English Channel. He felt as though he was drowning, drowning in worry and fear. Finally, he stood and looked at himself in the mirror over his dresser. At that moment the words of the family's priest, Father Lévesque, spoken in the Bernard's front room two years ago as Jack's mother lay grievously ill upstairs, echoed in his memory: *You must prepare yourself.*

~ *18* ~

It was a Friday afternoon in late October. Claire and Fergal boarded the Westfield car after school. They had taken only a few steps down the aisle when Claire yanked on Fergal's arm, pulling him abruptly into a seat behind the motorman.

"Wha–" blurted the boy.

"Shhh," interrupted Claire in a whisper. "See those two men back there?" Fergal started to turn but Claire grabbed his arm. "Don't look, Fergal. One of 'em's Jake Muller, Sarah's brother. The other one I don't know – but he and Jake was at that special ceremony for Stephen and the other soldiers who died – at Elmwood Park – and they were acting like it was a joke." Fergal's eyes met Claire's and he nodded but did not speak. Claire continued: "Why would Jake and that guy be hanging around together? And where are they going?" Again Fergal's eyes met Claire's. "That's what *I* wanna know."

Fergal sat on the edge of his seat, his watch in one hand, his lips moving all the while as the trolley jolted along Northampton Street, then turned and climbed slowly through pastures and fields on its way to Westfield. Claire could see the suspicious pair reflected in the window next to her and she stared at them as if trying to divine some secret plan or motive.

Nearly ten minutes went by as the car moved steadily down the tracks, waiting only briefly on a siding for a Holyoke-bound car to pass. Finally, it screeched to a halt at the Pequot Park station. In summer this was a popular destination for picnickers, boaters, and fishermen, but it was deserted now. The two young men stood and moved up the aisle past Claire

114

and Fergal, carrying fishing poles. They quickly exited the car, the door slammed shut, and the car began moving.

"They're going fishing. Look, they've got fishing poles," observed Fergal.

Claire rolled her eyes at the boy's ignorance. "Really, Fergal, who goes fishin' this time a year? My brother always said there was no point even bothering after the leaves fall. Not until the ice comes in. Plus they got no tackle boxes – no gear – when you go fishing you have all sorts of stuff, and bait, ya know? No, they ain't goin' fishin', Fergal, but there's definitely somethin' fishy about them." Claire stood, stepped past Fergal into the aisle, then pulled on his coat sleeve. "C'mon, follow me."

"But – you said—"

"Oh, come on, boy." Reluctantly Fergal rose and followed her to the front of the car. Claire spoke to the motorman. "Sir, pardon me, sir, but we were supposed to get off back there."

The man shook his head. "No stops between stations. Next stop Southampton Road."

Claire was nothing if not quick on her feet. "But I – I think I'm going to be sick–" She held her hand to her throat and grimaced. The car lurched to a halt.

"Git," replied the annoyed motorman with a wag of his head. Claire and Fergal quickly stepped down from the car and ran along the tracks back to the stop, then turned and hurried down a gravel path they had seen the two men following. Soon it ended on the shore of Hampton Ponds. It looked like their trail had suddenly gone cold.

"Well," began Fergal, "we better go back and catch the next car."

But Claire had not given up. A narrow, obscure path led away from the water into the woods and she started to follow it. "They must've gone this way, Fergal. Let's go."

Again Fergal began to protest, then he stopped, staring at something in the woods a short distance off the path. Two

115

fishing poles apparently had been discarded. "See, Fergal, I told you, they weren't goin' fishin', those two," whispered Claire. "That was just a cover. Come on, follow me. And be *quiet*." She plunged further along the trail with Fergal following uneasily.

The trail soon ascended through dense woods and the two moved more slowly, Claire looking around constantly, Fergal wheezing and groaning with every step. Finally, the path rose directly up a steep, rock-strewn slope studded with dwarfed pines and aspens. Claire set her bookbag on the ground, then proceeded. Fergal followed, still shouldering his rucksack. The footing was difficult and they made slow progress, but finally they scrabbled to the top and found they were standing on a high ledge overlooking a deep cleft filled with huge boulders.

"It's that old quarry, Fergal," whispered Claire. "My father brung me here once. It's where they got stone when they builded the trolley line."

"Built," replied Fergal, "when they *built* the trolley line."

At the near end of the quarry stood a ramshackle building with a rusted tin roof. Voices could be heard from inside. Carefully Claire scrambled down a narrow, steep path that ended directly behind the structure. Fergal followed, still looking uneasy. When at last they were near the building, they approached cautiously. Claire stepped up to the rear wall and found a crack that afforded her a view of the interior. Clambering onto a pile of lumber, Fergal located a similar vantage point a few feet away.

"Yeh, well, it's close ta three hunert miles each way," Manfred Becker was saying to Jake and Hank as they stood beside a flatbed truck with a canvas canopy over the bed. "So ya gonna need maybe four cans a gas. Plus ropes to secure the load – and to tie down the cover."

"Hey Manfred," began Jake. He seemed to be asking a question of the man, although his voice was thin and nearly inaudible from their vantage.

Manfred replied, "Well, once you're loaded up you gotta cover them boxes with a tarp, maybe two, then tie 'em down so they don't slide 'round. And lash down that cover, too. You don't want no one lookin' in, right?"

Just then one of the boards Fergal was standing on broke with a loud snap. He and Claire froze for what seemed like an eternity. Then the voice of the man resumed – maybe, just maybe, they hadn't heard the noise.

But at that moment a voice came from the corner of the shed. "Hey, what the–" It was Jake. Claire and Fergal bolted, scrambling frantically up the same steep slope they had just descended, Jake close on their tails. The footing was even more difficult for him and he slipped several times, allowing the two youngsters to reach the lip of the quarry and disappear down the outer slope. They scurried downhill as fast as they could and only after several minutes when they were finally on even ground did they pause, breathing heavily.

"Phew, that was a close call," Claire was saying. But just then Jake emerged from the brush and charged at the pair. He reached Fergal and grabbed him by the arms. Claire was already out of sight down the trail.

"I got your little friend and I'm not lettin' 'im go 'til you get back 'ere," hollered Jake in Claire's direction. "What's her name?" demanded Jake, shaking Fergal by the collar.

"C-C-C," replied Fergal, but he was unable to form a word. Just then Claire re-emerged from a thicket.

"Let him go," she shouted boldly, then paused. "Please."

"Hey, I know you, don't I?" asked Jake when he got a good look at Claire. "You're the Bernard kid, Jack's little sister?" Claire nodded. "I remember, you were on the Westfield car. What the hell you two doin' followin' us? Snoopin'?"

Fergal was shaking his head but he was still in such a state of fright that he was unable to reply. Claire spoke, a note of desperation in her voice. "We – we – were thinkin' of goin' fishin' on Saturday and – and – well – we saw you guys with

117

your rods and thought maybe we'd follow and – and – you know, see where the good fishin' spots was." Fergal nodded in agreement. "Please, Jake, let him go. We'll go away and not be b–b–botherin' you guys again, we promise." Jake glowered at Claire, then at Fergal. "And whatever you were doin' in the quarry, it's no never mind to us. None at all. We'll just be goin' along an'–"

Jake seemed to relax. Perhaps it was the realization that Claire knew his name that made him change his tone. "You're right, it ain't none a your business. Anyway, we're just doing some work for the guy what owns the quarry, that's all. No big deal. So just scram, you hear me, *scram*. And if I ever see you two snoopin' around again, or if I find out you tol' anyone you saw me here, I'll find you both 'n give you the wompin' you deserve. Understand?"

He released his grip on Fergal's collar and the boy nearly collapsed, his legs were shaking so. Claire took him by the arm and began leading him down the trail.

"Thanks, Jake, s–s–sorry to be such bothers," replied Claire without looking back.

Claire retrieved her bookbag, then they made their way back along the trail to Hampton Ponds. They followed the shoreline to the far side where Claire knew it was little more than a ten-minute walk to Southampton Road and home.

"Follow me, Fergal, we're practically home," offered Claire. "This is a good trail," she added, trying to make casual conversation that might lighten the mood. "I know 'cause Jack uses it to go fishing a lot." She was hoping Fergal would begin to relax, but he didn't reply. "Isn't it a nice trail, Fergal?"

Finally she turned and looked into the boy's eyes. Only then did she see tears streaming down his freckled cheeks.

"Don't cry, Fergal, we're practically home." But sensing the depth of his distress, she took his hand, stroked it, and spoke softly to him. "Fergal," she began, "I'm sorry about all that, I really am. I know, I promised you no more—"

"Investigating," interjected the boy tearfully.

"I know, I swore—"

"On a stack a bibles—"

Claire huffed. "Okay, you're right – I swore – I did. Please, Fergal, don't tell my father. If he finds out, I'll be back at St. Agnes in a heartbeat. And I'd hate that – and I'd miss all my friends at Forestdale." Fergal looked up into Claire's eyes. She realized that she had struck the right note. "Like *you*, Fergal. I mean, *you* and *me*, we're such – such *good* friends and – I – I wouldn't want—" Finally the boy's tears were abating.

"I mean, I'd miss—" She paused and looked squarely into his eyes, sincerity oozing out of every pore. "I wouldn't want anything to – you know – separate us." She smiled and looked up softly, pleadingly. Fergal nodded, the faintest smile emerging through his tears.

The two walked on, now side by side. Claire was realizing that she'd forged a powerful hold on this boy, but one that would require nothing less than her eternal devotion. Well, she thought, I guess I can do that!

~ *19* ~

The Wellington household was somber as each day passed without a word about young Tom. Anne's job was her one consolation. She could throw herself into her work and be caught up in the whirlwind of visitors, questions, and tasks. At times she found she had been so preoccupied that she actually felt normal for perhaps an hour or two. Then when the pace slackened and she had time for her own thoughts, the burden of anxiety and sorrow descended once again.

Twice every day Jack went to the mailroom, hoping against hope for some good news from Anne. But her letters were consistently somber and increasingly pessimistic. Then one day Miss Hulbert called to Jack as he was about to leave for a class.

"Mister Bernard, a word, please." Jack was expecting her to lecture him on running in the hallway or some other infraction. "You have a letter here, just arrived, Special Delivery."

Jack's heart was suddenly in his throat as he accepted the small envelope and immediately recognized Anne's handwriting.

> *Dear Jackie,*
> *We have had some news about Tom, although*
> *whether it is good news or bad we cannot tell. A*
> *Navy man came to visit Mother and Father this*
> *afternoon. They have received a report from a British*
> *army office. One of their soldiers was captured by*
> *the Germans in a battle near Ostend in Belgium. He*
> *was being transported by train to a German prison*
> *camp when the train derailed. The soldier escaped.*

When he was back in England he reported that there were several other prisoners on the train as well. One of them was an American sailor named Tom Wellington – he said he remembered the name because of the Duke of Wellington. He also said Tom was injured and in pain. In the confusion following the accident the soldier never knew what happened to Tom.

Oh Jackie, we do not know what to think of this news. Please write soon.

Love,
Anne

Jack folded the letter, placed it in one of his books, and headed off to class. But trigonometry was the last thing on his mind that morning.

~ *20* ~

Nearly a week had passed since the Wellington family received the fragmentary report of Tom from the British soldier. At first there was hope, but as the days ticked by with no further word, hope soon gave way to despair. And fear. Was it possible Tom had survived the torpedoing in the English Channel, been captured by the Germans, but died in a rail crash in Belgium? Or had he been recaptured after the crash, then transferred to one of those terrible German prison camps? Could they dare to hope that he too had escaped, despite his injury, as had the British soldier?

It was nearly midnight on Friday, October 26, when a knock came at the Wellingtons' front door. The arrival of an official Department of War telegram convulsed the entire household. One of the maids brought the envelope to Helen Wellington who was still awake in her study. She woke her husband, spoke to him softly, then carefully opened the envelope and read it.

Jack had arrived home that evening unannounced. Anne's letters had seemed increasingly glum and while he was feeling the pressure of approaching mid-term exams, he had decided on the spur of the moment to make the trip. He and a classmate from Wilbraham shared a cab to Union Station in Worcester, then took the train together to Palmer. From there Jack was able to catch a trolley to Chicopee, then on to Holyoke and finally Westfield.

After completing a few chores the next morning, Jack departed for Holyoke. When he arrived at the Wellington home he was concerned to see an official Navy motorcar pulled under the portico at the front door. He knocked on the door, then waited alone and shaken. Finally a maid opened the door. As soon as he stepped into the foyer, he could hear a commotion in the parlor. As he entered he saw Anne embracing her mother in tears. When she saw Jack she ran to him.

"Oh, Jackie – Jackie – it's – it's unbelievable. Mr. Warren – er – Lieutenant Warren, has just brought us wonderful news. It's Tommy – he's alive, Jackie, he's alive. He turned up at a British field hospital in France, someplace called Amiens, with another sailor."

"A soldier, an American soldier," interrupted the Lieutenant.

"They say he injured his arm – but he's going to be all right." She hugged Jack tightly and whispered in his ear, her voice trembling with emotion: "Tommy's alive, Jackie – *he's alive.*"

She handed Jack the telegram and led him into the library, then watched as he read it, tears streaming down her face.

WASHINGTON, DC   OCTOBER 26, 1917, 22:40 EST

TP WELLINGTON 125 THE HIGHLANDS HOLYOKE, MASSACHUSETTS USA

THE NAVY DEPARTMENT HAS RECEIVED INFORMATION THAT YOUR SON

SEAMAN THOMAS P. WELLINGTON 3RD IS PRESENTLY IN BRITISH FIELD

HOSPITAL AMIENS FR RECOVERING FROM INJURIES SUSTAINED IN THE

PERFORMANCE OF HIS DUTY AND IN THE SERVICE OF HIS COUNTRY. WILL

FURNISH ADDITIONAL INFORMATION AS SOON AS AVAILABLE.

    VICE ADMIRAL G. K. JOHNSTON, NAVAL HEADQUARTERS

Jack smiled. "I knew it, Annie, I just knew Tommy would pull through." Anne was smiling, too, through her tears. Jack was studying the globe. "Amiens — it's way to the north of France, close to the border with Belgium. How the heck did he get there? It's gotta be fifty miles from the English Channel – and more than a hundred miles from Ostend."

"I don't know, Jackie, I don't know." She paused, then hugged him. "Tommy's coming home."

When Anne had finally recovered her composure, they rejoined the rest of the family in the parlor, Helen, Thomas, Sr., Richard, Charlotte. One by one the members of the staff appeared, Mildred, Morwenna, Bromley, and several others offered their heartfelt congratulations. A bottle of champagne was opened and Mr. Wellington offered a toast to their son.

After a while Anne led Jack into the glasshouse that adjoined the parlor. "I've got to tell Carolyn, Jackie, as soon as possible. I know her mother said she would be arriving home from school around four o'clock. Perhaps I will walk to her house and be there when she arrives home. Will you come with me?"

"Sure, Annie, if you'd like me to."

Anne and Jack sat in wicker chairs on the porch of the Calavetti home at a few minutes before four, anxiously awaiting Carolyn's arrival. Her mother, Nina Calavetti, was not home yet; she often worked at the Women's Home until six on Fridays.

"Remember, Jackie, we're not supposed to know about the engagement." Jack nodded. "Oh, Jackie, Carolyn will be so excited. She was devastated when Tommy went missing. That afternoon in Amherst when I told her—" Anne shuddered at the memory. "It was awful, Jackie, just awful. It seemed like her whole world was tumbling down upon poor Carolyn." She paused, recalling the emotions of that day. "I hope I shall never again have to face such a task, of delivering such terrible news to a dear friend."

Just then an unfamiliar motorcar rolled up to the curb. Carolyn was seated in the passenger seat, but she was turned away from them, apparently in conversation with the driver. Several minutes went by as Anne and Jack waited for Carolyn to step out of the vehicle, but she seemed to be deep in conversation. Finally Anne could wait no longer. She rose from her chair, stepped off the porch and walked toward the motorcar, Jack following close behind.

"Carolyn?" she called out from the sidewalk.

Only then did her friend turn toward Anne. "Anne, dear," replied Carolyn with surprise, fairly leaping from the vehicle to the sidewalk. "I am — it is so—" Just then she saw Jack. "Oh, my — Jack. What's the occasion?" Suddenly her expression turned somber.

"Carolyn, we have the most wonderful news. Tommy — he's okay."

Carolyn flushed. Just then the driver exited the motor and stepped up onto the walk. He was a tall, slender young man with dark hair. "Anne, Jack, this is a classmate, Roger — Roger Bancroft. Roger, these are my friends, Anne Wellington and Jack Bernard."

"How-do," replied Roger, smiling and extending his hand to Jack. "Who is Tommy?"

~ 21 ~

Claire and Fergal had barely stepped off the trolley on Sargeant Street one morning the following week when several classmates surrounded Claire.

"Isn't that wonderful news about the sailor from Holyoke?" offered Yvette Lemieux. "It was in this morning's paper. Everyone was sure he was dead after his ship sank. But he's alive. Haven't you heard?"

"Yes, of course she's heard, haven't you, Claire?" replied Sarah. "He's a friend of her brother's, is he not?"

Claire nodded and smiled proudly. "My brother Jack was visiting his girlfriend, Anne Wellington, when they got the news about her brother. Jack called us on the telephone and told us all about it."

"You must have been worried sick about him, Claire, weren't you?" asked Yvette.

Claire shrugged. "Everyone was. But Tommy Wellington is very brave and clever. I suspect he could get himself out of nearly any mess, any day, anywhere."

"They say he escaped a Kraut prison. Killed a bunch of guards, then got away," interjected a tall boy who had been listening. It was Arnold Wilmot, one of those responsible for the paint-splattering incident.

"No, that's not what happened," replied Claire, throwing the boy a withering glare.

"Is so," was Arnold's reply.

Fergal spoke up. "Tommy Wellington was captured in the English Channel after his ship went down. Some Germans in a boat saved him. He was in a train on his way to a prisoner-of-war camp. According to the newspaper, the train was derailed. That's when he escaped."

"Oh, is that so?" replied Arnold in a mocking tone.

Fergal nodded, then continued. "I read that the Belgian resistance movement has been very effective against the Germans. Every night they sneak out and damage roads, bridges, even train tracks. It makes it difficult for the Germans to get supplies to their front lines."

"Well, ain't you a regular know-it-all?" replied Arnold derisively. As he spoke he reached over and grabbed Fergal's rucksack from the bench. "Say, Dooley, whatcha got in here?"

Claire spoke up sternly. "Put that down, Arnold."

"Ooh, what's in it, Fergal, secret messages an' – an' – stuff?" He opened the rucksack and started pawing through it. "Let's see what ya got here. Oooh, a couple books –a pair a spectacles – for Mister Four-eyes, a course – and a jackknife." Arnold opened the jackknife with some difficulty. "What's the knife for, Fergal? Let me guess, you like whittlin'." Fergal shook his head. "No? What for, then, eh Fergal?"

Claire spoke louder. "Arnold Wilmot, put the knife away before you hurt yourself. And give the rucksack back to Fergal."

"Say, I bet I know what the knife's for," continued the boy, ignoring Claire's warning. "For carving in a tree, maybe a heart, maybe *Fergal loves Claire*. Hah-hah, that's it – *Fergal loves Claire*, right? Or – maybe *Claire loves* –" At that moment Claire hauled off and slapped the boy hard across the cheek, so hard it could be heard by other students some distance away.

"Ow," screeched Arnold. He started to speak: "Why you – b–" Just then the pain suddenly rendered him speechless. His face turned bright red and a single tear puddled under each eye. He stood and turned away to hide himself from the gaggle of curious classmates that had gathered around them.

"Ha-ha, Arnold, she smacked you good," taunted another boy.

Then an eerie silence fell over the group. It was only a few seconds but it seemed like an eternity as everyone awaited the tall boy's response. Finally, Arnold made a half-turn toward Fergal and threw the rucksack at him. "Take your damned rucksack." With that he stood and walked away, still obviously smarting from the blow.

Fergal had rearranged the contents of his rucksack, lifted it to his shoulder, and quietly climbed the front steps to the school just as the bell rang. Several girls meanwhile were gathered around Claire congratulating her. Claire was grinning, feeling pretty good about herself, except, perhaps, for a tiny, niggling worry about the possibility that Mr. Patton, the principal – or, worse yet, her father – might get wind of yet another round of fisticuffs.

~ 22 ~

On Friday, the second of November, Helen, Thomas, Sr., Anne, Jack, and Bromley stood on a dock in New York City in the midday sun, a cold wind blowing off the water, its gusts sweeping dust and grit into swirls along the pier. Before them loomed the massive gray hull of the *USS Mercy*, a hospital ship that transported the injured from Europe. Steel gangways pitched steeply from the ship's deck to the dock below. Down those narrow walkways clambered uniformed sailors, medics, officers, and dockworkers. The injured servicemen were smiling as they descended, scanning the crowd of many hundreds that had gathered, perhaps looking for loved ones. Nearly all were sporting bandages, splints, crutches, or canes, but were walking proudly despite their infirmities. The Wellingtons, Jack, and Bromley, watched anxiously for Tom.

Soon a more somber procession began as stretchers were carried cautiously down the gangways. These injured were barely visible, each heaped with blankets and secured with straps. Their attendants were unsmiling, intent on their tasks. Anne clutched Jack's arm nervously.

After nearly half an hour the parade of injured slowed, then finally ended. Tom's would-be greeting party stood confused and uneasy. Helen had just stepped forward and spoken to one of the officers on the dock who was holding a long sheaf of paper, possibly a manifest, when Anne heard a familiar voice behind her and turned. There, not twenty feet away, stood Tom, smiling and waving, his left arm suspended in a bulky white cast.

"Tommy," shouted Anne and she ran toward her brother. But then she stopped short, not sure she should touch him lest she cause him pain. Tom stepped forward, smiling. "Hi, Annie. Little hug for your brother?" And he embraced her vigorously with his right arm. Soon all were encircling Tom, laughing and smiling. Tom explained that he'd disembarked by the forward gangway, the longest and steepest, not wanting to be in the way of the more seriously injured sailors.

"You look just fine, Son," observed Tom's father.

"Thin, though," added his mother. "Haven't they been feeding you?"

"I'm fine, Mother, really. A few days of rest and I'll be good as new."

"Your arm, dear, is it mending all right?"

Tom shrugged off the question. "It's fine, Mother, really. Thanks for coming to meet me, all of you. Jack, what about your studies, old buddy?"

Jack shook his head, "They can wait." And he patted his friend's shoulder. "Welcome home, sailor."

"Welcome 'ome, Master Tom," added Bromley, clutching his black cap with one hand and extending the other in a vigorous, heartfelt handshake.

"Annie, what's a matter, cat got your tongue?" teased Tom.

Anne smiled, but tears were streaming down her face. She took her brother's hand and squeezed it. "It's just so good to see you, Tommy – so good."

Tom smiled at his sister, then diverted his eyes. "How's Carolyn?"

~ 23 ~

Anne stood by her bedroom window watching anxiously as Tom ambled down the flagstone walk toward Beech Street. It was a miracle, she thought, that he was home safely and, to all appearances, in good health. Still she was uneasy. It had been nearly midnight by the time the family had returned to Holyoke after first delivering Jack in Westfield. Tom had quickly fallen asleep and seemed to have slept long and soundly despite the cast on his arm. Anne and her mother knew this as they had checked on him hourly throughout the night.

It was nearly noon when Tom finally appeared in the breakfast room. Several of the other staff members had come in to greet him and welcome him home and he smiled and thanked them politely. Mildred, the family cook of nearly twenty years who had always been very close to Anne and Tom, had greeted him cheerily, then stood smiling, dabbing at her eyes with a lace handkerchief before she excused herself suddenly, trying valiantly to control her emotions.

With a fork in his one free hand, Tom began spearing at his breakfast while his sister and mother looked on. "You know, you don't have to watch over me every minute," he commented after a while. "I can still eat without help." He smiled at them. Helen's expression must have caught his eye. "Mother, I'm fine." After he had completed his breakfast, he made a telephone call in the library, then spoke to his sister.

"Annie, I'm going for a walk – to see Carolyn. Just to say hello, that's all. I won't be long."

Anne smiled at her brother's casual air knowing it was all a front. "I'm sure she'll be happy to see you. Say hello to her for me, won't you? Tell her I can't wait to see her."

Now he was off and Anne stood watching him, wondering.

When she opened the front door to greet him, Carolyn Ford was unsteady on her feet. But there he was, Tom, the old Tom except for the cast so far as she could tell – that self-assured stance, that smile, that swath of black hair with its unstudied wave. He stepped inside. She closed the door quietly behind him.

"Dear Thomas, how wonderful it is to see you," she whispered, then forced a smile.

He took her hand. "Carolyn, how are you? You look – just as pretty as I remember—"

He kissed her lightly on the cheek, then took her in his arms and they embraced. It was a warm embrace, but brief, as Carolyn began to shake and she stepped back. "I'm sorry, Thomas, I must have a slight case of – of nerves."

"Where's your mother?"

"Like I told you on the telephone, she's off at the Temperance Union meeting until three."

"Then no need to be nervous, right?" Tom leaned in and kissed her again, this time tenderly on the lips. A pink glow spread across her face. They sat in the parlor, Tom in the heavy oak Morris chair by the fireplace, Carolyn poised anxiously on the davenport. She was trying to appear calm and self-composed, but she was studying Tom's every word, gesture, facial expression. She smiled, then looked down at the cast.

"How is your arm?"

Tom shrugged. "It's okay. Just takes time – you know – to heal."

Carolyn looked up into Tom's eyes and paused, weighing her next words. "Is it broken?"

Tom nodded and chuckled. "Yeh, you could say that."

Carolyn winced. "It's going to heal, though?"

"In time, sure."

"Does it hurt terribly?"

Again Tom shrugged. "Not too bad, no – not at the moment."

"What – what happened?" asked Carolyn with some hesitation. Tom shook his head. "Please, Thomas." Again she hesitated. "Please tell me about it."

Once again Tom shook his head. "Let's forget about it, okay? I have. So, how's college life?"

Carolyn sighed. "It's fine. It keeps me busy, you know. And the dormitory is very commodious. We each have our own room but there's a lounge on the first floor where the girls gather before and after meals."

"Do you like them – the other girls, I mean?"

Carolyn smiled. "Oh, yes, they're good gals, you know. Some of them could sit and talk all day."

"How about you, do you join in?"

"Some. But a lot of their talk is about their beaux–"

"Ahh, their beaux. Well, I hope you don't go on too much about yours."

Carolyn blushed, then shook her head. "Not too much. Only Darthea Farrell knows about us. She's from Ludlow. She caught me with my ring on one day – so I had to tell her."

"About that," Tom began.

But Carolyn interrupted. "How about if we go for a walk?"

Bundled against a sharp November wind, the couple set off through the Highlands, pausing for some time on a bench in Lincoln Park in the warm sun. Children were giggling and shouting as they took turns running, then sliding across the newly formed ice on the skating pond.

"Remember when we used to skate here at night?" asked Tom. "Annie, Jack, you and me? Mother would bring a lantern and blankets for us when we got cold."

Carolyn smiled at the memory, then corrected him. "*You* skated, Thomas, I just slipped and fell and then got up and fell

133

again, as I recall." She blushed, then smiled. "And you made fun of me," she said with mock offense.

"You wouldn't let me hold your hand – that's what I remember. You preferred skating alone and falling to holding my hand," Tom chided.

She squeezed his hand and smiled shyly. "Well, I got over that in time, didn't I?"

Tom held her gaze. "Yes, you did – fortunately for me." He lifted her left hand and looked carefully at the ring. "You know, thinking of you – the memory of you at the Depot that day, wearing that ring and smiling – it got me through some dark days, Carolyn – it kept me going."

"Was it terrible?"

A brief wave of pain rippled across Tom's face, quickly replaced by a smile. "It's all in the past now – forgotten." He paused and patted her hand. "Whatta you say we just think about the future?"

"Well, what about it?" replied Carolyn.

"Well, what's next – for us, I mean?"

"Thomas, I have still a year-and-a-half to go at Mass. Aggie. Then I'll need to find work and start saving. And you, Thomas, once you're well?"

"When my leave is over I'll probably–"

"Your – leave?" Carolyn interrupted.

"Yeh, I'm on medical leave – until my arm is healed. When I'm better I'll return to active duty."

Carolyn was stunned. "But – after all you've been through – they want you back?"

"Well, no, I mean – actually it's up to me. If I wanted I could get a medical discharge, but if the whole thing isn't over by then I'm hoping – well I don't think they would allow me back on a ship, but maybe I could work on a base stateside, maybe in Newport – or New York – or Norfolk, Virginia. As long as the war's still on – I want to do my part."

Carolyn was shocked at this revelation but relieved that Tom's plans did not include returning to the war zone. "I – we are all so proud of you, Thomas – your bravery – and valor."

Tom shook it off. "Not all that brave, Carolyn – believe me. There were other folks who were far braver."

"Like who?"

Tom shook his head, then lifted her ringed hand. "Speaking of bravery – does your mother know yet?"

Carolyn looked down at her hand. "Not yet. I wear it on my silver necklace. I know it's there, close to my heart, you know – but no one else does – except for Darthea."

"Soon, though? I mean, we have to tell her eventually, don't we?"

"Yes," replied Carolyn, "of course."

Soon the young couple were strolling along Hampden Street back toward Carolyn's home. She was speaking with animation about her dormitory room, her dorm mates, and her studies. At one point she realized she had been going on at some length and she turned and looked at Tom's face. It was pallid and tense.

She stopped, turned toward him, and looked squarely into his eyes. "Thomas, are you all right?"

He brightened momentarily. "Oh, sure, I'm just tired is all." But almost immediately his color grayed and the tension in his face re-emerged. He was breathing hard, it seemed, almost panting, even though the walking was easy. When they were finally at Carolyn's front door he spoke quickly.

"Well, I'll say goodbye for now, Carolyn." He leaned forward to kiss her lightly on the cheek. As he did so she could see that his smile was shaky and his cheek was cold against hers.

"Thomas, shall I walk you home?" He brushed off the offer with what was meant as a casual gesture, but it seemed to her hurried, forced. She watched him make his way to the corner where he turned and was quickly out of sight. She let herself in the front door, then stood by the window looking after him, worried.

"Oh, there you are." Carolyn flinched visibly, then turned to her mother who had suddenly appeared in the hallway.

"Mother, I – I didn't know you were home."

"Yes, well, the meeting was brief today. I fear some of the ladies are thinking more about the holidays than about the evils of drink right now." Their eyes met briefly. "Is something wrong? You seem at sixes and sevens."

Carolyn was struggling to maintain her composure. "Just a bit overtaxed – studies and all that. And then Thomas Wellington dropped by."

"Ah, yes, Helen told me they were meeting him in New York City yesterday. How is he?"

"I – I'm not certain. I thought at first he seemed fine, but–"

"Well, he's been through a lot, no doubt. But he's not your concern, after all," she added curtly. "Perhaps you should rest for a while?"

Carolyn nodded, turned, then climbed the stairs. In her room she lay on her bed, thinking about Tom.

An hour later Carolyn and her mother were having supper. "I do hope you're not overdoing, dear. Why don't you stay another night, get caught up on your sleep, and take the electric back to Amherst in the morning?"

"I really must go back tonight, Mother. I have studying to do. Marilee Spears is giving me a ride in her new motorcar."

Nina shook her head. "The way young women gallivant about these days is a fright. It's not right, I say, it's just too hard on their delicate constitutions."

Carolyn knew enough not to argue with her mother about what was and was not proper for a young woman. But she was determined to return to school that evening, to the freedom and excitement she found there. After supper she packed her small valise and was sitting in the parlor awaiting the arrival of her friend when the knocker on the front door sounded. It was Anne.

"Hello, Anne. It's wonderful to see you. But I'm sorry to say I have to leave. Merilee is coming by any minute now. She has a new roadster and she insists on taking me whenever she's on her way to Amherst."

"Oh, dear," replied Anne. "I'm so sorry. This weekend just slipped by and I so wanted to talk to you, to hear all about college."

"It's going splendidly, Anne, really. I'm learning so much and the gals in the dormitory are ever so jolly. We just laugh and laugh. I'm sorry I haven't written – I've just been so busy."

Anne was looking carefully at her friend's face that shone in the gas light of the parlor. "And Tommy came by this afternoon, I understand. I'll bet you two had a good deal to talk about. Isn't he looking well?"

Carolyn's smile faded as she replied. "Well, yes – quite well, uh, for the most part."

Anne knew her friend and could tell that there was something amiss. "Carolyn, dear, did something happen – with you and Tommy?"

Carolyn looked up and into Anne's eyes. Just then a motorcar pulled up in front of the house and a horn sounded.

"I'm sorry, Anne, but that's Merilee. I have to go." Nina appeared and saw Carolyn off at the door. Anne and Carolyn walked down the front walk together and greeted their former classmate. After Carolyn placed her valise behind the seat, she turned to Anne.

"Tommy – he, well, he – at first he was just fine, but we went for a walk and suddenly he seemed to change, to tire, to turn ashen – it was like I was looking at a different person. Did you see him when he got home, Annie?"

"Well, no, I didn't. He went straight to bed and slept right through supper. Mother was just about to take his meal up to him when I left to come here. But I'm sure he's fine, Carolyn, I know he is. Perhaps he was just – tired."

Anne stood watching as the roadster sped away.

Back home Anne sought out her mother. "Mother, is Tommy all right? I mean, did he seem himself when you brought him his supper?"

"Why, yes dear, I guess so. He was sleeping and I hated to wake him. I left his tray thinking he'd be famished when he woke."

Moments later Anne rapped lightly on Tom's door but there was no reply. She rapped again, then carefully turned the knob. The room was dark and her brother was fast asleep and breathing evenly. His face was a peaceful mask, she thought. On a table by the window rested the tray with his supper, apparently untouched. Next to the tray stood an empty glass tumbler half full of water. Beside it lay a small envelope surrounded by bits of white powder. Anne backed out of the room and closed the door softly.

Anne lay in bed that night for the longest time, her mind unwilling to settle. On the one hand she was feeling an enormous relief to have her brother home and safe. But Carolyn's words kept coming back, haunting her, raising her anxiety about Tom's convalescence. And the fact that Carolyn and Tom continued to keep their engagement a secret from her, from everyone, was a source of worry to her as well. She finally rolled over, gently lifted a copy of *The Forsyte Saga* from her nightstand, and began to read.

An hour later Anne was fast asleep, the reading lamp still lit on her nightstand, the book inverted on her lap. She was dreaming of the English countryside swaddled in green, then of a forest that at first appeared bright and full of light but soon became dark and forbidding. Out of the darkness there came a sound, a voice, low and slightly musical at first, but soon louder, more strident. Suddenly it transformed into a sharp, mournful keening. Anne woke, momentarily disoriented. She shook her head, not sure if she was still dreaming. Silence.

She stood, wrapped a flannel robe around her, opened the bedroom door, and stepped into the hallway. Still all was quiet. She waited, perplexed, then turned to re-enter her room. Just then the shrieking resumed from the far end of the hall, Tom's room.

She rapped on the door. "Tommy," she whispered, then entered. Tom's bed was empty, the blankets and covers strewn across the floor. Her brother was crouched in the far corner, his face buried in a pillow that now muffled his wailing. She knelt beside him, touched his shoulder, and spoke softly: "Tommy, Tommy – sssh – it's all right, Tommy. It's Anne – you're all right."

The crying at last ceased as Tom looked up into the dim light from the open door and recognized his sister.

"Annie, what are you—"

"Shhh, it's okay, Tommy. It's okay." He was breathing rapidly, almost panting now. "Come on, why don't you get back in bed?" Slowly he stood, struggling at first to get his balance. Then he sat on the bed staring at the floor. Anne sat next to him. Then she stood, took a glass of water from the supper tray, and filled it from a china pitcher. "Here, have some water." Tom took several small sips and seemed to calm. Finally Anne spoke. "What is it, Tommy? Are you all right?"

"Just a nightmare 's all." He ran his hands through his thick hair. "I'm okay. Sorry if I woke you." After several more minutes he smiled at Anne. "Really, I'm fine."

Just then Morwenna, the maid, appeared at the door in her nightgown. "Miss Anne, is there something the matter with Thomas? Anything I can do for you?"

Anne shook her head and smiled weakly. "No, thank you, Morwenna. He's fine. Just a bad dream. Go back to bed, please."

Morwenna smiled. "Well, if you're sure, miss. Goodnight, Miss Anne, Master Thomas." She turned and left

Anne stroked her brother's hair. "Maybe you should have something to eat. It looks like you haven't touched the meal Mildred sent up for you."

"Nah, I'll just go back to sleep, thanks." Anne retrieved the bedclothes and remade the bed as Tom stood watching groggily. Finally, he apologized to Anne, crawled into bed, and closed his eyes. Anne retreated, closing the door behind her. She was shaken but relieved that Tom seemed to have recovered.

Anne was awake early the following morning. As she prepared to leave her mother greeted her in the foyer.

"You are up early, dear."

"Yes, Mother, I've got so much work to do. I thought I'd go into the Home this morning."

Helen looked into her daughter's face. "Did you not sleep well, dear? You look fatigued."

"Well, no, I – it took me a long time to fall asleep." Anne looked into her mother's eyes. "Tommy – was having a nightmare last evening, Mother."

"Oh, dear, the poor boy." She exhaled, a worried expression creasing her face. "I didn't hear a thing. Perhaps it's just a touch of dyspepsia, or–"

"I looked in on him and he was – he was curled up on the floor – he looked like a frightened animal."

"I checked on him just now and he was sleeping soundly. Perhaps we should just let him sleep."

"Mother, I fear Tommy is suffering — from the sinking of his ship, the deaths of so many of his shipmates, and his captivity. I wish he'd talk to us about it. It might help him."

"I'm trying not to think about it, Anne dear — I'm trying to put it out of my head."

"That's just it, Mother, don't you see? No matter what he does, Tommy *cannot* put it out of *his* head."

~ 24 ~

The morning sky was just beginning to lighten to a dull gray as Hank maneuvered the truck up the narrow farm lane that led to the quarry. "Let me do the talkin'," insisted Hank as they pulled to a halt. "Nothin' happened, everything went like clockwork, right?" Jake nodded.

Manfred had been waiting for them just inside the quarry gate and he approached them with a forced nonchalance in his step. Only when he was a few steps away from the pair did he speak. "So, ya made it, eh?" He lifted a corner of the tarp and peered beneath it. "Any trouble?"

Hank shook his head. "Smooth as silk. They was waitin' for us at that pull-off, just like you said. Didn't take more 'n five minutes to load. Then we was on 'r way."

Manfred was looking at Hank as he spoke, measuring every word, every look, every move he made. Hank stood implacable, unsmiling. Then Manfred turned abruptly to Jake. "Problems?"

Jake shook his head and spoke nervously. "No s-sir, n-none."

"You sure, kid? You look a little off ya feed."

"It's just that we're tired, Manfred, been drivin' for hours," replied Hank. "We gotta get goin'. I work the second shift today. Can we have our money?"

"What's ya rush?"

"I – it's just kinda creepy out 'ere. What if someone sees us?"

"Keep cool, kid, no one ever comes here these days. And so what if they did? I'm in the quarry business and thinkin' of reopenin' this place – no crime in that." He looked on the two with a suspicious eye that made them squirm. Then he reached inside his jacket. Jake recoiled. But when he withdrew his hand it held a wad of bills. He stuffed several in Hank's hand, then turned, smiled, and did the same for Jake.

"Thanks," began Jake. Then he looked down at the money in his hand. Slowly his eyes rose and met Hank's, then shifted to Manfred. "But Manfred, that's–"

"I know – I said twenty-five each. But you done such a good job, I decided to sweeten the deal."

"But – fif–?" Jake could barely say the word.

"Yeh, that's right, fifty bucks each."

"Wow," replied Jake.

"Okay, thanks, Manfred. We betta be goin'," blurted Hank.

"Wait jus' a minute, boys." He pointed to the bills in their hands. "That little bonus there, it's like what they calls a retainer."

Hank and Jake looked confused. "Huh?" replied Hank.

"For another run."

Jake nodded but Hank shook his head slightly. "Ah, I don't know, Manfred, I—"

"What, you already backin' out? I gives you a bonus and a minute later you tellin' me ya done?"

Jake was tugging at Hank's sleeve and shaking his head.

"No, no, not at all, that's not it. What do you wan' us ta do? You name it," Hank assured him.

"That's better," replied Manfred with a smile. "I'll let you know – look for you at Bruno's – week, maybe two."

It was a cold, snowy night later that week when Jake and Hank were waiting outside *Das Bierhaus*, gyres of snow swirling about them.

"Can't we go inside?" complained Jake. "I'm 'bout to freeze out here."

"That's what Manfred said in his message, meet 'im on the sidewalk."

Just then a figure approached out of the blowing snow. "Hey, Manfred," began Jake, smiling. "Some weather, eh?"

The man stared blankly at the pair, then tipped his head toward the bar entrance. They followed him inside and took seats at their usual table in the shadows. The older man carefully removed his coat and hat, shook off the snow, and placed them on an empty chair. Then he sat, looked around, and spoke calmly.

"So, ya think ya ready for 'nother job, eh?" Both nodded. "Well, great, that's just great. Oh, but, 'fore I forget, one small piece a business from the last job."

"What's that?" asked Hank.

"A small matter of the copper."

"What copper?"

"Border Patrol – pulled you over – just below the border. *That* copper."

Hank swallowed hard. "Where'd you hear that, Manfred?"

"Let's just say a little birdie tol' me – a little birdie at police headquarters. Says they got a call on the telephone the other day from the border cops – pulled over this truck – Massachusetts plate, they said – acting suspiciously."

"Listen, Manfred, it was nothing – he just wanted to tell us our headlights was out is all. We thanked him, then took off."

"Yeh, so I heard. Gave 'im a good chase."

Jake chuckled. "Yeh, we left 'im in our dust."

But Manfred was not amused. "Just a little race with the coppers, eh? What are you guys, schoolboys on a lark? You get stopped by the cops, then you take off – and you never think to tell me?" Hank and Jake sat silently. "So the way I see it, you're incompetents, liars, and crooks. You got yourselves stopped by the cops – then decided not to tell me – then the other day you stand there smilin' and takin' my money like you were some kinda heroes."

"We – we figured we shook 'im, we got away, so it was no big deal."

"No big deal? All of a sudden we got both the Holyoke cops *and* the U. S. Border Patrol lookin' for that truck. And when they find it they're gonna look for those two jamokes who were drivin' it, and then the guy who stole it. No big deal, eh?" Manfred shook his head. "Right from the start I shoulda recognized you for what you are – a couple a losers." He stood up, then leaned over and scowled at the pair. "Nice knowin' ya."

Hank spoke up. "Wait, Manfred. Listen – we're sorry – we shoulda tol' you about the copper, okay? Come on, Manfred, give us another chance. We'll show you, I promise."

Manfred stood in silence for what seemed like a very long time. Finally, he cast a stern glance at each of them. "Well, okay. But first things first. Number one is the truck."

"What about it?"

"You gotta ditch it."

"Ditch it? Whatta ya mean, Manfred? Where?"

"Somewhere it won't be found. And remember, you guys're in this thing now, you're in it *deep*. But if all goes well, I'll think about lettin' you make another pickup – or delivery." With that Manfred rose, tossed some coins on the table, shrugged into his overcoat, and left.

Hank and Jake sat in silence sipping their beers.

"Ya think we're in trouble, Hank? With the cops, I mean," asked Jake.

Hank shook his head. "Naa. That copper didn't even ask our names, remember? And it was pretty dark so he could barely see our faces."

~ 25 ~

Claire and Fergal were seated near the back of the Westfield-bound trolley after school several days later. Claire was absorbed in a serial in the *Daily Transcript* of earlier in the week while Fergal sat next to her fidgeting and looking at his watch again and again. Suddenly the car drew to an abrupt halt. The power had been lost, the motorman explained, the third time that day on the line. All the riders could do was sit in the cold and wait, looking out on pastures covered with a thin veil of snow. Claire seemed oblivious to the interruption and continued reading. But Fergal's squirming finally got to her.

"Fergal, can't you sit still? You're distracting me – I'm trying to finish this serial about a girl who lived in Lexington during the Revolution." She could see that he was agitated with the delay. "Here, what if I hold the paper up like this? Then you can read the front page, okay?"

He nodded nervously, turned in his seat, and tried to find something of interest to read. Several minutes had gone by when he seemed alarmed by something he saw, a news story and a photograph.

"Uh," he began, "C–Claire—"

"Please, Fergal, don't talk – I'm at the best part now – the battle has just started and the girl—" Her voice trailed off as she continued to read.

The boy let out a stifled grunt. He looked at Claire anxiously, then back to the newspaper. Finally, Claire looked over the newspaper at him and spoke with annoyance. "What is it, Fergal?"

"A — a truck." As he spoke he pointed to a story on the front page that Claire had ignored in her haste to find the latest installment of the serial. She turned the paper over and looked at the story Fergal was fingering, then read the headline: "*Truck Pulled from River*. Uh-huh. What about it?"

"That's the truck that was in the barn – at the quarry."

Claire rolled her eyes. "Fergal, don't be ridiculous. Most of it's under water – all that's showin' is the back end."

Fergal pointed to the license plate that was clearly visible. "That was the number plate on the truck: 7-1-9-1-7."

"Now how could you possibly remember that, Fergal?"

"It's a palindrome – the same, forward or back, like *Madam I'm Adam*." He pointed to the digits as he read them in reverse: "7 – 1 – 9 – 1 – 7. And it has the year in it, too – 1917 – see?"

Suddenly Claire was interested and she read the story aloud.

> It appeared that the vehicle had rolled into the river at the site of the old dock at Smith's Ferry, about three miles north of the Holyoke Dam. A neighbor reported hearing a commotion about 2:00 am Tuesday. On looking out his window he observed two men walking casually up the street from the dock. The Holyoke Police Department is investigating.

Their eyes met. "Gee, Fergal, do you suppose the two men could have been Jake and that other guy?" Fergal's brow knitted. "Maybe it was an accident—"

"Or," added Fergal, "maybe they had to get rid of the truck – for some reason. Maybe Jake's mixed up in something illegal."

Late that afternoon Claire was doing her chores in the barn, tossing feed towards the chickens, then watching with

147

amusement as they scrambled, shoving one another aside with surprising force just to get a few extra morsels. It reminded her of the behavior of certain pupils in the lunchroom at school and she laughed at the thought, scolding the birds for their rudeness. She turned and suddenly, there was Fergal, a newspaper in one hand.

"Fergal – what are you doing here?"

"Look," he began. He raised the paper toward her but leaned away, as if not wanting to get any closer than necessary to his sometimes pugnacious classmate.

"What is it?" Claire responded as she took the paper. Then she saw the story and read the headline aloud. "*Abandoned truck connected to Border Patrol investigation.*" Her voice became hushed. "Holy moly, Fergal." She gestured to him to follow her through the rear door of the barn where they would be out of sight and earshot of her father and sister. Then she continued reading, still in a low voice.

> *The Ford truck found last week in the river north of the city may have been involved in criminal activity. According to Holyoke police, a United States Border Patrol officer encountered the vehicle traveling along a country road in Pittsfield, New Hampshire, on the night of November 4. Because it was operating without lights the officer stopped the vehicle. The driver claimed his lights were not working properly and promised to have them repaired right away. The officer then asked what they were hauling in the back of the truck. At that, according to the officer, the men ab–*

"Absquatulated," said Fergal. Claire looked up at him in astonishment. "Absquatulated," he repeated.

"What does it mean?" she demanded.

"They took off," replied Fergal.

"Well, why doesn't it just say, *They took off?*" she complained. Then she continued.

> The vehicle proceeded along the narrow road at great speed. The patrol car gave chase but the truck eluded them. Border Patrol investigators plan to visit this city to examine the abandoned motor vehicle.

"Goodness, Fergal, that was what Jake and his friend were up to, the trip they were talking about with that man." Claire was looking around anxiously as if weighing their options.

"M-maybe we should tell your fath—"

"Shhh, Fergal. No. We're not telling my father or anyone – not yet, anyhow. We don't know, maybe it was perfectly innocent, maybe they were hunting up there, you know? Or visiting family."

"But why did they absquatulate?" asked Fergal. "It sounds like they had something in the back of that truck they didn't want the Border Patrol to find."

"I don't know, Fergal, but if Jake was in that truck and people find out, it will only make things worse for Sarah. Let me think, I just have to think about it." Her rosy face contorted as she contemplated this new development while Fergal stood silently, looking increasingly apprehensive.

~ 26 ~

Tom and Bromley were in the Wellington garage, leaning over the fender of a shiny new motorcar, a 1917 Hupmobile roadster, staring at the engine.

"That there, Sir, 'at's whatcha call the carburetor. It's where the gas and the air get mixed. Very tricky device – very tricky. Don't go messin' with 'at would be my advice. Otherwise you get a mixture that's either too rich or too lean. Either way, you got trouble."

"What's all that there?" asked Tom pointing toward the rear of the engine.

"Oh, that's the clutch, sir, and the gearbox. The clutch I can fix, need be. But the gearbox, well, let's just 'ope she don't need no fixin', sir."

"Wow, Bromley, there's so much to know about motors these days, eh? How'd you learn so much? From books?"

Bromley shook his head. "Nay, nay. The old fashion way. Me pa, 'e had a livery down Springfield. Since I was knee-high he had me workin' on wagons and buggies. Then he got one o' them steamer cars and he'd spend hours out in the barn tryin' to make that ting go." The old man laughed. "Gracious me, I'd love to see 'is eyes if he could 'ave a look at this machine. He'd be flabbergasted, I do believe, sir – downright flabbergasted."

Just then Anne appeared at the garage door. "Sorry to interrupt. Any luck teaching my brother about motors, Mr. Bromley?"

"Oh, aye. He'll do jus' fine, miss. Well, I got an appointment for your father's car down at Mosher's. Better be on me way." Bromley started the long, elegant Pierce-Arrow in the next stall, backed it out into the driveway, and drove off.

"So, Tommy, now you have this shiny new roadster, where'll you be off to? Taking Carolyn for Sunday drives? Say, maybe you could be her chauffeur – pick her up in Amherst on Friday afternoons, bring her home, then take her back on Sundays. Her mother would be relieved – anything to spare her daughter from riding the electrics." She smiled at Tom.

"Maybe I could, Annie, maybe I could. I don't know about that girl, she doesn't seem to want to spend a lot of time with ole Tommy these days. Always studying, you know?" Tom closed the hood, picked up a rag and began wiping the gleaming red fenders. Anne watched him for a moment, weighing her words. Finally she spoke.

"I haven't had much chance to talk with her either, Tommy. I think we've spoken only once since you came home. And she was upset then."

"Upset?"

"Yes, it was the first time you went to see her after you got home. She said you – she thought you were acting like you were frightened, or anxious."

Tom shook his head. "Probably just nerves, you know, first time seeing her after months. Anybody'd be – anxious."

"It's just that, well, you – sometimes at night you get in a state."

"A state?"

"Well, I heard you calling out, crying– "

"Crying?" Tom shook his head. "I have not been crying. When have I been crying?"

"Tommy, I'm just thinking maybe your – the ship and the – torpedo – and the rail crash – all that. Maybe it's had more effect on you than you realize."

"Listen, Annie, I know you read a lot of books and magazines and newspapers. So just because you read about that Dr. Freud guy you consider yourself some kind of an expert?"

"Tommy, no, I don't consider myself an expert. I just think–"

Tom interrupted, picking up a tin of wax. "Listen, Annie, I got a lot of work to do here, okay?"

Anne's expression hardened. "Fine, then, I'll leave you to it," she replied curtly. Then she left the garage without another word.

A few minutes later she returned. "Tommy, I'm sorry, I know you are busy. I just wanted to tell you that Jack has been asking about you in his letters. I told him about your new motor and he said he'd like to see it. Maybe – maybe you could drive it over to Worcester one day and take him for a ride."

Tom did not reply but continued polishing his new car.

~ 27 ~

Jack was seated by a window in the foyer of his dormitory staring intently at his trigonometry book. All it took was the sight of a single trigonometry problem, even an easy one, to sour his mood, and he had before him ten problems to complete before tomorrow morning's class. He was worried.

Just then a gleaming red roadster pulled up to the curb. Its driver stepped onto the walk, looked around, then approached the front entrance with a familiar self-assured swagger and casual air despite the small cast on his left forearm. Book in hand, Jack rose and stepped out of the front door.

"Hey, Tommy. How are you doing?"

Tom smiled and spoke slowly. "Just fine, Mr. Bernard, just fine."

"Wow, look at that car. Anne told me about it but, wow, what the heck is it?"

"A Hupmobile, Jack, a brand new 1917 Hupmobile. It's got all the latest features, buddy. Electric starter, Zenith carburetor, water-cooled motor, four cylinders – you won't believe the power, Jack, you won't believe it. How about we take it for a ride?"

Jack nodded. Tom offered him the keys. "Eh, no, I don't think so, Tommy. I wouldn't know how to operate such a machine. You drive."

"Okay, Jack, okay." For the next half hour, the roadster careened along country roads through Holden, Paxton, and Boylston. Tom was obviously very proud of his new motorcar and spared no effort to show Jack its many features. As for Jack, he was unnerved by Tom's driving, swerving around curves, passing other cars, a smug smile on his face as if he was in some kind of road race. Finally, they returned to campus and parked in front of Jack's dormitory.

Tom gazed up at the ivy-covered building. "Nice lookin' digs, Jack. Very nice."

"Yeh, well, I barely have a chance to look around and admire the scenery these days." Jack raised the heavy tome.

Tom chuckled. "Jack Bernard – always got his nose in a book."

Jack nodded ruefully. "Yeh, well, that's why I'm here, ya know."

"What? You're not trying to say that this place is getting the best of you?"

Jack shrugged. "So, what's new with you, Tommy?"

Just then their conversation was interrupted by shouts from a group of young men playing football on the lawn of the laboratory building across the street.

"Looks like some of your classmates find time for something other than studies. Hey, want to give your old pal a tour? I want to see if this place is good enough for Jack Bernard. Nothing but the best–"

Jack interrupted. "Sure, Tommy, sure. Come in, have a look at my room first."

The two friends looked in briefly on Jack's room. It was littered with books, notepads, and crumpled up papers. On Jack's desk Tom spotted an ivory slide rule in a slim leather case. He picked it up, staring at the intricate scales and minute numerals. Then he threw a quizzical expression Jack's way.

"Slide rule," explained Jack. "You musta learned how to use one back at Dorchester," referring to the private preparatory school Tom attended.

"I guess so, Jack. Lot of that's just a blur these days. *The dim, dark past,*" he added with a sardonic smile.

154

An hour later they sat staring at menus in a restaurant near the campus that catered to students. Tom had already made a dent in a tall dark lager while Jack's beer was untouched. "Go ahead, Jack, whatever you want, Delmonico steak, pot roast dinner. You name it – my treat."

After they had ordered, Jack leaned back in his seat and looked his friend in the eye. "So, what's new with you, Tommy? How's Carolyn?"

"She's doing fine. She likes college life all right. She's studying up a storm in Amherst, just like you. Seems to like it. She doesn't say as much, but my guess is she's just relieved to be out from under her mother's thumb, you know? She's got all these girlfriends she likes a lot, and she's always talking about some lecture or play or concert. I'd say she's having a grand time."

"What's her place like? Is it nice?"

"Well, I don't know. I haven't been over to see it yet. Not sure I'm going to, either." Jack was surprised. "Listen, Jack, I might as well tell you. I broke it off with Carolyn. Seems like we live in different worlds. And I figured it would be hard on her since I might be shipping out again."

"Huh?" replied Jack, his jaw dropping in disbelief.

"Yeh, I'm thinking of re-enlisting."

"But haven't you done your part? I mean—" He glanced at Tom's cast, but he was thinking of everything else Tom had been through.

"I'm not saying I'd be serving on a ship, Jack. I could, I swear I could, but they probably wouldn't want me, you know. I'll never be a hundred percent." He raised his cast. Then he sighed. "I'm hopin' maybe I can work on a base – stateside, I mean – like Newport or Norfolk or somewhere else. "

"But why, Tommy? Haven't you done enough?"

"We're still at war, Jack, them damned Krauts are marching through Belgium – and France – and Poland – the bastards." Tom's face was suddenly bright red, his jaw set. He was obviously trying to rein in his emotions. Finally he continued. "And I don't feel right sitting home while other guys are doing the fighting for me." He looked up just then and saw Jack's smile vanish. "No – no – Jack, I didn't mean it like that. Come on – you don't think I was talking about you? I mean, you have a – a proven condition. Your own doc said it."

Tom was referring to Jack's recent illness. Jack had been accepted for admission to Worcester Polytechnic Institute at the end of his senior year of high school. But despite a generous scholarship, he was worried about his family and chose instead to work at Wellington Textiles for a year to save some money. That spring, while working in the dyehouse, he suffered several seizures. The initial diagnosis had been epilepsy, but in time it was determined that the episodes were triggered by a noxious solvent, benzene, used to scour wool. Eventually the family physician, Dr. Gibson, concluded that Jack was not suffering from epilepsy and should remain healthy so long as he avoided benzene. But Jack was shocked to learn that his medical condition made him ineligible for military service. The Army draft began that summer. Tom had immediately enlisted in the Navy. But there would be no draft notice for Jack, nor would he be eligible to enlist in any military service according to Dr. Gibson.

Jack shook his head. "You know, I think 'bout that every day, every single damn day. Here we are – me and these other college guys – what are we doin', anyways? Playin' ball – drinkin' beer – jokin' around – you know, it's all so jolly. Meanwhile, thousands a guys are in them trenches, or on ships like you were, never knowin' —"

Jack wished he hadn't carried the conversation in that direction and quickly changed the subject. "So, how's your arm doin'?"

"Better, Jack, much better. Another few weeks it'll be like new, I bet."

"Good, Tom, that's good." Tom was nodding but looking away.

Tom paused. "Say, how are your sisters? Claire's at Forestdale now, right? Just like her big brother."

"Yeh, she sure is. But she doesn't have much to say about it. You know how it is for new kids? Remember how you came to my rescue in grade eight?"

Tom shook his head. "I can't say as I do, Jack. What – did I save you from drowning in the river or something?"

"Nah. There was these two Irish boys and they were gettin' on me in the schoolyard, about bein' French. You told 'em to get lost. That was the first time we met, Tommy, ya know that? Wow, that's a lot of years we been friends."

"Well, I bet Claire's got some friends at Forestdale that will make her feel at home."

Jack chuckled. "The only one I know of is a neighbor from Westfield – Fergal – Fergal Dooley." Jack shook his head and smiled. "Bit of an odd duck. I don't think he's about to rescue Claire – or anyone."

"And Marie?"

"She's working for the telephone company in Westfield four days a week, mostly mornings. It's all right, I guess, and it means she can be home by the time Claire gets back each day. My dad and our neighbor Felix have opened a garage business, right in our barn. That's keepin' them pretty busy."

Just then a group of young men entered the restaurant, laughing and talking loudly as they seated themselves in the next booth. "Everyone at WPI seems to be havin' a jolly time, Jack, everyone except you."

"Yeh, well, it's hard, Tommy. I'm just not sure if I'm smart enough, you know? I want to do well, get decent grades, and that means I don't have too much time for gay-blading. I am playing intramural football, though, and that's fun, but it ends soon, before exams. Meantime, I gotta–"

Suddenly Tom's eyes were flashing. He was listening intently, not to Jack but to one of the students in the next booth expostulating loudly about the war: "We got no right stickin' our noses in over there," the fellow was saying. "What do we care what happens to Belgium? Who ever heard of Belgium, anyway? The Jerries are only defending themselves is all. They're just doin' what anyone would do. The Brits and the French, they're pathetic. They deserve what they get."

At that Tom rose from his seat, turned, and roared at the young man, "You don't know what the hell you're talking about, buddy."

The student rose to his feet. "Yeh? And who are you?"

"A guy who knows a hell of a lot more than you do about the war in Europe."

"Since when?" The young man shot a dismissive look at Tom, then turned and smirked at his friends. Tom reached out and grabbed his sleeve, spinning him back toward him. At that the fellow raised his right arm. Tom drew back his right arm, about to throw a punch, but his elbow caught Jack square in the mouth.

Jack dropped to his knees, his hands clutching his jaw, a thin stream of blood trickling from between his fingers. Unaware, Tom proceeded to pummel his opponent with punches. Despite his cast he knocked him to the floor in front of the booth. His companions rose as one and lunged on top of the two in an effort to separate them.

Tom was roaring. "You make me sick, you lousy college good-for-nothing. You think you're so smart, but you know nothing, you hear me? Nothing." He turned toward Jack who by this time was seated in the booth holding a blood-soaked napkin to his lip.

"What – Jack, you all right?"

"I'm okay, I'll be all right." He looked up and into his friend's face. "Forget it, okay?"

158

Tom turned and glowered at his nemesis who was by now standing surrounded by his chums.

"Tommy, forget him, eh? C'mon, sit down and relax."

The other fighter was quickly ushered away to another room, but not before the fellow let loose several obscene phrases at his attacker. At that Jack pleaded: "Let's get outta here, Tommy." Then the two exited, Tom tossing several bills onto the table as they departed. Out on Highland Street Jack began to lead Tom to his dormitory. But at the front walk Tom stopped.

"Listen Jack, I gotta get going."

"Geez, Tommy, you shouldn't be drivin' all that way back to Holyoke alone, in the dark. Why don't you stay the night? You can sleep on the floor in my room – there's some cushions in the lounge you can use for a mattress."

Tom shook his head. "Uh-uh. I betta go."

Jack sensed that Tom was still angry. "C'mon, Tommy—"

Tom stood stone-faced. "See ya." He began walking toward his car. Then he paused and turned. "Listen, Jack, you – er – won't tell my sister about this, eh? She wouldn't understand."

"Understand?"

"What – what I went through. What it's like – "

"What *did* you go through, Tommy? You know, you've never told me—"

Tom stood impassively, his lips frozen in a tight moue. "I gotta go."

~ 28 ~

Manfred Becker stood on the sidewalk in front of Paddy's puffing on a cigarette. He looked up Suffolk Street, then down, then turned and entered the bar. He was surprised at how many imbibers he found at midday, some standing or leaning on the bar, others seated at several small tables along the wall. He ordered a beer, then stood holding his drink only a few steps from the door, waiting.

A Victrola in the back room was playing sweet, sad songs that seemed to reflect the melancholy mood of the patrons, the city, the nation: *Homeward Bound, I Didn't Raise My Boy to Be a Soldier, Keep the Home Fires Burning*. The war that America had entered only six months earlier, the Great War, the one that so many Americans were so confident could be wrapped up in no time, was not going well. Reports of casualties among American forces appeared in the newspapers daily along with news of Navy vessels torpedoed or damaged by mines, some alarmingly close to the east coast. The patriotic fervor that had gripped the nation in the early months of the war was fast turning to doubt, dread, fear. Was it possible that the Central Powers – Germany, Austria-Hungary, and their allies – were about to succeed in their dastardly mission and overrun France, Belgium, and eventually England? How many American soldiers, sailors, marines, would be sacrificed before the fighting was over? Would it all prove futile?

Manfred had almost finished his beer and was getting restless when a dark figure appeared in the doorway. It was Werner. Manfred pulled on his coat, looked around blankly, then stepped out onto the street. Leaning against a telephone pole, he pulled another cigarette from his coat pocket, lit it, and took several long pulls. Only then did his eyes rise.

"Lovely day in Holyoke, eh Becker?" observed Werner.

"Yep, just hunky-dory, as the Yanks say." There was a long pause. "So, what's up? Your message sounded like something was happenin'."

"Vell, you could say that, *Mein Herr*. You could say that." He flicked ashes from his cigar onto the sidewalk. "Here's vat. The boys in New York are gettin' nervous." Manfred listened impassively. "Feds and cops, they're all over the city. They say that copper Tunney ees putting the 'eat on. Give him a few more veeks, he'll have all our connections in the harbor cut off."

"So, what're you sayin' – the plan is dead?"

Werner looked around, then shook his head once. "Nope."

"What, then?"

Werner lowered his voice. "They vant to move it up a veek. This veekend, Sunday morning – early – before the noose gets too tight, before it ees too late."

"That's impossible, Werner. The stuff's still in crates. It'll take days. Can't be done."

"It must be done, that ees all there ees."

Suddenly Manfred's tone changed. He spoke more calmly, as if buoyed with new confidence. "Listen, I been tinkin'. The drive from 'ere to Jersey – with all those fireworks – that's a big gamble, a real big gamble. All it takes is one copper along the way who needs to make his quota of stops for the night. Or a blowout, ya know? The truck flies into the ditch, the stuff's blown to smithereens, and the driver's off to the Pearly Gates."

Werner shrugged. "That ees the business ve are in, *Mein Herr*, like it or no. Chance ve take."

"I gotta better idea." Manfred nodded toward the Flats, the lowest section of the city along the banks of the Connecticut River. "There's dozens of mills within a mile of where we're standin' right now – paper mills, textiles mills, foundries, gunworks. They're wide open. It'd be a cinch."

Werner shook his head slowly. "Forget it, Becker, just forget it. Arms, troops, ships – American ships, British ships – big ones – that ees vat they are lookink for. They vant to shake Vilson and his generals – make the people start to doubt him. They are not interested in poppink off some two-bit factory makink lace doilies – or toilet paper."

Becker's voice got lower, more intense. "Wellington Textiles, they got big contracts with the War Department." He looked squarely into Werner's eyes. "I know that place inside-out, Werner. Sittin' ducks."

Werner was shaking his head, but Becker persisted. "You gotta admit, this New Jersey trip is risky. So why risk it at all? Why not find a much easier target right here in our backyard?"

Finally Werner nodded. "Maybe so, maybe so." He took a long draw on his cigar, then blew out a swirl of smoke. "There ees a big meetink in New Haven tomorrow night. I vill see what they say about this idea. No promises, but vee vill see."

It wasn't much, but it was enough to give Manfred some hope. Hope that he'd be back in the big leagues, not just some small-time errand boy. The failure of the Springfield arsenal plot was still fresh in his mind. It wasn't his fault, he was sure, but he was being blamed. He had to erase that, maybe with something bigger, much bigger, something that, when it was successful, would be to his credit, his and nobody else's.

Several days later, Werner left a message under Manfred's door, dashing his hopes:

> *Visited Uncle Boris in NH. Staying with original plan. Meet him for breakfast tomorrow 5 am, Paddy's.*

Early the next morning a rusted old ice truck bounced along a rough, snow-covered farm lane in the darkness, its headlights only dimly illuminating the way ahead. The road followed the edge of a field of corn stubble, then entered a stunted forest. Shortly it came to a halt before a rusted iron gate with a hand-made sign reading *Keep Out*. The driver climbed out, unlocked the padlock, and swung the gate wide. A few hundred yards further the truck turned sharply and entered a deep cleft in the hillside that widened into a bowl-shaped excavation, the old Martinson Quarry as locals called it after the original owner. The truck pulled up to a building in the center of the quarry that once had been a stable and warehouse for the quarry operation. The driver exited the truck, slid the old stable door open, then pulled the truck inside.

"Back here, *Mein Herr*," instructed Manfred to his passenger. He led him through a door into a windowless room at the rear of the shed. Old quarry tools were strewn about – saws, sledges, crowbars, spikes, mallets, wedges – as well as several heavy sleds that once carried huge loads of stone drawn by a team of horses. The quarry had been a busy place back when the trolley lines were under construction in Westfield, Holyoke, and Springfield. The rock was dense, volcanic, but fortunately had parallel joints that made it easy to crush into trap rock, the preferred material for railroad and trolley line beds.

He lit a single kerosene lantern and held it high as the pair looked around. In one corner a dusty canvas tarp lay over a dozen or so heavy wooden crates. "I haven't touched 'em since they was delivered," explained Manfred. He lit several more lamps and hung them from the ceiling. He and his guest pried the lids off two boxes. One contained dozens of lengths of lead, each a tube about six inches long.

"Ahh, seegars," observed Manfred. The man nodded. "You seen 'em before?"

Again the man nodded. "Uh-huh."

Another carton contained large tins with wide, tight-fitting lids marked with the letter D. Inside was an innocuous looking powder.

"What's 'at?" asked Manfred.

"Picric acid – Explosive D, they call it," replied the man. Then he added, "Nasty stuff."

Another carton held four glass bottles, each filled with a clear, syrupy liquid and fitted with a white ceramic plug.

"And these?"

"Sulfuric acid."

"Then how da these things work?" asked Manfred at last.

The man held the end of one of the lead pipes up to the lantern, revealing a hollow chamber inside. "See that tube in there? See how this end is smaller?" Manfred nodded. The man opened another box that contained hundreds of copper disks. He picked up one and tried to insert it into the lead chamber. At first it resisted. He found a hammer and a short, blunt nail and used them to force the slug into position.

"First you solder the slug in place. So, now there are two chambers with the slug between 'em. See?" Manfred nodded. "The picric goes in the small chamber. Seal it with wax, then molten lead. Then about four ounces of sulfuric goes in the other chamber. Seal it, too."

"That's it?"

"Well, yah. But once it's loaded it's like a fuse. The acid eats through the copper. When they mix – kaboom."

"How long?"

"Depends."

"On what?"

The man reached into the carton and picked out several copper disks. "There are three sizes of slugs – thin, medium, and thick. The thin ones take about twelve hours, medium about a day, the big ones at least three days. Those British munitions ships that sank last summer off Long Island? Couple hundred a these in the hold of each ship. Three days, almost to the minute from when those Micks loaded them with cargo — kaboom." The man looked up at Manfred and smiled.

"Did you invent them, *Mein Herr*?"

The man shook his head. "A guy by the name of Scheele – Walter Scheele. Ingenious, eh?"

Manfred nodded. "So what're you gonna do with 'em here?"

"Well, they gotta be ready to go late Saturday. So Wednesday I start loading the picric and sealing the one end. It's slow work." He paused and lifted the lids of several more crates. "At least a couple hundred here. Saturday morning I load the sulfuric in the other end, seal it up, and pack 'em. They'll be on their way to Jersey that night, loaded on ships the next day. All's gotta work like clockwork."

"But wouldn't it be a lot easier to do the loading in Jersey, close to the docks?"

"Ya, sure, but there's Feds, Bureau, troops all over the place down there these days. Too much risk." The man smiled and seemed to relax. He leaned against one of the stacks of boxes, then gazed around the room. "This place safe? I mean, we have to worry about someone getting in here?"

"Naw, never seen nobody 'round 'ere. And the place is locked up tight."

"Well, it's pretty good cover, really. Anyone find the stuff here probably figure it was left behind from the old quarry operation. Smart move, Becker, smart move."

"Yeh, well, that's what I figured. Anyway, the stuff'll be gone by Saturday night, right?"

"Ya. That's the plan." The man began opening other crates and examining the contents of each. After several minutes he looked up at Manfred. "Why don't you get going, then, huh? No need for you to hang around. I'm just gonna look over the stuff and see what I need to bring Wednesday."

"Okay, just snap the padlocks behind ya, eh?"

"Ya, okay, right. You got a key for me, so I can get back in when I need to?"

"No need. I can meet you here. That way I can help."

The man shook his head. "Better I work alone. I need to concentrate. Besides, no point us both gettin' blown up, right?" he added with an eerie smile.

"Okay, if that's what you want. But I don't have no extra keys. I'll hang the padlock so it looks like it's locked. Doesn't matter no how. Like I said, nobody comes 'round here."

The next afternoon Claire and Fergal stepped off the trolley at the Southampton Road stop. Side by side they made their way along the road toward home. As they approached the Bernard farmhouse, a truck passed them, splashing water from a puddle that they had to jump to avoid. The driver seemed to enjoy this and was smiling and laughing as he passed.

"C-Claire," began Fergal. "Did you see that guy in the truck?"

"Huh?"

"From the quarry – he was the guy we saw at the quarry – that Manfred guy. I'm sure of it. He had that beard and the same kind a hat."

"Oh, my god, Fergal. Do you think he's headin' to the quarry?"

"Maybe." Fergal nodded. "Maybe so."

"We gotta find out, Fergal. We gotta go to the quarry."

Fergal hesitated. "But, you – you swore – remember? No more investigating."

"Oh, come on, Fergal. We'll just have a quick peek."

A few minutes later they were following the narrow path that led to Hampton Ponds. Then they were climbing the trail to the lip of the quarry looking down on the shed. Fergal was uneasy but Claire was determined to have a close look. She started down the steep gravel-strewn section of trail toward the rear of the shed and Fergal followed nervously.

Peering through the same openings as before, they could see the truck, the one that had splashed them, its two rear doors open. As they watched the sinister-looking man emerged from another room carrying wooden crates, crates that appeared to be loaded with short lead pipes. They watched in silence as he made several trips carrying more crates.

Finally, he closed the storage room door, slammed shut the truck's rear doors, then climbed in. The engine gave a few weak sputters before it started, then backed out of the shed into the gray late day. The truck halted, the man climbed out and closed the shed doors, then drove away.

"Wha-whatta you think's in those crates, Fergal?"

The boy shrugged his shoulders.

"Maybe it's the stuff Jake and that other guy went to New Hampshire to pick up," offered Claire. "Spirits, maybe. I read that a lotta guys are sellin' liquor that's smuggled over the border from Canada. They don't pay any taxes and they sell it to whoever makes 'em the best offer."

"I'll bet there's more inside," replied Fergal, peering through the gap in the siding.

"He probably keeps this place locked up pretty tight," observed Claire. Their eyes met. At their feet lay a pile of old, weathered planks. Claire idly kicked at the pile, then picked up a long, narrow plank that had been cut at an angle, forming a point at one end. She inserted the pointed end into the narrow opening in the side of the shed and used it like a pry-bar. A strip of loose siding yielded and began to bend, opening up a small gap.

Meanwhile Fergal disappeared around the corner of the building, only to reappear seconds later with an iron pipe that had been lying on the ground beside the shed. He used the pipe to pry another board loose, but the gap produced was not as large.

"Look, Claire, you hold that board against the wall. I'll use it like a f–f–fulcrum." She did as he instructed and the gap suddenly widened. Claire began to pull on the loose board. It started to split. "Careful," warned Fergal. "We don't want to break it or someone will find it." He released the board, moved the fulcrum up, then pried once again. Now the entire board began to yield, not merely to bend. At the bottom the gap was over six inches wide and over a foot long. "Once more," said Fergal. And again he moved the fulcrum up and pried.

"That one too, Fergal," suggested Claire pointing to a small gap beneath the adjacent panel. In a matter of minutes they had the second board jutting out alongside the first. Fergal wedged another board under the two panels to keep them open. Then he stooped down and, twisting as he pushed with his feet, inserted his skinny frame through the opening. Claire watched in amazement. "Oh, my god, Fergal, you did it. Let me—"

Fergal reached one hand back through the opening. "Claire, my rucksack." She handed it to him and then, with a little effort, she too was inside.

Inside it was dark, very dark. The only illumination was a narrow shaft of daylight that entered through the crack they had just opened and a similar wedge of light that came through around the large sliding doors on the front of the building. As they peered into the darkness, vague shapes gradually came into view – a tractor, a winch, some old wagon wheels, and, on a shelf, three kerosene lamps, their glass globes blackened with soot. The air was thick with the smell of kerosene, dust, and musty old wood.

Fergal rustled through his rucksack and withdrew a book of matches. Soon one of the lamps was producing an eerie glow along with dense sooty smoke. He turned a knurled knob on the lamp – the flame brightened and the smoke disappeared. Now the full dimensions of the room were visible. It was mostly empty except for the tractor, winch, wheels, plus a pile of canvas tarps and a number of greasy canisters that might have held oil, kerosene, or gasoline. At the rear was a door that appeared to lead to another room.

"Whattaya think's in there?" asked Claire. They approached it slowly. A padlock hung from a hasp. "Darn, it's locked."

Fergal reached out, grasped the padlock in one hand, looked closely at it, then gave it a twist. The lock yielded. "Nope, just looks like it is." He removed the padlock and slowly opened the door. The pair stepped inside.

They gazed around at more old quarry equipment. Claire was the first to see the boxes. "Wait a second —"

The boy raised the kerosene lamp above the boxes.

"What is all this stuff, Fergal?"

He placed his rucksack on the floor, then lifted the lid on one of the crates. "Lead pipes. Hundreds."

Meanwhile Claire opened another crate containing large glass jugs. "Look, Fergal, maybe this is booze, eh?"

"I dunno." He pointed to the markings on the outside of the crate and read it. "H – 2 – S – O – 4."

"What's that?" asked Claire.

"Acid – sulfuric acid."

Claire looked at him in amazement. "What's it for?"

"Printers use it, engravers. My da has a bottle he uses for sterilizing when he dehorns the oxen. Stinks something awful."

Then Claire's eye fell on one of the tins. "Picric. What's picric, Fergal? Maybe they used this stuff in the quarry?"

The boy shook his head and shrugged. "Maybe." He looked around the room at the old quarry tools and implements, all coated with a thick layer of dust and laced with cobwebs. "But these crates – I bet they haven't been here long. See?" He dragged one finger across the top of one of the crates, then held it up to the lantern. "They're clean, no dust."

Just then a low rumble could be heard from outside.

"Fergal," whispered Claire with alarm, "the truck. He's back. We gotta get outta here."

"But—" Fergal carefully replaced the lids on the three crates they had disturbed. Then he pulled the tarp over it. The rumble was getting louder. They stepped through the storage room door. Fergal paused and replaced the padlock in exactly the position it was in when they found it. Claire went straight for the opening they had made in the rear wall, but Fergal went first to the shelves where he snuffed out the lantern and placed it back where he had found it. Then he headed toward the entry gap. They could see the headlights of the approaching truck shining through the gaps around the shed doors.

Claire wriggled through the opening and turned to help Fergal when he whispered. "My rucksack – I forgot – I gotta get it."

"No, Fergal, it's too late."

But the boy disappeared back across the room toward the storage room door just as the truck came to a halt in front of the garage doors. In a moment he came out of the storage room carrying his rucksack. Again he closed the door behind him and carefully arranged the padlock. He was halfway across the larger room when the garage door rattled, then slid open.

The man paused, sniffing as if he detected an odor in the still air inside the shed. Then he went back to the truck, climbed in, and drove it through the doors into the shed. He climbed out and sniffed again. Barely ten feet away, Fergal was crouched behind the rusted tractor. The man went to the storage room door, removed the padlock, and disappeared inside. This was Fergal's chance, maybe his only chance, to escape undetected. In seconds he slipped through the opening in the wall. Claire was crouched in the shadows outside, holding her breath with fear for the boy.

They both knew there was no chance of closing the pried boards without making noise. Fergal took one of the pieces of lumber from the pile and laid it against the wall to hide the opening. Silently the pair climbed the steep path to the lip of the quarry. The moon was just beginning to peek over the eastern

170

horizon, allowing them to move quickly without stumbling. They watched as the truck departed once again.

"Oh my goodness, Fergal, I've never been so scared in my life. I was sure he was gonna see you," exclaimed Claire as they walked side by side along the wider path that led around the west side of Hampton Ponds to Southampton Road.

She looked up at the boy. His eyes briefly met hers, then darted away. She reached out and grasped his arm, bringing his march quickly to a halt.

"It – it was – I mean – Fergal–" She paused. Their eyes met. "You are something, Fergal Dooley, really. You know so many things, and you're smart and clever – and brave."

Fergal looked again into Claire's eyes, then down at the ground, then into her eyes again. "We're a good team, you an' me." He smiled.

"Yes, Fergal, we are a good team – a really good team."

When they reached the Dooley farm, Claire spoke up. "Well, Fergal, I'll see you tomorrow morning."

"I'll walk you home," replied Fergal. "You shouldn't be going home alone. My aunt says a girl should be escorted to her door."

Claire was about to protest, but decided against it. They walked together along the road.

"Fergal, your aunt, you never call her by name. What's 'er name?"

"Beatrice. Aunt Beatrice. She's my ma's sister."

They continued walking. But Claire was thinking, trying to choose her words carefully. "What happened – I mean, where's your mother, Fergal?"

"She stayed in Ireland. She was sick and they put 'er in a home."

"Does she ever write to you?" Fergal shook his head. "You must miss 'er." Fergal nodded. "I miss my mom, too," she added wistfully. She sighed. "You know, her voice, how warm it felt when she held me. And the treats she used to make me."

"Treats? Like what?" asked Fergal.

Claire thought for a moment. "Ginger snaps. I loved them. She'd have a plate of ginger snaps waiting on the kitchen table after school. Sometimes when I'd get home, even before I opened the door, I could smell 'em. I miss that, Fergal, I really do."

The next morning Charles Bernard was emptying the ashes from the kitchen stove when he heard a rap at the door. "Morning, Fergal."

The boy stood on the step looking up at Charles, clinging to his rucksack. "Morning, sir. Eh, may – may I – speak with Claire, sir? It's – we – I gotta ask 'er about – Latin – homework." His eyes fell.

"Yeh, sure, come on in." Charles turned toward the back hallway and called to his daughter, "Claire, you got a visitor."

In a moment Claire emerged from her bedroom. "Fergal – whatta you doin' here?"

The boy stood silent, his eyes shifting from Claire to her father, then back to her. Finally he spoke. "I – I had a question – about – our Latin exercises."

"Oh, yeh, okay. Well, let's go out to the barn. You can – show me there." Charles sensed there was something going on, something the two did not want to share with him.

Moments later Claire and Fergal stood at the rail of the sheep pen in the barn. Fergal pulled a heavy tome from his rucksack and balanced it on the rail. "You gotta see this, Claire. It's a cyclopedia of my da's." He quickly flipped to a page that he had marked and read:

Picric acid, derivative of phenol, toxic yellow crystalline form used as a dye or mordant for cotton and wool.

Claire nodded. "So, maybe that guy sells it to the mills. Jackie worked for a while in the dyehouse at Wellington Textiles. They use some awful stuff in those places, you know, to clean the wool and set the dyes."

"But look at this, Claire," added Fergal as he continued to read:

Also used as an explosive agent; when ignited it burns firstly with characteristic inky black smoke, finally detonating with surprising violence.

Their eyes met, then Claire spoke: "Maybe they use it in the quarry – you know, for blasting–"

Fergal nodded. "Yes, that's probably right."

~ 29 ~

Thanksgiving Day dawned bright and cold, the first rays of sun just illuminating the treetops as Marie Bernard emerged from the kitchen door, wrapped a woolen scarf around her neck against the chill, and shambled toward the barn to gather eggs. Her father, brother, and sister were still fast asleep. Jack had arrived by train the previous evening. Before retiring, he and his father had prepared a large turkey from a neighbor's farm to be roasted in the coal-fired oven. Claire had been charged with the task of cleaning, cutting, and peeling vegetables, an assignment she carried out more or less willingly.

When Charles and Evelyne Bernard first arrived in Holyoke from Québec in 1901, Jack was just a toddler and Marie still a babe in arms. The young couple had all they could do to put a regular meal on the table in those days, much less the expansive feast expected on Thanksgiving. A few years later when the family was in better circumstances, Charles would tell the children of that meager first holiday meal, about how little they had to put on the table beyond a few root vegetables, and about how stunned they were to hear a knock at their door and to discover a neighbor, *Monsieur* Gilbaut, offering them an enormous ham shank.

This particular Thanksgiving Day would be celebrated across the country with something less than the usual enthusiasm. On the minds of most Americans were the thousands of their countrymen caught up in the horror of the war in Europe. To make matters even more grim, many families had been ravaged by sickness and death of young and old from pneumonia, scarlet fever, and the Spanish influenza.

The Bernards attended the first of two masses at St. Agnes Church in the morning. Back home, everyone pitched in for the final preparations of the midday meal. A particular tradition of the Bernards before partaking of a holiday meal was an extended grace in which each family member contributed words of special thanks. Charles began by remembering his wife, Evelyne, her parents and grandparents as well as his own, all now gone but not forgotten. Marie offered a prayer for their sister, Thérèse, who had passed away of diphtheria over a decade earlier. Claire gave thanks for their neighbors, Felix, Madeleine, Émile, and Elaine Bousquet, and asked God to watch over them and soothe their grief on this first Thanksgiving without Stephen. Finally, Jack offered thanks for the return of Tom Wellington to his family.

Just as the meal was nearly over, a motorcar pulled into the yard. "That'll be Anne," said Jack. He had invited her to join them for their Thanksgiving dinner, but the Wellingtons would be celebrating at home with Anne's Uncle Richard and his wife Charlotte. Anne had agreed to drive to Westfield later in the day to join Jack and his family in their Thanksgiving dessert consisting of several pies Marie had baked for the occasion.

Jack stepped through the kitchen door just as Anne emerged from her motorcar. He smiled as she approached him, a wicker basket in one hand.

"What in–" she began, peering at his face. She placed her free hand against his chin and gently turned it, examining his injury. "What happened to you?"

Jack shrugged. "Oh, just a little header in practice the other day. It's nothing." Quickly he changed the subject. "Did you have a good Thanksgiving dinner?" Anne proceeded to describe the feast at the Wellington household in detail.

Inside, Anne greeted Marie in the kitchen, then placed the basket on the Hoosier cabinet. "This is from Mildred, her pumpkin spice pie." Claire quickly pulled Anne away to the parlor where she proudly showed off her needlework projects, tatting, knitting, embroidery.

A few minutes later everyone was seated around the kitchen table as Marie served up slices of pie and Claire poured coffee. When Anne asked Claire about school, she received a sharply-worded critique on her teachers, the principal, and certain of her classmates. Marie spoke briefly of her work at the telephone company, then launched into an animated description of her volunteer stints serving meals to nearly one thousand men several times a week at Camp Bartlett, just a mile up the road from the Bernard farmhouse.

"Jackie, you've been very quiet," observed Anne at one point when the conversation lagged. "Tell us all about your classes. Are they going well?"

"So-so," he replied. "Chem and rhetoric are fine, but the trigonometry has me buffaloed most of the time."

"According to Tommy you do nothing but study. He said your room was piled high with books and reams of paper. Do you like your school chums, Jackie?"

"Oh, sure, they're swell."

At that Claire spoke up, a devilish twinkle in her eye. "Funny how he gets along just dandy with all those new friends at college, then his best friend in the world comes to visit and pokes him in the kisser, eh?"

"What?" cried Anne, looking with shock, first at Claire, then at Jack.

"That's who give him the fat lip — Tommy," revealed Claire gleefully.

Jack glared at his younger sister, then turned to Anne smiling. "It was an accident. I – I surprised him 'n he turned all of a sudden. It wasn't his fist, it was his elbow."

"I thought you said–" began Anne. Just then Marie offered more pie and coffee and the matter was dropped, although Jack had a feeling his reprieve was only temporary.

When it came time for Anne to take her leave, she thanked Charles first, then Marie, then Claire. Jack helped her into her overcoat and walked her to her motorcar, hoping she'd be on her way without further discussion of his injury. But he was not to be so lucky.

"Jackie, I am annoyed at you," she began, pursing her lips and planting her hands firmly on her hips. "You lied to me about your lip. You told me it happened playing football when it was Tommy – Tommy hit you. Explain, please, why you felt it necessary to conceal this from me."

"It was nothing, Annie, really, just an accident."

"Jack Bernard," she replied adamantly. "I want to know the truth. What happened between you and Tommy? I noticed he was in a foul mood the morning after his trip to Worcester. Did you two fight?"

"No, Annie, we didn't fight."

"Well what happened then?"

"But he made me swear I wouldn't tell you, Annie."

"All the more reason to tell me, Jackie. I have to know what's going on with my own brother."

"Okay, okay. Tommy got into a tussle with someone in this restaurant where we went for supper. The guy was loud and going on about how America had no right being in the war in Europe. Tommy just flew into a tirade. He started throwing punches at this guy and I tried to stop him. And I took an elbow, that's all."

Anne was upset. "Oh, Jackie, I am so sorry. He – it's how he seems to be these days. Any little thing can set him off."

"Annie, please don't tell him I told you. He'll never speak to me again."

"I'd better be going," replied Anne. But she was upset, that was clear, upset and more worried than ever about her brother.

~ 30 ~

The next day Jack had planned to devote entirely to chores: a thorough mucking out of the animal pens, dressing the vegetable gardens, and helping his father to rig up a winch in the new garage. Shortly before noon a familiar motorcar pulled into the driveway.

"Tommy," said Jack to his father. He dropped his tools and walked out of the barn to greet his friend as he stepped from his motorcar. Just then Charles emerged from the barn and tipped his hat.

"'Lo Thomas, good to see you, son. On the mend?"

Tom smiled and nodded. "Yes, sir, definitely."

"And your folks, how a' they? Bet they're pleased to have you back home." Charles winced. "So a' we, son, be sure o' that."

"Well, sir, it is certainly good to be back in Holyoke." He looked up at the sign over the barn door. "How's the new business going?"

"Eh, well, we're keepin' the wolf from the door, least for the time bein'. Helps to have this guy 'ome to do some of the 'eavy liftin', though." He nodded toward Jack who shrugged. "Course, he has to spend a lot o' time with his books – and that sister a yours," added Charles with a wink to Tom. Then he turned to Jack. "'Nough for now, Son – I'm all done in. Anyways, I'm sure you and this guy got some catchin' up ta do. Nice to see you, Tom," he said, patting him on the shoulder. With that he shuffled off toward the kitchen door.

Jack showed Tom around the barn. It looked very different from the way he'd seen it just a few months earlier, now that it

179

had been converted to an automobile repair shop. They examined the new addition Charles and Felix were working on, a single story wood-frame garage. Finally, they sat in the workshop where the wood stove was producing some much-needed heat.

In the corner Tom noticed Jack's ice-fishing gear: tip-ups, tackle, auger, ax, sled. "Looks like you're all set for fishing." Jack nodded. Tom's expression softened as he looked at the gear. "We had some great times, you and me, out at Hampton Ponds, fishing through the ice, eh, Jack? I remember the first time I heard the ice boom — God, was I scared."

"Yeh," replied Jack, smiling. "You started runnin' for the shore. I had to go chasin' after you shoutin' that we weren't gonna fall in. You looked like you seen a ghost," added Jack, laughing.

"Yeh, I bet I did — I bet I did look like I'd seen a ghost."

"I got an idea, Tommy. I have about two weeks off around Christmas. How about if we go fishin', just the two of us? Like the good ole days."

Tom nodded. "Yeh, Jack, let's do it. That'd be swell. Maybe before Christmas, okay?" Jack nodded. There was a long silence. Then Tom spoke again. "Listen Jack, about what happened the other day — in Worcester. I wanted to ap—"

Just then Claire appeared at the workshop door. "Hi, Tommy."

Tom looked up at her and smiled. "Hi, Claire. Wow, you look like you've grown a foot since I saw you last. How are you? I hear you're going to Forestdale these days. Following in your big brother's footsteps, I guess?"

Claire shook her head. "More like trying to stay outta them," she replied, shooting a wry look towards her brother. "Say, maybe you boys can explain something. In the mill, do they use some stuff called picric acid, like for dyeing?"

Tom shook his head. "Never heard of it. Jack?"

Jack nodded. "I have. Mr. Sullivan, the dyer I worked for, he told me 'bout it once. It's a yellow powder – some mills use it as a mordant for setting the dyes. But I never seen it at Wellingtons'. Why do you wanna know?"

"Oh, it's not me. Fergal – Fergal Dooley – he was reading about it for school and they were saying about how it was used for dyeing fabric. Well, I betta get to my chores." Claire turned to leave, but just then Fergal appeared, rucksack in hand. "We gotta go," she commented as she tried to push him back through the door.

"Hey, Claire, aren't you gonna introduce your friend to Tom?"

Claire turned and sighed. "Tommy, this is Fergal Dooley. Fergal, this is Tommy Wellington. He's in the Navy." Fergal looked uncomfortable but managed a smile and a nod.

Jack continued. "Hey, Fergal, Claire says you were wonderin' 'bout picric acid, huh? I was just tellin' her how they use it in some mills for fixing dyes – you know what I mean?"

Fergal nodded. "Yes, sir. It's a mordant – to make the dyes fast. It's sometimes called phenol."

Jack was impressed. "That's right, Fergal. Say, are you interested in chemistry? 'Cause I have some college books you might want to look at."

"Come on, Fergal," interjected Claire. "We got Latin exercises to do, remember?"

But Fergal wouldn't budge. "Claire and I found a lot of it in a shed at the Martinson Quarry," he added. He paused when he saw Claire was looking at him intently, her eyes flashing. "That's–"

"They're not interested, Fergal – come on, let's go," interrupted Claire as she again tried to push him backward through the workshop door.

"The quarry?" replied Jack, his eyes shifting from Fergal to Claire. "What the heck were you two doin' in that place?"

"Just lookin' 'round, that's all," explained Claire.

Jack was alarmed. "Just lookin' around – in an old quarry?"

Claire turned and faced her brother squarely. "Well, maybe it's good that we did. There was that picric stuff, and some sulfer—"

"Sulfuric acid," interjected Fergal.

"Yeh, sul-fer-ic," repeated Claire.

"And pipes – lead pipes, hundreds," added Fergal.

Jack looked mystified. "Picric and sulfuric acid." His eyes met Tom's. "That's bad stuff."

Claire was suddenly worried. "Please, Jackie, don't tell Daddy. I promise we won't go near the place again."

Jack smiled. He enjoyed watching his little sister squirm. Lately she was getting too big for her britches, or so he'd been telling Tom, and needed a comeuppance.

"Claire, if Dad finds out I know about this and haven't told him, then *I'll* be in dutch."

"He won't find out if you don't tell him, pleeeease."

Finally, Jack relented. "Okay, but maybe we should go over there and see what's goin' on. Tommy?"

"Yeh, sure."

They all clambered into Tom's motorcar, Jack and Claire in the passenger seat next to Tom, Fergal wedged in the narrow space behind the seats that was meant for one or two valises.

The roadster made its way slowly along the narrow road beside the cornfield, then through the open gate and into the quarry. As it pulled up in front of the shed a figure could be seen in the shadowy interior.

"Uh-oh," said Claire. "It's probably that guy Manfred that Jake and his friend were workin' for. We betta not–" But as she spoke the figured emerged into the light.

"Professor Smith?" called Jack as he and the others climbed out of the roadster, surprise in his voice. The man seemed momentarily taken aback. "Remember me, sir? Jack Bernard."

"Ah, yes, certainly, of course."

"This is my friend, Tom Wellington, Anne's brother." He turned and spoke to Tom. "Professor Smith is a geologist – a paleontologist, actually. We ran into him when we went up to Smith's Ferry to see the dinosaur tracks."

"How do you do?" replied the professor.

Tom smiled and shook the man's hand. "Pleased to meet you, sir."

"Hello, Professor Smith," chimed Claire.

"Ah, Miss Bernard, nice to – to see you again. And your friend, there–"

"Fergal – Fergal Dooley," she added. Professor Smith smiled at Fergal who nodded his head several times, his expression brightening briefly. "What are you doing here, Professor? Looking for more dinosaur tracks?" asked Claire.

"Why, yes, yes indeed. Always exploring about, I am. A geologist cannot bear to be far from rocks, you know?" He smiled at Claire.

"My father brung me and my sister and Jack here once to look for geodes. I always wanted to have a geode."

"Ahh," replied the professor. "And were you successful?"

Claire shook her head. "Uh-uh. But we found some garnets. One of them was big as an agate, I swear." She made a circle with her thumb and index finger to suggest the size of the rock. The professor nodded.

"I spose you're lookin' for dinosaur tracks, Professor?" asked Jack.

"Well, ya, sure. You know, there are tracks just a few miles to the east so this seemed a likely spot. And you, more prospecting?"

Jack shook his head. "No, sir. My sister here and Fergal had this crazy notion–"

Claire interrupted him, speaking loudly. "Yeh, we thought the same as you, Professor, that maybe there'd be tracks here. Right, Fergal?" She looked at Fergal who seemed perplexed and was shaking his head. "Can we look with you?"

"Oh, well, I've already had a look around. Not much to see, really. I must be going now."

"What's in the shed, Professor? Anything?"

"No, no, nothing at all, really. Except some old quarry equipment, that's all. Well, very nice seeing you again, Jack, Miss Bernard, Fergal. And nice meeting you, Mr. Wellington." With that he made his way down the road toward the gate.

"So," began Jack as he entered the shed, "is this where you found that stuff?"

"In here," replied Claire as she and Fergal led Jack and Tom into the storage room at the rear of the shed. "It was right here," explained Claire to Jack and Tom, pointing to one corner. "Right, Fergal?" Fergal nodded. "See those canvas tarps? They were covering it. How many crates do you think there was, Fergal? Ten, twenty?"

"There were seventeen," explained Fergal. "Four big ones, seven smaller ones, plus six flat ones."

"And the picric?" asked Jack.

"It was in the big crates, three tins in each."

"The sulfuric?"

"It was in the smaller cartons – four each – large glass bottles with ceramic stoppers," explained Fergal. He sniffed. "You can still smell it, that sulfur smell, like rotten eggs."

Tom spoke up: "What about the flat cartons? What was in them?"

"Pipes," replied Claire.

"Lead," added Fergal, "they were made of lead."

"How do you know they were lead?" asked Jack.

"I tested one with a magnet. Most lead is non-ferrous – it's not attracted to a magnet." Jack looked at Claire in amazement.

"He always has a magnet in his rucksack, you know, in case he needs it," explained Claire.

"How big were these pipes?" asked Tom.

"They was oh, maybe just like this long," replied Claire, demonstrating with her open hand. "Maybe four inches, right Fergal?"

"They were six inches long," replied Fergal, "and about one and a half inches in diameter."

"Yeh, okay, six inches."

"Like this?" asked Tom. He'd been looking under the pile of tarps when the toe of his shoe struck something hard. He picked up the object and looked at it.

"That's one of 'em!" replied Claire. Fergal nodded.

"Whatta ya think, Tommy?" asked Jack.

"Well, it looks like it's some kind of casing for blasting. You fill it with gun powder or TNT–"

"Or maybe picric," interjected Jack.

"Maybe," replied Tom. "There'd have to be a fuse attached. Then you just slide the pipe into a hole drilled in the rock – or a crack – light the fuse, then get the hell out."

Jack was examining the lead pipe carefully. "It's got two chambers." He looked at Tom and shrugged his shoulders.

Tom turned toward Claire and Fergal. "It looks like someone's been storing quarrying supplies here, that's all. Dangerous stuff, but that's what you expect in a quarry. What makes you think there's anything suspicious going on here?"

"Nothin'," replied Claire. "Really, nothin'. Well, let's go."

But Fergal spoke up. "We saw these three guys here a couple weeks back. They had a truck – a Ford – and they were talking about making a trip to Canada to get some stuff. "

"Who were these guys? Was that professor one of them?"

Claire shook her head. "Just some guys, maybe gonna reopen the quarry is all. C'mon. Let's go."

185

Fergal continued. "And we didn't have any idea then that they were doing something illegal. Not until they found the truck in the river."

"What?" replied Jack. "A truck in the river?"

Fergal explained about the photograph in the *Daily Transcript*, how the vehicle had been discovered, and how he could be certain it was the same truck they had seen in the quarry.

"You remembered the number on the license plate?" asked Jack, astounded.

"Uh-huh. Anyway, there it was, the same truck we had seen here, being pulled from the river. And then a few days later the paper said the Border Patrol was after these two guys who were driving that same truck. They said they were acting suspiciously and transporting contraband."

"Contraband?" replied Jack and Tom simultaneously.

"And then, just the other day," Fergal continued, "we saw that same man driving a rusty old ice truck, a McIntyre, on Southampton Road. We went back to the quarry and there he was, loading some of the crates into the ice truck."

Fergal was whispering something in Claire's ear.

"What?" demanded Jack. "Fergal?"

"It's about the – professor," the boy explained. "I think he was lying."

"Lying?" replied Jack. "When?"

"Just now. When he said he was looking for tracks in this rock, dinosaur tracks."

"Well," replied Jack, "it makes sense."

Claire rolled her eyes at her brother. "You can't be serious, Jackie?"

"Whatta ya mean, Sis?"

"You were at the professor's lecture, weren't you?" She turned to Fergal who was shaking his head. "Tell him, Fergal."

"Tracks are made in soft sediments – sand, mud – from the bottoms of lakes, rivers, and streams," began Fergal. "When creatures walk in them, they leave impressions – tracks. If the sediment hardens up it preserves the tracks." He paused, looking up at the ledges above them. "This is trap rock. It's volcanic – formed millions of years before the sandstone with the tracks. Maybe hundreds of millions. No dinosaur would leave tracks in these rocks, no matter how big he was."

Jack looked embarrassed and nodded. "Yeh, okay, I suppose you're right, but–"

Then Claire spoke up, pointing to the rim of the quarry high above them. "From up there you can see the smokestacks of Holyoke one way and the river and the whip factory in Westfield over the other way. You showed me that yourself once, Jackie – remember? Those sediments where the tracks were made, those were all down in the valley, not up high like this."

"But the professor seemed to think–"

"Couldn't you tell, Jackie? It was a lie. He wasn't here to look for dinosaur tracks. That's obvious."

"Why would he lie about that, Claire?"

"I don't know." She turned and her eyes met Fergal's. "That's what we gotta find out."

"We gotta tell Dad about this, Claire," said Jack a few minutes later as Tom pulled his motorcar into the Bernard's yard. "Maybe it's all perfectly innocent, but that business about the truck in the river's got me wonderin'."

The three climbed out of the roadster. Tom said, "I gotta get back to Holyoke, Jack. Sorry I couldn't be much help, but let me know what you find out about all this." The gears clashed as he threw the Hupmobile into reverse, backed out of the yard, then sped away.

Charles was in the barn repairing the broken wheel of a farm truck when Jack appeared. Claire and Fergal stood behind

Jack as if seeking protection from him as he presented this startling information to his father. He began by trying to explain what had led to their trip to the quarry, what they had found there, and why he thought they should be concerned. "I thought, well, maybe we should go to the police station and talk to the cops, you know?"

But Charles' thoughts were in another direction entirely as he looked past his son and stared at Claire.

"What in the name of all that's good and holy were you and Fergal doing at the Martinson Quarry?" was Charles' first response. In the end, however, he agreed with Jack. They should go to the Westfield Police Station first thing the next morning and report what they had seen at the quarry.

"Fergal, I think you and me better have a talk with your father." Fergal's face turned a ghostly white.

~ *31* ~

The Dooley place was just a few farms along Southampton Road from the Bernards' home, yet Charles Bernard and Eamon Dooley were practically strangers. In the two years since the Dooleys had moved in, the men had doffed hats rarely, once when Eamon drove his team past the Bernards' farmhouse hauling a wagonload of onions and turnips, another when their paths happened to cross at Lyman's Feed and Grain. Even then they acknowledged one another with the briefest of nods, a grunt or short "how-do," nothing more. Eamon was quiet, sullen really, and Charles felt no need to say more.

So it was that not a word was exchanged between the two men during the ten-minute ride into Westfield in Charles' truck. In the back sat Claire and Fergal, equally taciturn. Only when they pulled up at the curb in front of the Westfield Police Department did Eamon speak.

"Don't know what any of this got to do with my boy," he grumbled to Charles as they stepped out of the truck.

"I'm sure it won't take long," replied Charles. "There's probably nothin' to it."

In the few seconds Claire and Fergal were alone in the back of the truck Claire whispered to Fergal: "Let me do the talking, do you understand? *You don't say a word.*" The boy looked briefly into her eyes, swallowed nervously, then looked away.

Inside Charles spoke to a clerk at the front desk. "My daughter and her friend here, they seen some suspicious goings-on up at the Martinson Quarry – thought it oughta be reported."

"Have a seat," the clerk replied curtly. "I'll see if someone can 'elp you."

The four sat in silence on two hard wooden benches against the wall, Charles and Claire on one, Fergal and his father on the other. Claire and Fergal exchanged glances, the men sat in stony silence.

Soon a rotund, ruddy-faced man in a uniform appeared. He spoke first to Eamon. "Yes, sir. What's the problem here?"

Eamon merely grunted, then nodded toward Charles.

"Charles Bernard, officer. Up on Southampton Road?"

"How-do. Sergeant O'Malley."

"This 'ere's Eamon Dooley. Our young-uns 'ere seen some fellas up at the old quarry in Rock Valley. We – er, Dooley and me — thought you folks might wanna know 'bout it." He turned and looked at Eamon who looked away with an expression of indifference.

"What kind of goings-on, Mr. Bernard?"

"Well, apparently the children were at the quarry a few weeks ago and saw three men talkin'."

"Uh-huh."

"This here's my daughter, Claire." She looked up at the officer briefly. "And this is Fergal, Fergal Dooley." The boy stood, cap in hand, his face looking sallow. "Tell Officer O'Malley what you saw. Go on, now," urged Charles.

Claire spoke up immediately while Fergal sat, eyes downcast. "We was comin' home from school on the trolley 'bout a month ago and we saw these two guys gettin' off near Pequot Park. They was carryin' fishin' rods. We thought it were odd and decided to follow them."

"And what seemed odd about two men going fishing?" inquired the sergeant.

"For one they had rods but they didn't have any other gear. Plus everyone knows there's no use fishin' Hampton Ponds after the leaves fall, not 'til the ice comes in."

The sergeant glanced briefly from Claire to Charles, then back to Claire. "So you followed them."

"Yes, sir, and we saw where they dropped their rods in the woods. So we figured the rods were just a cover."

"Cover?"

Claire nodded. "To make it look like the guys was goin' fishin'."

"And where did they go, miss?"

"We followed the path from the pond up to the quarry. They was talkin' to this guy in a shed. We watched 'em from the back, through a crack in the boards."

The officer looked up at Charles, then at Eamon, then back to Claire. "Did it ever occur to you, Miss Bernard, that you and your friend were trespassing on private property?" Claire shook her head. "There are signs all around. It's not a safe place for children to play—"

Claire's jaw jutted out, her lips pursed tightly. "We weren't playing, sir."

"—and that you might be in danger, following men you don't know and spying on them?"

She threw the detective a determined look. Then she raised her eyes toward her father and her expression changed. "We thought it might be important, that they might be – up to something."

"Men working in a quarry, that doesn't sound like anything so serious, now, does it?" Claire shook her head. The sergeant looked at Charles, then at Eamon. "So, that's it?"

"No, sir," continued Claire. "We heard 'em talking like the two guys was takin' a trip, somewhere in New Hampshire. Near the border, he said. The old guy he told 'em the trip would take 'bout six hours. In the back of the truck was a couple of big metal cans he said had extra gas. And he told 'em they had to be back to 'olyoke before daylight."

"Okay, so they were planning a trip of some sort, picking up something in New Hampshire. Still, what makes you think there was anything suspicious about all this?"

"The guy said they'd need a couple a sheets a canvas to cover the back. *You don't want no one seein' what you got back there,* is what he said."

"Hmm," replied the sergeant.

Claire looked to Fergal, then continued: "Few weeks later we – Fergal saw a story in the paper 'bout a truck they found in the river – the one was stole in Westfield."

Sergeant O'Malley nodded. "Uh-huh. Yes, I'm familiar with that incident. What about it?"

"It was the same truck we saw in the shed at the quarry."

The sergeant rolled his eyes. "Now how on earth could you know that it was the same truck?"

Claire glanced at Fergal. "Tell 'im, Fergal."

"The number – on the license plate," began Fergal. "It was 7–1–9–1–7."

"It was, was it?" replied the sergeant, chuckling. "And how the he – how in tarnation could you remember that?"

"He remembers things, sir," Claire replied. "Fergal remembers *everything*." She turned and looked directly into Fergal's eyes. "Right, Fergal?"

The boy nodded but did not speak. Claire continued: "Anyway, there it was, gettin' pulled from the river just a few weeks after we saw it at the quarry. And then, a few days later, the paper said the Border Patrol was after these two guys who were driving the truck. They said they was acting suspiciously and transporting contraband."

The sergeant looked surprised, his eyes shifting from Claire to Fergal to their fathers.

"We still didn't think much 'bout it, sir. Not 'til a few days later. We was walkin' home from the trolley an' this truck went by and splashed us. The guy looked like the one we saw at the quarry."

"And that was just this week?"

Claire nodded. "Tuesday. We followed the trail past the pond and up to the quarry. The guy was there but he left and –

well – after he was gone we got into the shed. We found a loose board on the back and we sprung it open. There was a small room with boxes and crates – chemicals and pipes – lead pipes."

"Chemicals? What kinds of chemicals?"

Claire looked at Fergal. "Tell 'im, Fergal."

"Tins of picric acid and big glass bottles of sulfuric acid. The bottles had white stoppers that looked like porcelain."

"We heard a truck coming and we got out just in time. It was the truck that splashed us."

"It was really rusty and made a funny sound – *clunk, clunk, clunk*," added Fergal.

"And what was this man doing?"

"He was loading some of the crates from the storage room."

"What happened then?"

"He got in the truck and left. Then we left, too. When my brother Jack got home from college – he's in college – he's gonna be an engineer – we asked him about that stuff. He said those acids are probably for dyeing wool. Maybe they was sellin' it to the mills."

The sergeant turned to Fergal. "And I suppose you remember the license plate on this truck, as well, young man?"

Fergal shook his head. "No, sir. There was no plate. But it was a black McIntyre, sir, 1910, it looked like an old ice truck with two doors on the back. And the motor made that *clunk-clunk-clunk* sound."

"Okay," began the sergeant. He paused, looking at the two men. "I'm not sure any crime's been committed here. Those guys may've had a perfectly good reason for going to New Hampshire, getting the goods, then bringing them back to Holyoke. Maybe they're in the chemical business and usin' the shed at the quarry to store merchandise until they sell it."

"But why'd they ditch the truck is what we couldn't figure," replied Claire.

"Well, we'll look into it. The truck was stolen, that much's true – don't mean those guys stole it. Maybe they bought it from the thief not knowing it was stolen. So we need to talk to those three. Do you know their names?" He looked at Claire.

"The old man, they called 'im Manfred. That's all we know."

"What about the two younger ones?"

Claire shook her head. The sergeant sighed, then looked up at Charles, then Eamon. Finally, he turned and looked sternly at Fergal. "What about you, young man? Do you recall anything about those two younger men?"

Fergal looked first at Claire. She glared at him stern-faced.

"Don't look at her, son, look at me," demanded the sergeant. "What about those two other guys?"

Fergal was uncomfortable and he twisted his cap with both hands. "One was named Hank."

"Uh-huh, Hank. Okay. Do you know his last name?"

"Köhler – Hank Köhler, I think."

"And the other?"

"Jake – Jake Muller." Fergal was careful to pronounce the name properly.

"Muller?"

Fergal spoke slowly, softly. "*Mule* – er, sir, it's pronounced *Mule* – er."

"Muller, Mule-er, what's the difference? He was there," replied the sergeant with annoyance.

"He attended Holyoke High School for a few years. Then he worked at Wellington Textiles." Fergal's eyes left the police officer and fell downward. He couldn't look up at Claire and suffer the withering glare he knew would still be directed toward him.

"All right, then," replied the sergeant. He turned to Claire. "Do you have anything to add?" She shook her head.

The sergeant asked Claire and Fergal to wait outside, then spoke to Charles and Eamon. "Every few years some kid falls or drowns in one of those quarries up on the mountain. It's not a place for kids to be, understand?"

Eamon Dooley stood impassively while Charles responded. "I can guarantee you my girl won't go anywheres near there ever again, sergeant." He turned and looked at Eamon who merely nodded.

Meanwhile Claire stood on the sidewalk, hands on her hips, her back to Fergal.

"I – I—" began Fergal.

Claire turned and glowered at him. "What is the matter with you, boy? Don't you ever think before you go flappin' your gums? Tellin' him about Jake? Now he'll probably get arrested and the kids at school will be even meaner to Sarah. And how d'you know Hank's name?"

"I saw it on a letter at that boarding house. I'm sorry, Claire, I'm sorry. It's just – I forgot – I mean, I wasn't thinkin'."

"Yah, well, I guess you wasn't," retorted Claire. "Really, Fergal Dooley, I don't understand how someone who's so smart can be so – so *stupid*."

Fergal was stung by Claire's words. His chin began to quiver and he turned away from her. "I – I just don't like fibbin'." Then he turned and looked into Claire's eyes that were still red with anger. "I'm just not good at it – like you." He looked down.

~ 32 ~

Snowflakes drifted lazily out of the gray sky as Anne and Jack walked down Appleton Street that evening.

"Do you realize that this is the first time we've been out together, just the two of us, since you left for Worcester in September, Jackie? What with you gone for weeks at a time, my job, and then Tommy's situation, we've hardly had any time together in months." Anne stopped, turned, and tugged on the lapel of Jack's woolen coat. She looked up into his face where the gas lamplight gave his skin a particularly healthy, robust glow. She spoke softly. "I've missed you, Mr. Bernard," then leaned against him and kissed him softly on his cold cheek.

Jack smiled but pulled back. "Well, I've missed you, too."

"Really? Truly? From the sound of it you have been so absorbed with your studies and football that a girl begins to wonder if you ever think of her when you're away."

He shook his head. "Are you joking?" They started walking again, Anne's arm wrapped around Jack's waist so that she could hear every word. "I never stop thinking about you, Annie. Sure I keep busy, but you wouldn't want me mooning all the while, would you?"

Anne looked up at Jack with a roguish grin. "I suppose not – well, maybe an occasional sigh – a wistful note of longing – just once or twice each day."

Again Jack laughed. "The days aren't so hard." He looked briefly into Anne's eyes. "It's the nights – they're the times I miss you the most. It's awfully lonely in my little room, with only my books to keep me company."

They turned onto High Street. "Maybe, in the new term, I could – come for a visit – for a weekend? How would that be?

I've only been to Worcester once and I'm dying to see your campus, your dormitory, and all that. What do you say? I could take the train, or maybe Tommy would drive me in his motor – I mean, and drop me off."

Jack nodded. "That would be wonderful, Annie, really. The other boys in my house think I'm making up stories about my sweetheart. I'd love for them to meet you after all."

Minutes later they entered O'Shaughnessy's, one of the most popular restaurants in the city. Jack took their coats to the cloakroom while Anne stood in the foyer gazing at a painting of a serene Irish landscape. As Jack turned he glanced into the bar. Through the smoky haze he spotted a familiar face. He returned to Anne and they were seated by the headwaiter.

O'Shaughnessy's main dining room was elegantly furnished with dozens of round tables of dark walnut, each covered with a crisp linen tablecloth and a small centerpiece of silk flowers in a china vase. Tall windows framed by heavy damask drapes looked out on High Street, separated by large potted ferns in ornate ceramic pots. Three massive wrought iron chandeliers hung from the pressed metal ceiling, casting a soft, mellow light over the entire room.

As they perused their menus, Anne turned, opened her purse on the seat beside her out of view of anyone, and removed something. She reached for Jack's hand as she whispered. "Jackie," her gaze leading his eyes to her hand. It held a five-dollar bill. She nodded to him. Jack blanched shamefacedly, but quickly took the bill, glancing around briefly to assure that no one had witnessed the exchange. "Come on, Jackie, we talked about this, remember? I'm a working girl these days and you're a college man, so it only makes sense. Besides that, you deserve a treat once in a while – we both do."

Jack looked deflated. "I know," he replied with a slight nod. "It's just – humiliating, that's all, to have my girl paying the tab."

Anne took his hand in hers. "Once you graduate from college, Mr. Bernard, with all sorts of honors and accolades, you will have a fine job as the chief engineer for some great American manufacturer." She paused and Jack rolled his eyes. Anne continued: "And then you will be able to lavish all sorts of gifts and treats on your dear, sweet Anne, or–" Anne's eyes suddenly grew dramatically large in an expression of mock sadness, "or whoever your latest sweetheart may be by that time."

Finally, Jack cracked a smile and his face flushed. "You know, Annie, you're right. Who do you think the lucky girl'll be? Mary Pickford? Gloria Swanson? Or maybe Vivian Martin – she's kinda pretty, don't you think?"

Soon the waiter appeared and Anne ordered chicken pot pie, Jack the New England boiled dinner. While they waited for their meals, Anne began reminiscing. "Remember all those times we came here in high school? You, me, Tommy, and Carolyn – or whoever was Tommy's latest." Jack nodded and Anne continued. "It used to be crowded every night of the week. Now look at it. The bar is packed, but the dining room's practically empty." Again Jack nodded. "The war is having an effect on just about everyone, Jackie. It seems as though most of Holyoke's young men are in the service, and most of the girls are in the mills. Hardly anyone has the time – or the money – to go for an evening out. We're just lucky, Jackie, do you know what I mean?" Jack nodded but seemed distracted. "What's the matter, Jackie? Is something wrong?"

"No, no. Come with me, Annie, I want you to meet someone." He rose, took her hand in his, and led her back through the foyer to the bar.

"Mr. Sullivan," called Jack to a figure seated at the end of the bar. The man turned on his stool. He was tall and lanky with a ruddy face, shining green eyes, and a tangle of coarse, black hair. He smiled broadly when he recognized the young man before him.

"Well, Jack Bernard, as I live and breathe. Shore I 'aven' seen ye 'round in a few shakes. How ye doin'?"

"I'm fine, sir. I'd like you to meet my girlfriend, Anne – Anne Wellington." The man jumped quickly to his feet. "Anne, This is Mr. Sullivan, Frank Sullivan. He's the dyer at Wellingtons'."

"How d'y do, miss?" he replied, doffing his cap.

Anne smiled. "Very well, thank you, sir. And you?"

"Oh, can't complain, really. Very nice to meet you, miss. Known your da and your uncle for a long time. In fact, Mr. Richard 'e 'ired me 'isself, 'e did – in New York. I was workin' for a silk mill in Paterson, New Jersey. He come lookin' fer me, wantin' me fer dyer at his mill in 'olyoke." Anne smiled and the man continued. "Been at it ever since – nigh on fifteen years now." He nodded at Jack.

"Mr. Sullivan's a walking encyclopedia when it comes to scouring, mordanting, dyeing, all that," explained Jack. The man grinned.

"So I've heard many times from my father and my uncle," replied Anne with a smile.

"Can I offer you folks drinks?"

"Oh, no, thank you, sir – we got a table waiting for us in the dining room. Then a show at the Bijou."

The man nodded. "Well, off ye go, then, young folks, an' 'ave yourselves a wonderful evenin', now. Pleased to 'ave met ye, Miss Wellington."

"Say, Mr. Sullivan, maybe you can solve a bit of a mystery for me. Picric. Picric acid." Anne seemed puzzled as Jack continued. "I remember you talkin' about it in the dyehouse, sir. Do you ever use it these days?"

The man shook his head and took a brief sip of lager from a tall glass on the bar. "Nay, uh-uh. They use it some as a mordant with cotton and flax." He turned to Anne. "Fixes the dye, you know." Then he turned back to Jack. "But ain't used so much with wool 'ese days. Tricky to work with. Every batch come out bit diff'rent." He shook his head. "Too much bother. We got lots o' betta tings for our purposes. Why?"

"There's an old trap rock quarry near our place, in Rock Valley."

"Oh, aye," replied Mr. Sullivan.

"My sister and her friend were snoopin' around there a while back an' they come across a big stash of picric in a storage shed there. They were asking me and Anne's brother what it was used for."

"Oh, well, sure, it's an explosive. They might a used it in the quarry back in the day. But that place has been shuttered for at least ten years, ain't it?"

"And they found some sulfuric acid, too, and lots of lead pipe. I just wondered—"

Mr. Sullivan interrupted Jack. "Wa – wait a second, son. Lead pipe – whatta yeh mean? Long pipes, like water pipes?"

"No, sir. Short, like this." From his coat pocket Jack produced the pipe Tom had found in the storage shed.

The man looked aghast. "Jesus, Mary, and Joseph," swore Mr. Sullivan, grasping it from Jack's hand. He lowered his voice and looked around. "Where 'n hell'd ya get that ting?"

"Huh?"

"It's what they calls a seegar. That's nothin' they'd a used in that quarry." He lowered his voice. "What ye got there's a weapon, son, a weapon o' war." Jack was stunned. "Them's what the Jerries been usin' on American ships, and factories, an' armories."

"Are you sure?"

"Look at it. See? The picric goes in one chamber, sulfuric goes in t'other, copper slug in the middle. When the acid eats through the copper and the two mix, boom – one 'ell of a bang." He turned to Anne. "Pardon me French, miss, but it's true. One mighty big bang-up there."

"How do you know so much about 'em?" asked Jack.

The man winced, then spoke gloomily. "They used 'em in Dublin – the Easter Rising. That's how me brother Daniel died, one went off too soon. Listen, son, if I were you I'd chuck that ting in the river, I would. You don't wanna have t'explain to no one how you come by 'at. Understand?"

Jack nodded. "Okay, yeh, right away. Well, thanks Mr. Sullivan. We'd better be goin."

"Okay, nice to see ya, son – miss. But be sure an' take my advice, 'ear? Nobody trusts nobody nowadays, not when there's a war on." Jack nodded.

Back at their table in the dining room, Anne looked perplexed. "Jackie," she whispered, "what was all that about? What were you and Tommy doing in that quarry?"

"He came by yesterday afternoon. I wasn't expecting him, you know, after the other day in Worcester – he just showed up. Well, we were talkin' about this and that when Claire and her friend Fergal appeared. They told this story about what they'd seen at that old trap rock quarry off Southampton Road. About these guys they saw there, and chemicals, and these lead pipes. Tommy drove us over to have a look. We were thinking it was just old quarrying supplies. But what Mr. Sullivan said 's got me thinkin'."

"You mean about that pipe – that seegar? Do you believe it, Jackie?"

"I – I don't know." Just then the waiter appeared with their meals, interrupting their conversation. Jack took several mouthfuls of corned beef before he spoke again. "You know who we saw at the quarry? Professor Smith."

"Oh?" replied Anne. "I suppose he's looking for more ancient footprints, hmm?"

"I don't know, Anne. I just don't know. That's what he said, but Claire and Fergal had their doubts."

"Well, what do you mean, Jack?"

He shrugged. "Oh, nothing. So, what else is new? Any word from Carolyn?"

"Well, yes, Jackie, I visited her yesterday. It was the first time we had really talked in ages."

"About school?"

"Yes. She loves Mass. Aggie. It sounds like she has made many friends there. And she enjoys her studies as well. I'm so happy for her. To be honest, Jackie, I'm a little jealous. I love my work, honestly. But more and more I am beginning to feel the urge to be back in school myself. Do you understand?"

Jack smiled and nodded. "Of course. You love your books and literature so much. Why wouldn't you want to continue your education?"

"But Jackie, she told me something else that was shocking. She and my brother – they are no longer keeping company. That's how she put it."

Jack nodded. "Yeh, Tommy told me last week. He said he broke it off with her." Anne was shaking her head. "What?" asked Jack.

"Jackie, according to Carolyn *she* pitched *him*."

Jack was startled by this revelation. "Well, that's not what *he* said."

"Of course not, Jackie."

"The way he talks everything is hunky-dory."

"That's just it. He walks around smiling like everything's fine. But everything is *not* fine, Jackie. For one thing he has these nightmares, or whatever they are. He shouts – shrieks, sometimes – in his sleep. One time I found him cowering on the floor in his bedroom with a blanket pulled over his head."

Jack shook his head. "I can't imagine–"

But Anne continued. "And Jackie, he's got a bottle of whiskey in his room, I saw it by his bed one night. He has a drink, then he takes some sleeping powders they gave him after his surgery."

"It's probably what he went through, you know?"

"And that," she added. "He refuses to talk to us about it. I mean, his ship was torpedoed and sunk, somehow he survived. The lieutenant – you met him that day – he said Tommy was captured by the Germans, then put in a boxcar on a train that was in a wreck. He broke his arm in the accident. A few weeks later he turns up in a British field hospital. That's all we know. He simply refuses to talk about it."

She leaned toward Jack and continued in a whisper. "I know – I understand that those are terrible memories that he wants to be rid of – I don't blame him, really, not for a minute. But I am just not sure he should be – you know – bottling them up inside. What I mean is, they could all come spilling out one day. That's why Carolyn broke it off with him, I'm sure of it. The way she told it, it sounded like she was frightened for him – or *of* him."

Several minutes went by, the couple enjoying their meal in silence, each contemplating the state of Tom's mind. Finally Anne broke the silence. "It worries me, Jackie, it just worries me. I'm just afraid something will happen that will set him off."

~ 33 ~

"Heavens, Tommy, you look dreadful," commented Anne when her brother appeared in the parlor late the next morning holding a cup of hot, black coffee.

"Yeh, well, I barely slept – bit under the weather."

"What time did you get in? I was up reading until after eleven and didn't hear you."

Tom took a seat by the fire, sipped his coffee, then sighed. "Late. Digsy and a couple of his buddies were passing through. We had a bit of a Dorchester reunion."

Anne knew all about Tom's old roommate, Chester Arthur Digsworth the Third. The two had been roommates at the Dorchester School in Greenfield. Any reunion, any event of any kind involving Digsy, could mean only one thing: excessive consumption of alcohol.

"Really?" replied Anne. "How is old Digsy these days?"

"Always the same. That fella has a magic formula for high living: pretty girls, fast cars, and the finest gin money can buy. Yup, Digsy's got it all."

Yes, Anne was thinking, Digsy does have it all, all except for even an ounce of self-respect. "Well, I hope you are taking it easy on the Digsy formula, Brother."

Tom sat impassively, sipping his coffee. "You and Jack have a good time?"

"Oh, yes, we had a lovely time. We very nearly had O'Shaughnessy's dining room to ourselves, but it was just fine. I understand you paid Jack a visit on Friday?"

"Yep, just dropped by to shoot the breeze."

"And ended up going to some quarry with Claire and that friend of hers?"

"Yep. Those kids had been nosin' around in that place a few weeks back and saw some suspicious activity–" Tom rolled his eyes. "Probably nothing to it. What'd Jack tell you about it?"

"Well, he went on and on about acid and those lead pipes."

"Yeh, well, just a lot of old quarry supplies is all."

"He also introduced me to his old boss from the dyehouse, Frank Sullivan. Do you know him?"

Tom chuckled and nodded. "Yep. Let me guess, he was bendin' over the bar?"

"Yes, well, so he was, but he seemed very nice. Jack had one of those pipes and he showed it to him. The man practically jumped out of his skin."

"Oh?"

"He said that pipe is something called a seegar – it's used to make a bomb – that they used them in the rebellion in Ireland – and they are very dangerous. He warned Jack not to carry it around or even show it to anyone. He acted like, well, I don't know, like it might be part of a plot."

Tom clutched his coffee cup like it was a lifeline and seemed uninterested in continuing the conversation.

Anne rose and looked down at her bedraggled brother. "Maybe you could spend some time with Mother and Father today." The maid had just brought in the morning edition of the *Daily Transcript* and placed it on the end table. Anne picked it up and handed it to her brother, but as she did so she smelled alcohol. "Better get yourself cleaned up first," she added wryly, then left the room.

His coffee cup in one hand, Tom held the paper with his other hand, scanning the front page idly. Then something caught his eye. He began reading.

"Jesus–" he swore softly to himself. Then he called out, "Annie." He set the cup down, rose, ran into the front hall, then climbed the wide stairway to the second floor. At his sister's

205

bedroom door he spoke again. "Annie." He tapped lightly on the door and she opened it. "Tell me again what Mr. Sullivan said about that lead pipe."

"What? Why?" asked Anne. Tom stepped into his sister's room and began to read the story to her:

NEW JERSEY BOMB PLOT AVERTED
Federal agents describe large
cache of deadly explosives
Holyoke man among those arrested

A truck loaded with explosives was stopped by Federal agents in Passaic, New Jersey, Saturday night. Three men were arrested at the scene. Soon after nearly a dozen accomplices, many German nationals, were also brought in from neighboring towns. Press reports indicated that some of the men arrested were from Holyoke although they have not as yet been identified.

"From Holyoke?" replied Anne with alarm. Tom continued reading:

Hundreds of lead pipe bombs were found in the back of the truck. Agents described them as cigar bombs containing acids that when mixed explode violently. One agent speculated that the bombs were destined for a British naval vessel docked in New York Harbor and carrying weapons and ammunition headed to France. "Those cigars are small, but they can produce a very violent explosion," remarked the agent. "They could easily have destroyed a ship full of armaments."

"Tommy, are you thinking those guys that Claire and Fergal saw were – German spies? Saboteurs?"

Tom nodded. "And the Holyoke cops and the Westfield cops didn't know a thing." Then he read the last paragraph:

Agents of the Bureau of Investigation were reportedly staked out at an isolated farmhouse awaiting the arrival of the truck. When asked about the arrest and the alleged plot, Holyoke Police Chief Hanrahan denied having any knowledge. "Whatever was going on, the Bureau chose not to inform us."

Barely a half hour later Jack and Tom were talking in Tom's motorcar that was parked in the Bernard's side yard.

"*Jésus-Christ*," swore Jack softly in French. "That's it, then, Fergal and Claire were on to something, something big."

"Yeh, and those cops, Jack, they didn't believe them. They refused to take them seriously."

"We don't know that, Tommy. The sergeant said they'd look into it. Maybe–" Jack was re-reading the story. "Wow, Tommy, this is amazing. A German sabotage plot right under our noses. Come inside – wait 'til Dad and Claire hear about this."

Claire was not surprised at the news. "So the guys they arrested in the truck musta been the ones we saw at the quarry the first time, Manfred, Jake, and his friend. Those two were workin' for Manfred – they picked up the stuff in New Hampshire. So that was the plan from the start, to store it at the quarry, then deliver it to New Jersey."

"When you and Fergal went to the quarry the second time, you said the picric and sulfuric were all in tins and bottles, right?" asked Jack. Claire nodded. "And there were those lead pipes, the seegars, too. So they must have loaded those seegars right there and they were already on their way when we went there."

"Gee, that musta been dangerous for those guys, carrying all those loaded bombs. Couldn't they go off anytime?" asked Claire.

Jack interjected. "Mr. Sullivan said if they use the biggest copper disks there's maybe five days before they start exploding. But accidents could happen, it's true. That's how Mr. Sullivan's brother was killed in Ireland – one went off too soon."

"If it was so dangerous, why didn't they arrest those guys before they left Holyoke?" asked Claire.

"Probably because they figured they were only minor players," explained Tom. "The agents were betting that if they let them go they'd lead them to bigger fish in New Jersey and New York, maybe disrupt other plots. This is probably just a small part of something much, much bigger. Those Krauts, they're capable of anything – believe me, anything."

"I'm sure glad you and Fergal didn't tangle with that gang, Claire. They must be some nasty guys."

Claire had something else on her mind. "There's one thing that I'm still wonderin' 'bout, Jackie," began Claire. "It's the professor."

"Yeh, what about 'im?"

"He had to be lyin', about the quarry, about why he was there." Their eyes met. "I – I just wonder if maybe, somehow, he–"

"Well, he *is* German," replied Jack. "Remember the night of the lecture, that guy from the *Transcript* practically accused him of being a foreign agent."

Tom was suddenly interested. "Lecture?"

"Yeh, the professor gave a talk at the Women's Home, about the dinosaur tracks. Annie introduced him. It was in September, while you were – away."

"You're telling me that guy, that so-called professor, the one who was hangin' around the quarry when we got there, that he's a Kraut?" Tom's face was suddenly deep red.

"He was born in Germany, Tommy, but he's been in America for a long time. I'm sure he would never–"

Tom shot Jack a sharp look. "I better be goin'." And he quickly stepped out the kitchen door and was walking toward the Hupmobile when Jack caught up with him. "Tommy, where are you goin'?" Tom had opened the motorcar door and was about to get in when Jack grabbed his arm. "Tommy, come on, let's talk about this, eh?"

Tom yanked his arm away from Jack. "No time for talk, Jack, no time for any more goddamn talk."

"Claire, dear, may I come in?" asked Marie as she rapped softly on her sister's bedroom door.

"Uh-huh," came the muffled reply. Marie opened the door. Claire lay on the bed in the dimly lit room, facing away from Marie. Marie sat on the bed.

"Claire, what's the matter? Are you upset about those men?" There was no response. "Father told you to stay away from that place, remember?" She paused. "You know, as a young woman you have to be more careful – about, well, about avoiding men in – in certain situations."

Finally Claire spoke. "It's not that, Marie."

"What is it then?"

"It's Sarah. Once everyone knows her brother was involved in that business, and was arrested – a spy or conspirorator – or whatever they call 'em – they'll – things will be even worse for her – and the other German kids in school."

"I'm sure the teachers and your principal – Mr. Patton – will see that does not happen."

"Sometimes it seems like they don't care, like they're just as mean – not, you know, in what they say so much as what they do – or *don't* do. Some of them I think feel the same as those awful boys."

"I'm sure that's not so, Claire."

"But what should I say to her, when I see her? I don't know whether I should bring up Jake, or make believe it didn't happen. I could just pretend I hadn't heard, I suppose. But once his name is in the *Transcript*, everyone—"

"Well, Claire, as her friend I think you should try to offer her some words of sympathy – of consolation." Marie paused, thinking. "Perhaps you could simply say you are sorry for all she and her family are going through, without mentioning Jake by name or those awful men and that terrible plot."

~ 34 ~

Three Holyoke Police Department patrol cars tore down Lyman Street, sirens blaring. The lead car pulled to an abrupt halt in front of a seedy tenement in the section of Holyoke known as the Flats. The other two cars soon pulled in behind it. More than a dozen neighbors had gathered on the sidewalk looking relieved to see the authorities arrive.

The police had received a frantic call from a resident a half hour earlier reporting a fracas in one of the apartments. He had heard loud shouting, threats, possibly a scuffle. All was quiet now, but neighbors were understandably worried about what was going on in the apartment on an otherwise peaceful Sunday afternoon.

Soon six burly, barrel-chested officers armed with nightsticks entered the building and climbed the narrow stairway to the third floor. A paddy wagon soon appeared on the scene and several more officers waited on the sidewalk.

Eventually the front door opened and a young man with dark hair appeared, escorted in handcuffs by two officers. It was Tom Wellington. The officers led him to the paddy wagon, shoved him in the rear, and slammed the doors. Then the vehicle sped off.

"Okay, folks, it's all over. You can go home now, understand?" announced a senior officer.

One of the patrol cars remained until the last of the crowd had dispersed. Nearly a half hour later, two more officers emerged from the building escorting another handcuffed man, this one gray-haired and wearing dark glasses, a worn woolen cap pulled down over his forehead.

A few minutes later the patrolmen climbed out of their wagon in front of the police department headquarters on Dwight Street. They opened the rear doors and assisted the gray-haired man in handcuffs from the wagon, then led him by the arms up the stone stairs. Several reporters were watching the proceedings as photographers snapped pictures.

"Mr. Wellington," said an officer to Tom as he sat in a barren interrogation room, "the Chief wants to talk to you hisself. He'll be right down."

A few minutes later Chief of Police Thomas Hanrahan appeared in the doorway. "Mr. Wellington – er, Seaman Wellington." Tom looked up blankly. The chief extended his hand and Tom shook it briefly, unsmiling. The two were acquainted. In fact, Chief Hanrahan had been instrumental in having charges dropped against Tom, charges of arson and manslaughter, two years earlier. "Nice to see you again." He pulled up a chair and sat across the table from him. "So, what's this all about? I can guess, but I want you to tell me."

"Listen, Chief, we're at war with those Huns. Sailors and soldiers are fighting right now, and many of them are dying, just to help the English and the French – our Allies – fight back the Kaiser's forces."

"I'm well aware–"

"And this guy, this so-called professor, he's part of that plot – the cigar bombs – in New Jersey. I'm sure of it."

"And what exactly makes you so sure of this, Seaman?"

"He's German – a geologist – worked in mines – knows explosives. And he was at that quarry, the one where those seegar bombs were stored. I saw him there with my own eyes. The very next day those bombs turn up in New Jersey in the hands of German saboteurs." Tom laughed. "What more goddamn evidence do you need?"

"So you just decided to take matters into your own hands, is that it?"

"Well, you guys didn't seem like you were about to do anything."

"Seaman Wellington, how exactly did you know where the professor was living?"

"My sister. She had his address. I found it on her writing desk. She sent him a letter – I can't believe it myself – thanking him for giving a lecture at the Women's Home where she works. He should be locked up – in the deepest, darkest dungeon you've got–" Tom's face was getting red and the veins in his forehead were throbbing. He was practically yelling now. "Better yet, put him in front of a damned firing squad–"

"Listen, Seaman Wellington, I am well aware of your service and can understand the depth of your feelings on these matters. But we're only holding Professor Smith for his own protection. He has not been charged with any crime."

"But he's a traitor, a conspirator, a bomb-maker."

"Listen to me, will you just listen?" implored the chief.

~ 35 ~

A group of grade eight girls were seated together in the lunchroom. Julie Trottière was describing in detail a dress she and her mother were sewing. "It will be perfect for the skating party," she was exclaiming to all who would listen. Claire, Sarah, Yvette, and Charlotte were listening, but Claire's attention was directed toward Sarah.

She seems all right, Claire was thinking. She's smiling, her cheeks have their usual pink glow, her eyes are shining. But she must be hiding the hurt, the worry, the shame she and her family have been enduring since the events of the weekend in New Jersey. She is certainly making a good appearance of being perfectly content, despite the turmoil her brother's situation must have visited upon her family. Claire was also mindful of the insults and derision that would surely rain upon Sarah from certain grade eight pupils once the news was out. She wanted more than anything to speak to her friend, to console her, to reassure her. But Sarah and the others were now discussing hair styles, braids, curls, bows, combs, and all other matters related to personal grooming.

Finally, Miss Sussim appeared and escorted the class to the hallway outside their classroom where they donned coats, hats, and mittens, then proceeded to the snow-covered schoolyard. Most of the girls huddled in the entryway, not wanting to risk slipping on the frozen ground. Having had her fill of girl-talk, Claire stepped gingerly into the yard and looked around briefly. Fergal was standing alone by the fence, obviously trying to avoid her gaze. She turned in the opposite direction.

"You are a brave girl to be out here alone, Miss Bernard." It was Albert. Claire felt uncomfortable whenever they spoke. No matter where she looked, whether at his hair that fell softly against his face, or at his calm, shining eyes, or at his slender lips that always seemed to hold a smile, wherever her eyes fixed she felt she must surely be revealing all.

She tried to smile and formulate a casual reply, but found difficulty in doing both simultaneously. So she tried first to smile, then to make some kind of sensible reply. "Oh, I – well – er–"

Thankfully, Albert rescued her from her uncharacteristic stammering. "Have you chosen a topic for your essay yet?"

Claire was still stammering. "Oh, eh, well–" Not wanting to look completely foolish, she finally recalled something she had read in *St. Nicholas Magazine* a few days earlier. "I was thinking of perhaps, eh, animals – animal husbandry."

Albert seemed perplexed. "Animal husbandry?"

"Yeh, you know, how cows and sheep and other animals – have – h-husbands." Even as she spoke the words she knew it was nonsense. "What about you?"

"Oh, I'm writing about Mark Twain and how his childhood inspired his writing."

"That sounds very interesting. Much better than animal husbands–"

"Miss Bernard," he interrupted, "are you planning to attend the skating party?"

The question seemed to come out of nowhere and caught Claire unprepared. Albert was leaning toward her, apparently intent on either hearing a reply or otherwise sensing in her demeanor some trace, some tiny nuance of interest – or indifference. She paused and that had him worried, thinking that she was looking for a way to extricate herself from the conversation. He need not have worried. Her hesitation had to do with his eyelashes, long for a boy, and now sprinkled with snowflakes.

Finally she spoke. "Oh – why – yes, of course, everyone is attending."

He smiled. "Would you do me the honor of having a skate with me?" He paused, waiting for a reaction. "One, or perhaps two?"

Just then Sarah appeared smiling sweetly at Claire. "Come onto the step, silly," she pleaded, pulling Claire toward the entranceway where the other girls were huddled. She turned and spoke curtly to Albert: "Excuse us." Claire looked briefly at Albert, an expression of helplessness on her face, then allowed Sarah to lead her away. Albert turned and wandered off onto the snowy schoolyard looking disappointed.

Under the protection of the portico, Sarah brushed snow off Claire's coat. They both laughed. "I could tell you wanted to be rescued, Claire."

"Rescued?"

"From him," replied Sarah, nodding toward Albert who was now standing alone some distance away, the snow swirling about him.

Claire nodded. "Oh, *him*," she replied dismissively, but then looked away from Sarah lest her blushes give her away.

Sarah proceeded to prattle on in her usual light-hearted way about Latin, about geography, about Miss Sussim. Meanwhile Claire was not really listening but rather was carefully preparing her words, even as she gazed cheerily into Sarah's eyes. Finally, when there came a brief lull in the monologue, Claire spoke up.

"Sarah," she began, being certain to pronounce her friend's Christian name in the approved manner. Sarah returned Claire's gaze expectantly. "I – I wanted – well – I've been meaning to say – well – I'm very sorry for – for everything your family has been through." Claire paused.

Sarah looked confused. "Claire Bernard, what *are* you going on about?"

"I – I heard about that – that business in New Jersey – with Jake and Hank. I never thought–"

Sarah tossed her head back and laughed, her eyes shining in amusement. "Claire, dear, excuse me but I really have no idea what you are speaking about. New Jersey? Jake and Hank? Who's Hank?"

If Sarah is pretending, thought Claire, she certainly is doing a good job of it. "Sarah," resumed Claire, "I heard about the arrests – the plot."

"Claire Bernard, what nonsense have you been concocting in that pretty head of yours?"

"Well, isn't Jake – er – I mean – isn't Gerhardt – in jail?"

Again Sarah guffawed. "No he is *not*, silly. In fact, Gerhardt came to supper last evening. He tells us he has just received a promotion at Wellingtons' woolen mill. He's now the number one man in the warehouse – next to the foreman, that is. They think the world of him there."

Claire smiled, struggling to erase every trace of astonishment from her face and her voice. "Oh, well, I – I imagine they do, Sarah, of course they do."

"So what is all this business about jail and New Jersey?"

Just then the bell rang. For Claire the timing was a godsend. "Just a joke, Sarah, a foolish joke."

As the pupils assembled in two rows to re-enter the school, Albert suddenly appeared at Claire's right hand, smiling when she looked his way. "Don't forget – the skating party," he reminded her, punctuating his words with a discreet wink. Claire suddenly felt light-headed and for a moment feared she might lose her equilibrium, teeter, and faint right into Albert's arms, right there in the entryway.

Claire sat alone as the Westfield-bound car bumped up Sargeant Street. Across the aisle from her sat a dour-faced

Fergal, his lips moving slightly as each electric pole slipped past the window. Claire wanted to talk to him, to tell him what Sarah had said. Maybe he could help her understand how Jake could have returned to Holyoke, gone back to work, even earned a promotion to hear Sarah tell it, after the events in New Jersey. Could he possibly be out on bail already, after what he had done? Or could Sarah be fabricating all this to cover the worry and humiliation her family must be suffering at her brother's arrest?

But Claire and Fergal were no longer friends, that was clear, and the estrangement was painful for her to bear. They had not spoken since she yelled at him and called him stupid several days earlier at the police station. Yes, she was thinking to herself, he was a foolish boy – even stupid at times, just as she had said – but at the same time he was her partner, her fellow investigator, they had shared experiences and secrets known to no one else. She needed to talk to him.

Claire had been intentionally diverting her gaze, pretending to be absorbed with the snowy landscape that lay silently before her through the window. Near Pequot Park some men were harvesting ice on Hampton Ponds with long-handled saws. A team of oxen waited nearby with a heavy dray to haul the ice off to a storage shed several miles away. At one point she turned and glanced toward Fergal, but he was seated with his back to her, clearly unwilling to engage in a conversation with her.

When the car squealed to a halt at the Southampton Road stop, Claire stepped down to the snow-covered road, then set off without a backward glance. She could hear Fergal's boots crunching on the icy surface behind her. She was about to stop and wait for him to catch up to her so she could strike up a conversation as if nothing unusual had happened between them, but she couldn't – or wouldn't. When finally she reached her house she turned and strode up the driveway toward the barn, hoping Fergal would follow her, or speak. He did neither, but just continued trudging down the road.

Claire was angry. Fergal was being foolish and she wanted to tell him so. She wanted him to understand how stupid he could be sometimes. But she knew where that would lead.

"Fergal," she called to him. The boy just kept going. She started to follow him. "Fergal, you—" She hesitated. "Fergal, please let me talk to you – *please*," she begged, the last "please" spoken with special emphasis and a tone of urgency she hoped would elicit a response.

The boy took several more steps, snow and ice crunching under his boots. Then he stopped and turned but stood expressionless. Claire ran to catch up with him. Finally they were face to face, although he gazed downward as if he was examining the snow.

"Please, Fergal, won't you talk to me?" The boy stood motionless, but ever so slowly his eyes rose to meet hers. The wind was whipping around them. Nearby stood a small three-sided shed where canisters of milk were left for pickup. "Fergal, I need to talk to you. You have to listen to me." She stepped into the shed and Fergal followed, still looking uncomfortable.

"I talked to Sarah in the schoolyard this noon." Fergal did not respond. "I wanted to tell her how sorry I was, sorry about Jake, you know?" Fergal finally looked up and into her eyes. "I mean, imagine, her own brother, a German sympathizer, a traitor." Fergal nodded slightly. "But she acted like she didn't know what I was talking about." Again Fergal nodded. "She said Jake was at home for supper just last night. And that he's working at Wellington Textiles again and just got a promotion. I thought at first maybe she was pretending, but she's not the kind of girl to lie, you know?" Fergal seemed to understand. "Fergal, I'm startin' to think maybe those guys who were arrested in New Jersey, maybe they weren't Manfred and Jake and Hank. Maybe they were other Germans, secret agents, corn-spirters–"

"*Conspirators*," corrected Fergal. "You mean *conspirators*."

For a moment Claire was angry with Fergal. "Okay, okay, *conspirators*." Then she checked herself. "If they're still in Holyoke, like nothing happened, maybe they're up to something else."

Claire paused awaiting a reply. For a moment Fergal stood silently. Finally he nodded, then spoke. "I've been wondering about something. Remember the second time we went to the quarry?"

Claire nodded. "Yeh, what about it?"

"We saw that Manfred guy loading crates into his truck, right? Where'd he go with them is what I don't understand."

"He came back while we was still in the shed. We skedaddled, but he almost caught you," added Claire.

"Yes, he came back less than ten minutes later. What I wonder is if some of the bomb supplies went to New Jersey, but maybe Manfred took some of them away? If he did, the newspaper didn't mention it, maybe they didn't know about it. They made it seem like all the stuff was in that one load, the load that was delivered to New Jersey."

Claire turned and stared directly into Fergal's 's eyes. "You don't suppose Manfred has planted more of those cigar bombs, maybe right here in Westfield, or Southampton, or Holyoke? Jackie said the others were set to go off in three days."

"Maybe the police and those agents from the Bureau of Investigation don't know about it," added Fergal. Their eyes met. "We – we should tell them–"

"No, Fergal," replied Claire sharply. "We're not tellin' no one, not until we know for sure. Come on, we gotta go to the quarry."

Claire was headed toward Southampton Road but Fergal's feet were planted in the snow.

"Come on you foolish boy – there ain't much time." Fergal's head hung and he shook it once. "What's the matter, Fergal? We'll just have one quick look."

Still the boy would not move. "Come *on*," she shouted at him.

"*No*, Claire Bernard, I said *no*," shouted Fergal. His face was scarlet. Claire had never heard him raise his voice, never seen him angry before. "We promised the policeman – our das – Jack and Tom. We promised them. Remember?"

"Fine, then, I'll go alone," replied Claire, her face red with anger and her jaw set. She turned and took off in a run along the snow-covered road as Fergal watched.

~ 36 ~

Father, Father," called Marie from the kitchen door toward the barn. There was no reply. She quickly threw a shawl over her shoulders and shuffled through the snow to the workshop door. Inside she found her father turning a fitting on the lathe.

"There you are, Father – *Father*," she shouted. Finally he looked up, saw his daughter, and released the treadle.

"Oh, 'ello dear, you just get 'ome?"

"Yes, Father. Do you know where Claire is? I expected her to be doing her homework, but she's not in the house."

Charles looked perplexed. "Well, did you check the privy?"

"Yes, of course. Father, her coat isn't on the hook and I don't see her bookbag in her room. It's nearly five o'clock, where could she be?"

"Maybe she's over at the Bousquets. I'll run over and see." Moments later he returned, a worried look on his face. "Elaine says she saw Claire and Fergal comin' up the road from the car stand some time ago. We don't need a worry, dear, long as that boy's with 'er." He thought for a moment. "Tell you what, I'll run over the Dooley place, she's probably there."

He jumped in the Model-T. It rattled and gasped for several seconds, then started, and sputtered off down Southampton Road. In less than ten minutes he returned. He was stepping out of the motorcar as Marie emerged from the back door. "Did you find her, Father?"

Charles walked toward her shaking his head, carrying something under his arm. "The only soul at home was the lady,

222

Fergal's aunt, and she hadn't seen either of them. Now she's in a tizzy, too."

"What have you there, Father?" asked Marie.

"I found it settin' in the milk-stand, front of the Dooley's." He held it up. It was Claire's bookbag.

Marie crossed herself. "Oh, dear Lord, what has happened to her?"

"Now, now, don't be worrying. I'm sure she'll turn up any minute now." Charles stepped into the kitchen. "Can you help me make a telephone call, dear?"

"Master Thomas, sir," said Deidre, one of the Wellington maids, as he sat in the parlor reading. "There's a telephone call for you, sir."

Tom went to the library and lifted the receiver. "Hello? Oh, yes sir, Mr. Bernard, hello, there. What's wrong, sir? When? Oh, yeh, sure, I'll be there fast as I can, sir. Yep, meet you right at the quarry entrance on Southampton Road. Yep. Okay."

Fifteen minutes later Tom's roadster came careening up Southampton Road and pulled in behind Charles' motor.

"Any news, Mr. Bernard?"

"Nothing, Thomas, and it's gettin' dark and mighty cold. I'm just afraid those two have gone into the quarry again. I got two kerosene lamps and a couple blankets."

Tom nodded. "Okay, follow me, Mr. Bernard."

The two motors turned into the road leading to the quarry. The way was snow-covered but they were able to move slowly in the ruts made by other vehicles. They followed the edge of the cornfield, now covered with a blanket of snow. Then, just as the road entered the woods, they came upon a police vehicle blocking the way. The driver's door opened and out stepped an officer. He seemed groggy, as though they had wakened him from a nap.

"Officer, I'm Charles Bernard, this is Tom Wellington. We're lookin' for two young uns, my daughter, Claire, and her friend Fergal Dooley. They're both fourteen. Have you seen them?"

"Eh, nay, ain't seen a soul since I took over at noon."

"Can you let us pass, officer? We need to get into the quarry. They might be in there, one of 'em might be injured – er something."

"Sorry, sir, but my orders are to 'low no one in. It's a crime scene, you know. It's where those Krauts–"

"Yeh, we know," interrupted Tom. "But this is an emergency. You gotta let us pass." Tom was getting agitated. Finally Charles took him aside. Then they reversed their motors and headed back out to Southampton Road.

"Okay," began Tom when they had parked well out of sight of the officer. "Here's an idea. There's another way into the quarry. I remember it from when I was a kid, my brother took me in there once. It's off the trolley line – it's the way they hauled rock out of the quarry when the line was built back in the aughts. I'll drive around to Hampton Pond Road, follow the trolley tracks in my motorcar as far in as I can, then walk. Meanwhile you go in this way on foot, just give the good officer there a chance to fall back to sleep first."

"But maybe we should go to the station and file a report first?"

Tom shook his head. "All the way to Holyoke, or Westfield? It'd be an hour anyway before they get out here. We can be in that quarry, both of us, in ten, fifteen minutes."

Charles nodded. "Don't worry, sir, we'll find them, I promise."

~ 37 ~

The ice truck lumbered down the rough road in the darkness, its motor droning and straining through the snow and over the uneven terrain. Claire lay in the back, bound and gagged, tossing left and right as the truck lurched. She was straining at her bonds, but to no avail, tears of fear and frustration streaming down her cheeks.

Suddenly in the darkness the heap of tarps beside her moved. She thought it was just the motion of the truck until she heard a soft whisper.

"C-Claire."

She let out a muffled scream.

"Shhh, it's me, Fergal. Stay still." She felt his hands on her ankles, pulling at her bonds. Then she felt something cold next to her skin as the canvas tightened. Again a muffled scream.

"Shhh, don't move," he whispered. "I'm gonna cut the canvas with my jackknife – stay still." And in a matter of seconds the bonds on her legs fell away.

"Roll over," he whispered as he pried gently beneath her legs and back. "Okay, now hold still again while I free your hands." But at that moment the truck lurched again and she was spun over, her face now pressed against the cold wooden floor.

"Are you okay?" he whispered as he gently brushed the hair from her face. "Just another minute."

The bonds on her wrists were tighter and he struggled with his knife. At one point it nicked her arm and she whimpered, but then the ropes were cut. She sat up, groping at the gag, but Fergal was already untying it. Finally it fell away.

"Oh my god, Fergal." She was trembling. "Where — how did you?" she began in a shaky whisper.

Just then the truck's motor stalled. Fergal placed his fingers gently against her lips. "Shhh. Don't worry. We're gonna get outta here."

The motor cranked once again but wouldn't start. Claire and Fergal now were crouched before the latched doors.

"But how, Fergal? This door's latched from the outside."

"That one is," he whispered, "but not this one. I wrapped my cap around the latch before I shut it. All we have to do is push."

"Huh?"

Just then the cranking ceased and the men's voices could be heard, cursing loudly outside the vehicle. "God-damn piece of crap," spouted one of the men. "It's that starter. We're gonna need a tire iron. In the back."

"Get down," whispered Fergal. Claire lay down and he quickly pulled the oily tarps over them just as one of the doors opened.

Light from a kerosene lantern suddenly washed over Claire as she lay motionless. A hand removed a heavy iron tool that lay on the floor just beyond Claire's feet, then slammed the door. Claire and Fergal remained still, listening to the sounds from the front of the truck, not daring to move lest their captors returned for more tools.

They heard several sharp metallic whacks, some muffled conversation, then the motor cranked again. This time it started and the vehicle resumed its slow passage. The two were quickly at the door once more.

"Let's get out, Fergal, now."

"We can't," replied Fergal glumly.

"Why?"

"My hat, it fell off when he opened the door. Now both doors are latched."

A shiver of dread traveled down Claire's spine. "Whatta we gonna do now, Fergal?"

"I don't know."

The tires of the Hupmobile squealed as it turned onto Hampton Pond Road. It was headed south toward Westfield, traveling as fast as Tom could make it go on the bumpy route. Shortly he passed a vehicle parked on the shoulder and realized to his dismay that it was a Holyoke police car. In the mirror he could see the cruiser start, pull out onto the road, and follow him, its blue rooftop light flashing.

"Great," thought Tom, "just what I need." With that he accelerated and quickly left the cruiser in his dust.

The ice truck strained up a short, steep pitch, made a sharp turn, and began to accelerate.

"We just crossed the tracks – we're on Hampton Pond Road now," whispered Fergal.

As the truck accelerated, it became clear to the two that their situation was dire. Even if they could get one of the doors open, they might not survive a leap at this speed.

Just then a motorcar shot past them traveling in the opposite direction. But in an instant its brakes screeched, its tires squealed, and the car came to a halt. In a matter of seconds it had turned around and was now following behind them. It crept perilously close to the back of the ice truck, its horn sounding. The truck accelerated more.

Claire could hear rustling and clinking sounds. "What are you doing, Fergal?"

"My key ring. Maybe I can use it—"

Then she heard a clink as the boy looped the ring over the latch mechanism that held one door closed. She heard him grunting.

"Help me, Claire. Here, grab it and pull." Now they were both straining on the key ring and prying. At first there was no give, but as they worked the mechanism back and forth and up and down it began to yield. Finally, with a sharp report, the latch popped up and the door swung open several inches. Fergal reached out and turned the knob that released the other door. Now they could see the motorcar close behind, the police cruiser in hot pursuit, lights flashing.

The three vehicles were now hurtling down Westfield Road. At Northampton Road the truck slowed only slightly, turned abruptly, then accelerated once again. Suddenly the roadster pulled into the opposite lane as if to pass the truck, but the truck veered abruptly, cutting off the pursuing car. They passed briefly under an electric street light and the roadster was illuminated.

"Oh, my gosh, Fergal, that – that's Tommy's motor, the Hupmobile. Where'd he come from?"

The truck slowed and made another turn onto South Street, then accelerated once more.

"Whatta we gonna do, Fergal? I'm scared."

"As soon as he slows down, we gotta jump, Claire, we gotta."

Just then the truck slowed and began to make a sharp turn onto Race Street next to the canal. The roadster veered as if to pass the truck and cut it off.

"Claire – *jump now*," yelled Fergal.

Claire climbed through the door and for a fraction of a second teetered on the rear bumper. Then she jumped. As soon as her feet met the road she was flung backward, landing hard then tumbling on the gravel surface. In seconds Fergal, too, had jumped, somehow managing to keep his footing as the truck and the roadster sped away side by side up Race Street.

"Claire, Claire–" called Fergal, running to her and kneeling over her. "Are you hurt?"

The truck was careening toward the delivery entrance of the Wellington Textiles warehouse. But the roadster sideswiped it. The truck swerved out of control, then ran off the road, down a steep embankment, and into the canal. The roadster came to a halt and Tom emerged, his eyes on the truck that was floating and on two men struggling to climb out the windows as the water rushed in.

An eerie silence prevailed for several seconds. "Tommy," came a shout from behind him. He turned to see Fergal and Claire standing in the street, the police cruiser pulled up behind them. "Look out, Tommy," called Fergal.

Tom turned again and saw flames erupting in the back of the ice truck as one of the men flailed wildly in the water in an effort to move away from the vehicle.

Suddenly a ferocious explosion occurred in the truck. Flames shot in all directions along with fragments of the dismembered vehicle. The force of the blast knocked Tom, Fergal, and Claire off their feet. Regaining their footing, the three ran up the street away from the blast, a shower of glass raining down around them from hundreds of shattered factory windows above.

~ *38* ~

Marie sat on the edge of a chair pulled up next to Claire's hospital bed. She was stroking her sister's hair gently and looking uneasily at the bandages on her face and hands. She turned and looked up at her father, his face gray with shock and exhaustion at the events of the last few hours.

Marie had received a telephone call from Tom at the hospital shortly after the ambulance arrived. Minutes later her father drove up. Father and daughter had driven the few miles to the hospital without a word. The attending doctor was reassuring, explaining that Claire had suffered only bruises and abrasions from her hard fall from the back of the speeding truck. Nevertheless, they were stunned to see the girl lying in the hospital bed heavily bandaged. She had been given a mild sedative to help her sleep, and the doctor assured them she would be ready to go home in the morning if there were no complications.

Charles and Marie so far had received only a fragmentary account of what had occurred. Charles had tried to get more details from Tom, but while he was unhurt he was wan and disheveled and clearly in no condition to talk.

"You better get home, son," suggested Charles. "We'll be fine here. Claire's okay it appears. We 'preciate what you did for our girl."

Tom shook his head but could not respond. He turned and walked away down the long, drab corridor.

"Father, why don't you go home now, too?" suggested Marie. "I'll stay with her through the night."

"But I should be the one–" he began.

"No, Father, you need to rest. I'll be fine. Tom said Anne is on her way and will stay with us for a while. Now go, please, Father, and I will call you on the telephone in the morning."

Charles nodded, stepped shakily forward and stroked Claire's hair, then bent and kissed her forehead. He rose, looked away from Marie and up at the ceiling. "Okay, then, we'll see you in the morning."

As he walked down the long narrow hallway to the entrance, he encountered Anne.

"Miss Anne," said Charles, smiling briefly.

"Oh, Mr. Bernard. How is Claire doing, sir?" she asked.

Charles nodded. "Well, she'll be okay. They give 'er some powders jus' now so she's fast asleep."

"What were she and Fergal doing? How did they end up in that truck?"

Charles shook his head. "I don't know, miss. I really don't know. They went out to that quarry. I guess they had suspicions. Why they couldn't tell us and let the cops deal with it, I just don't understand."

"I talked to Jack on the telephone. He's taking the first train in the morning. I plan to stay with Marie and Claire for a while," added Anne.

~ 39 ~

Anne left the hospital around eleven while Marie stayed the night in Claire's room, sleeping on a cot brought in by one of the nurses. She woke every few hours to check that her sister was sleeping soundly and to ensure that the covers were secured snugly. She was watching Claire intently when she first opened her eyes the next morning. She leaned forward and stroked her hair.

"How are you feeling, dear?"

Claire seemed confused. "Where—" she began, struggling to make sense of her surroundings.

"Ready for some breakfast?"

Claire nodded. "I – I was having the strangest dream–"

Marie took her hand. "Shhh. You're all right, Claire. I'll ask the nurse if she can bring you something to eat, okay?" Soon she returned. "Here's some tea. They'll bring you some oatmeal shortly." She watched as Claire sipped the tea.

"Claire, dear, there are a couple policemen outside who want to talk with you. Shall I tell them to come in?"

Claire looked briefly at her sister. "When can I go home?"

"The doctor said last night that you could probably be discharged this morning after he sees you. Shall I tell the police officers to come in?"

With her sister's help Claire sat up in the bed, better prepared for company. Marie ushered in the police officers.

"Miss Bernard, I'm Chief Hanrahan, Holyoke Police Department. This is Agent Pierce from the Bureau of Investigation in Boston. How are you feeling today?"

Claire nodded. "All right, I guess."

"Good, good. You took a bad spill, I'd say," replied the agent. She nodded again but her face showed no emotion.

"Miss Bernard, we need to ask you some questions. We talked to the Dooley boy last evening and he told us what he could. We just need to get a few additional details from you."

Again Claire nodded, her eyes meeting Marie's.

"Don't worry," added Chief Hanrahan, "we're not going to scold you. You – well, you did something very brave. Your actions prevented what would have been a terrible disaster. If those bombs had exploded inside the mill warehouse or anywhere close to it, that building would have collapsed. I hate to think of the toll in lives and in property that would have resulted. You, your friend, and Mr. Wellington are certainly heroes."

"Miss Bernard," continued the agent. "Chief Hanrahan tells me that you and young Dooley first reported suspicious activity in that stone quarry several weeks ago. The Holyoke and Westfield police investigated and informed the Bureau and we were able to account for the explosives that had been assembled there – at least, most of it, in a truck that was stopped in New Jersey the following day. As you know a number of arrests were made and it was believed that the plot had been broken. What made you and the young man suspect there were more bomb-making supplies being held somewhere?"

Claire looked at Marie. "Go ahead, Claire, explain."

"Well, we saw that man with the beard, Manfred, at the quarry a few days before. He was loading some crates into that ice truck and hauling them away."

"What kind of crates, miss?"

"The ones with the picric and sulfuric acid." The two officers exchanged glances. "We watched him load 'em in his truck and take them away."

"Did you know then that those were bomb-making materials?"

Claire shook her head slowly. "No, sir. My brother thought maybe they were used for dyeing yarn and cloth – in the mills."

"Did you have any idea where this man took them?"

"No, but it wasn't far. He came back just a few minutes later. Fergal and I was inside the shed and had to run for it. We just got out 'fore he opened the door. We figured he was movin' them to another shed or someplace real close by."

"Miss Bernard, why didn't you mention this when you talked to Sergeant O'Malley in Westfield?"

"We – me 'n Fergal – we didn't think about it again until after he talked to us. We were just thinkin' about the delivery to New Jersey and–"

The agent asked: "Yesterday afternoon, at the quarry, there were two men, is that right?"

Claire nodded.

"Did you recognize them? Had you seen them before?"

"One, the skinny one with the beard, his name was Manfred. The other, the fat one with the red face, I never seen him before." Claire paused, looking briefly at Marie. "What – happened to them? Did you catch 'em both?"

"Oh, we got the big guy in custody. We fished him out of the canal and locked him up right away."

"And – the other guy? Did you catch 'im?"

The police chief shook his head, glanced first at Marie, then looked directly at Claire. "Well, miss, he – didn't get out of the truck before it exploded."

Marie took her sister's hand in hers and stroked it gently. The two officers again exchanged glances. "Well, I guess that's all for now, miss. We'll be on our way."

~ 40 ~

Helen Wellington arose early that morning and dressed quickly. She had been awake much of the night, worried about her son and how he would react to the events of the previous evening. She must have dozed off when he arrived home sometime after midnight. She had listened several times at his bedroom door but heard nothing other than loud snoring.

As soon as activity began in the kitchen Helen went looking for Mildred. A few minutes later the maid brought her tea in the parlor where she sat close to the warmth of the fire. On the tea tray was the morning paper. She took a sip of tea, then drew a deep breath, opened the newspaper, and read:

SABOTAGE PLOT IN HOLYOKE AVERTED
Wellington Textiles warehouse targeted
Two German spies responsible for the attack
One dead, one recovering from injuries at
hospital guarded by Bureau agents

An enormous explosion rocked Wellington Textiles on Monday night. The detonation could be heard for miles around. Many windows in the four-story warehouse were shattered, but miraculously no workers were injured.

The source of the explosion was reportedly an ice truck carrying hundreds of pounds of explosives that came hurtling through the city around six o'clock last evening. One witness reported that the truck pulled into the loading area on Race Street and was immediately rammed by a motorcar. The collision sent the truck plunging into the canal where it floated briefly before exploding, sending flames over one hundred feet in the air. The motorcar was operated by Thomas A. Wellington III, son of the mill owner.

Two men were seen struggling to exit the ice truck as it floated in the canal seconds before the explosion. One was rescued and rushed to City Hospital where he is currently recovering from burns, guarded night and day by federal agents. The injured man has been identified as Bertram Fischer, 42, lately of Willimansett. The second man, identified by authorities as Manfred Becker of Holyoke, is believed to have perished in the explosion. Efforts by the Holyoke Fire Department to recover the body were underway this morning.

Thomas Hanrahan, chief of the Holyoke Police Department, reports that an undercover agent of the Bureau of Investigation had infiltrated the circle of conspirators and kept the Bureau informed of the progress of the plot. Those efforts led to a number of arrests in New Jersey on Sunday and the seizure of hundreds of pounds of bombs and bomb-making materials.

Two children from Westfield first brought the plot to the attention of authorities when they observed unusual activity in the Martinson Quarry in Rock Valley. One, a fourteen-year-old girl, was reported to have been held by the Germans for several hours but escaped shortly before the explosion.

Anne appeared just as Helen finished reading the story and she could see that her mother was upset. Helen handed the newspaper to her daughter and waited as Anne read the account.

"Well, Mother, we can't expect them to pretend it didn't happen."

"I know, dear, I know. But I fear this will only serve to further inflame public sentiment against Germans, Russians, all foreigners. Lawrence Whittemore is already back on his self-declared pulpit." She pointed to an editorial with an even larger headline, PLOT DEMONSTRATES THE DANGERS IN OUR MIDST, much of which was a repeat of his customary diatribe against immigrants.

Anne nodded in agreement. "Claire Bernard says anti-German madness has infected Forestdale School. Even schoolchildren her age are spewing hatred toward one another. That is what got her involved in this awful business in the first place."

The last sentence of the editorial was devoted to extolling the heroism of the unnamed man who risked his life to infiltrate the coterie.

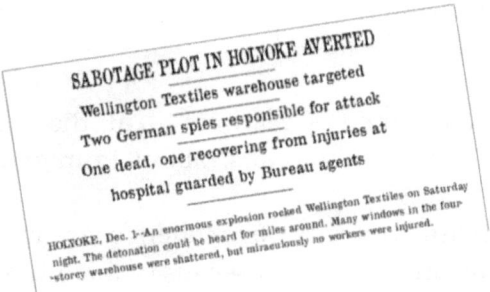

SABOTAGE PLOT IN HOLYOKE AVERTED

Wellington Textiles warehouse targeted

Two German spies responsible for attack

One dead, one recovering from injuries at hospital guarded by Bureau agents

HOLYOKE, Dec. 1-An enormous explosion rocked Wellington Textiles on Saturday night. The detonation could be heard for miles around. Many windows in the four-storey warehouse were shattered, but miraculously no workers were injured.

An editorial staff meeting was just ending at the offices of the *Holyoke Daily Transcript* on High Street. Lawrence Whittemore sat at his desk talking to one of his Assistant Editors when his secretary appeared in the doorway.

"What is it, Martha?" He could hear some kind of hubbub in the outer office.

"Sir, there are a – some ladies, sir – to see you."

Just then Helen Wellington appeared. "Mr. Whittemore, may we have a few minutes of your time?"

"Eh, do you have an appointment?"

"No, sir, we do not. But it is quite urgent."

"Martha, see if you can find a time tomorrow when Mrs. Wellington can come back and–"

Just then another woman appeared in the doorway beside Helen. It was Marjorie Reed, wife of the owner of the *Daily Transcript*. "Lawrence, I think you had better make some time now," she said indignantly.

"Well, eh, yes, of – of course." Helen and Marjorie entered the office and the secretary showed them to seats in front of the editor's desk. Whittemore sat, flushed.

"So, ladies, what may I do for you?"

"Lawrence," began Marjorie, "Mrs. Wellington and I have come to lodge a complaint."

"A complaint? Really? Against the *Transcript*?"

"No, Lawrence, not against the *Transcript*."

The man looked confused.

"Against you," she added.

"I see."

"We are concerned – alarmed – at the tone of your editorials these last few months, about immigrants, and all foreigners."

"Well, I assure you that our readers share my feelings — and it is also the unanimous consensus of the Editorial Board."

"You are stirring up anger and resentment, Lawrence – and suspicion. Turning neighbor against neighbor, friend against friend – needlessly."

"My dear ladies, I respect your concern for neighborliness, but our nation is at war. You do realize that?"

Helen's face was turning bright red. Marjorie spoke up. "Lawrence, Mrs. Wellington's son has only recently returned from Europe. He managed to survive a terrible U-boat attack. He spent many hours floating in the sea. He was imprisoned by the Germans, escaped, and made his way across enemy territory to Allied headquarters with a serious injury. Lawrence, Mrs. Welllington does not need to be reminded of the fact that we are at war, now, does she?"

The man mumbled and shook his head. In front of him was the morning's paper. "I trust you both are aware of the plot that was foiled, right here in Holyoke? A perfect example of the dangers about which I have been writing. We have traitors, saboteurs, in our midst. At least four German anarchists were living in our city, plotting horrific deeds against us, against our nation – and against Wellington Textiles, I would point out."

Helen nodded. "Indeed, Mr. Whittemore. But your editorials, your invective, are directed at all people of German extraction in America. There are thousands, I dare say millions, of people of German descent in America today and most are fine upstanding citizens. Yet you would make them all scapegoats for the acts of a few."

"We need to be watchful, Mrs. Wellington, in our factories, in our schools, in our shops, even in our homes. Those who wish us ill are everywhere, as this incident demonstrates."

Helen and Marjorie nodded, but Whittemore continued. "Fortunately, as you no doubt have read, we now know that a loyal resident of Holyoke infiltrated this group of traitors, gained their trust, and led them right into the hands of the police and federal agents."

Helen spoke up. "Well, he sounds like a model citizen—" Whittemore smiled. "Deserving of some kind of commendation by the mayor, perhaps by the *Transcript*?"

"I heartily agree, ladies, most heartily. Unfortunately, the authorities are keeping his identity a secret."

"Well, Lawrence, it seems a newspaper in New York City published the name of the individual in this morning's edition."

Helen rose and stepped to the office door, then opened it. A gray-haired man entered the room smiling, cap in hand.

"Mr. Whittemore," said Helen, "may I introduce Dr. Henry Smith. I believe you know him as Doktor Heinrich Schmidt."

"What is he doing here?"

Marjorie Reed stood. "Lawrence Whittemore, I believe you two have already met, hmm?"

"What is this all about?" demanded Whittemore in high dudgeon.

Marjorie replied. "Professor Smith, sir, is our hero."

Back home that afternoon, Claire lay in her bed surrounded by familiar objects, the sampler she had been working on, her collection of stuffed animals, her remembrance book. She reached for the framed portrait on her dresser and held it in both hands, gazing into her mother's eyes. Jack sat by her bed for a long time, telling Claire all about school, reluctant to upset her with questions about the events of the previous day. Just as he was leaving, there came a knock at the kitchen door. Marie came to Claire's bedroom door and tapped lightly.

"Claire, dear, Fergal's aunt is calling. She wishes to see you."

"Tell 'er I'm sleeping, Marie, please. I – I can't see 'er now."

Marie nodded and closed the door softly. A few minutes later she returned with a plate of cookies. "She brought you some ginger snaps. She said Fergal told her you would like them."

Claire looked at the golden morsels on the plate and smiled. "They smell awfully good, but I'm not hungry at the moment, Marie. I think I'll just have a little nap."

For nearly a half-hour Claire lay in bed, her eyes closed, her mind unable to find repose.

The next day when she was feeling better, Claire trudged down the road to the Dooley place. Fergal's aunt answered the door.

"Why, there you are, dear. I'm so glad to see you're feelin' better."

"Yes, ma'am, much better. Thank you for the ginger snaps."

"Oh, child, you're welcome. Fergal asked me to make 'em special, said you'd like 'em."

"Yes ma'am, they are my favorites." She paused, trying to look past the large woman. "I wondered if I could see Fergal, ma'am. I wanted to thank 'im, too."

Looking suddenly serious, the woman whispered, "He's out in the barn, doin' 'is chores. Go ahead, but be quick, okay? He's not feelin' too well right now. And his father'll be back shortly."

Claire walked across the snow-covered yard to the barn, slid the heavy door open, and entered. She found Fergal currying Castor, speaking softly to the huge animal. He was standing stiffly, wearing a worn muslin shirt that hung loosely on his shoulders.

"Hello, Fergal."

He turned slowly toward her, but as he turned he winced.

"Hello, Claire," he replied weakly. "How are you?" His voice was shaky.

"Okay," she replied as she removed her hat and scarf, brushed them free of snow, then shook snowflakes off her long black coat. "Fergal–"

The boy had resumed brushing the horse but she could see that it was difficult for him.

241

"How's Castor?"

"He's all right. He has the rheumatism, so the doc says. You can tell it hurts him in the cold weather. That's why we keep him in this stall with lots of hay. It's away from the doors and the drafts and he stays–"

But as Fergal was speaking Claire noticed something on the back of his shirt. It was a spot of blood. "Fergal," interrupted Claire, "you – you got some blood." She reached out, lifted his shirt, and recoiled at the sight. The boy's back was streaked with red welts, several of which were punctuated with spots of dried blood.

"I didn't know you was hurt, Fergal. You seemed fine after the explosion, I remember."

"Wasn't the explosion."

"What happened?"

"You betta go, Claire, before my da finds you here–"

The boy looked briefly at her. She had never seen so much sadness, hurt, and shame, all in one look. He turned away, sniffling.

Suddenly she understood. "Oh, my God, Fergal, did he–" she began, feeling queasy at the thought.

"Thanks for coming by, Claire," he sputtered. Then he resumed brushing the horse.

Claire stepped forward and placed her hand on his. He stopped brushing. "Thank you, Fergal–" He looked up. "For the ginger snaps – and everything."

He smiled briefly. "You told me once they were your favorite–"

"They are, yes. That was very kind of you." She hesitated, their eyes met, then she continued. "Fergal, what you did – it was very brave."

Fergal smiled briefly, then shrugged. "Yeh, well, my da doesn't see it that way. You betta go, Claire."

~ *41* ~

Anne was poring over a stack of invoices at her desk at the Women's Home when three quick taps sounded on her office door. She looked up and smiled. "Tommy, what are you doing here?"

"I was down at the mill talking to Uncle Richard and thought I might walk you home – if you're leaving soon?"

"Well, as a matter of fact I am."

The siblings walked slowly up Appleton Street. "Any news on your motor?"

"Well, *Messieurs Bernard et Bousquet* promise it will be good as new in another week. The front end took quite a beating in the collision."

"What were you talking to Uncle Richard about? Going back to work at the mill?"

"Well, yes, eventually. When the war is over."

"Oh? Well – that is wonderful news. But–" Anne stopped and turned to her brother. "What are your plans for now?"

"Well, Annie, I'm re-enlisting." Anne stood in silence, dumbfounded. Her eyes grew wide, disbelieving. "Yes, I leave the day after Christmas." He could see his sister's demeanor change, her color suddenly pale. "Don't look so glum, Annie, I'm just going back to Newport. It's a desk job. I'll be helping train new enlistees. Not that I'm an expert, of course. I'll mostly be helping with planning and scheduling. I'll be assistant to the Vice Admiral of the school."

"Well, if that's what you want?"

"No, Annie, it's not what I want. What I want is to get back in the war. But they don't want me. Damaged goods, you know? So this is the best I can hope for."

The pair resumed walking on the snow-covered sidewalk. "Besides, Eleanor's in Newport," added Tom.

"Eleanor?"

"Yeh, Ellie Russell. She's a yeomanette – she enlisted at the same time as I did, in Newport. I think she's a little sweet on me."

Anne sighed. "Tommy," she began, shaking her head in disbelief. "Have you told Mother and Father about your plans?"

Tom shook his head. "Tonight."

"My goodness, Thomas, you – are you sure about all this?"

"I know what you're thinking, Annie. Whenever you call me *Thomas* I can just feel it. You wonder if I'm thinking straight, after all I've been through – shell shock, nerves, all that. Well, I'm over it, Annie. I've put it behind me."

"Have you?"

"Yes."

"What about Jack?"

"He's coming home for Christmas next weekend, right? Well, we're going ice-fishing up at Hampton Ponds. I want to set things right with him, Annie – I do."

Anne nodded and smiled.

When Claire arrived home from school that day, Marie was at the door to greet her. "Claire, dear, Tom and Anne are here with a friend. They're in the parlor with Father."

Claire removed her coat and boots. She could hear voices and laughter from the front room.

"Ah, Claire, 'ello, dear. Come in, come in," said her father when Claire and Marie appeared at the parlor door. He rose from his chair and reached for her arm: "Look who's come to see ye."

"How are you, Claire?" asked Tom, rising and smiling broadly.

"You remember this gentleman," added Anne, nodding to the gray-haired man standing next to him. It was Professor Smith.

"Miss Bernard," said the professor softly. "Nice to see you. How are you feeling?"

"I'm okay," she replied, her eyes shifting from the professor to Tom and then to her father. "What–"

Charles spoke up. "Claire, Professor Smith asked to see you." Claire nodded but seemed confused. "He said he wanted a chance to, um–"

Uncharacteristically, the professor interrupted. "I wanted to speak with you once more before I leave. You see, in just a few hours I will be departing Holyoke to return to my family in Colorado." He paused, looking at the faces gathered about him. "I feel I owe you an apology, Miss Bernard. You, your friend – Master Dooley, is it? – and your brother Jack. That day at the quarry, I confess I was not entirely honest with you all."

Claire nodded.

"But I understand that you and young Dooley figured that out, eh? You were correct, it's not a place where we would expect to find fossil tracks. That rock is all wrong, and the site is much too high. Fossilized animal tracks, as you supposed, usually form in lowlands, in wet sediments on the bottoms of streams and lakes and so on. So you were right."

Claire wagged her head. "It was Fergal figured that out, really. Well, I guess we both did."

"So, you see, you were only following my advice, remember?"

"Advice?"

"*Air – oh – tes – ay pahn – da. Question everything.*"

Claire smiled shyly. "Oh, yeh, that European guy?"

"Yes, Euripides. Quite a guy he was, indeed. And you, Miss Bernard, are quite a young lady."

Again Claire smiled. But quickly her smile faded. "You lied because you were working with those awful men, helping them, making those seegars?"

The man nodded but shrugged his shoulders. "Well–"

Then Tom spoke up. "I think we misjudged the professor, Claire. I know I did."

"It is true, I am German. I was born in Hamburg, earned my baccalaureate degree in geology there, then completed my education in Scotland. Like many geologists I worked for mining companies at first and became skilled at using explosives in mining. I worked for coal mines in Scotland and England and briefly for a large mining firm in Colorado before being hired as a professor of geology at the University of Colorado."

"Soon my wife blessed me with two lovely children, a girl and a boy, Margarita and Frederick. They are of course adults today, both married. I have three grandchildren, ages five, seven, and ten. Alas, Frederick and Helmut, Margarita's husband, enlisted last spring."

"They are both soldiers, Claire, in the United States Army," added Tom.

The old man nodded. "We are naturally very proud, but very worried for them." He looked up at Anne. "But they believe in what they are doing – for America – for our allies. And so do I."

"Then why were you helping those men?" asked Claire pointedly.

"He wasn't helping the Germans, Claire, he was helping the United States," interjected Charles.

The man nodded. "I had a friend in Denver who worked for the War Department. He and his wife invited me to dine with them one evening a year or so ago. We talked about the progress of the war and in particular about German sabotage efforts in America. Those bombings were interfering with America's efforts to aid the British and French. After our country entered the war last spring, it seemed as though more sabotage might turn Americans against President Wilson, against the war. If they were successful, that is."

"I don't understand, Professor Smith. How could you help America?"

Again Tom spoke up. "Claire, Professor Smith agreed to work for the Bureau of Investigation – as a spy."

Claire's eyes grew wide. "A spy? Really?"

The professor nodded. "My friend had a contact, an employee in the German consulate in Manhattan named Kreitzer. I can tell you this now because he has since been arrested. But like many of them, he was actually working for Division IIIB – *Abteilung IIIB* they called it – a German sabotage ring. In the last year, since Black Tom, they have lost many men. The Bureau of Investigation and the New York Police Department rounded up dozens and put them in jail or deported them. So *Abteilung* was looking for new agents, new collaborators. I was introduced to Kreitzer as a German-American who was sympathetic to the cause and who possessed valuable skills with explosives."

"What Professor Smith did was extremely dangerous, Claire. He was very brave," added Tom.

The man smiled. "It had to be done. And it seemed I was best suited for the task, you see? I was already planning on spending time at Yale University in Connecticut, a sabbatical we call it, doing research on the fossil beds along the Connecticut River. Kreitzer believed I could blend in easily in Holyoke. He told me he had several men in the city who could be enlisted to deliver bomb-making supplies. I was to move to Holyoke, go about my research, and wait for further instructions."

"Which is exactly what he did," explained Tom. "He rented a room in the Flats and rode the streetcar up to Smith's Ferry to do his research."

Claire brightened up. "That's where we met you – me, Jack, and Anne."

"Indeed. Took me quite by surprise, you did," replied the professor with a laugh. "Other than the landlady where I live, you three were the first folks I had to speak with after I came to Holyoke. I was nervous."

Claire looked at the professor, her brow knitted. "Well, you had Anne and me fooled. It was Jack who thought you acted a little suspicious that day. I remember he said something about it coming back on the trolley."

The professor nodded. "Well, I was being truthful about my work. But I was trying very hard not to look or sound German, considering how suspicious people are these days. Of course, the night of my lecture, that fellow from the newspaper accused me of being a traitor. I had been reluctant to do that talk–"

"Yes, I remember, you told Anne no at first. But then a few days later you changed your mind."

"Well, she was so persistent and seemed genuinely interested in my work so finally I thought, how can I refuse her? The audience will be young ladies from the Women's Home, and I'll be discussing paleontology, not the war, or politics. I was not expecting the public to be in attendance. From that night on I was very worried that someone would report me to the police, or that the Division would decide that my cover had been compromised."

"You knew that guy Manfred?"

"Well, no, not really. I was told I would receive a message to meet someone when the goods arrived in Holyoke. I wasn't told his real name."

"So you put together those bombs from the stuff in that shed? Wasn't it dangerous?"

"Well, yes, of course. But what no one knew, not Manfred, nor the men from New Jersey who picked up the devices, was that they were harmless. You see, I did not use the sulfuric acid."

Claire was wide-eyed. "I thought that was the stuff that melted away the copper disk. So what–"

The professor nodded. "Water."

"Huh?"

"Yep, water. I filled the one side with water instead of sulfuric. No one knew, except, of course, my contact at the Bureau."

"Well, what happened to the sulfuric? There was a lot of it."

"That night I dumped all that acid on the ground behind the shed."

Claire smiled. "Fergal was right."

"How's that?"

"After you left us at the quarry that day, we were looking around and Fergal said he smelled sulfur. I told him he was imagining things."

"Ah, well, when sulfuric acid reacts with some kinds of rock it produces a disagreeable odor somewhat like rotten eggs. Very perceptive of him."

"But why'd the truck explode, then?"

"Well, miss, Manfred loaded those seegars himself, apparently. Before he brought me to the quarry, he must have already removed some of the supplies, sulfuric, picric, the lead pipes, and all."

"We saw him, Fergal and me," replied Claire, wide-eyed, "when we visited the quarry the second time. He was carrying crates from the storage room to his truck. We didn't realize it at the time, but he was already carrying out his plot."

The professor nodded. "You two were the only ones that knew about Manfred's plan, other than Manfred himself. And I had no way of knowing how much had been delivered from

Canada in the first place. I remember he asked a lot of questions about the seegars, how they worked, how they were assembled. I figured he was just curious."

The professor looked at Charles, Tom, and Marie, shaking his head. "That's one reason *Abteilung's* operations have been so successful in America. No one knows *everything*. Every worker has only so much information and no more. It means less chance of secrets getting out. But this time, Manfred used it to his advantage, and with near-disastrous results."

"So you knew about the shipment to New Jersey?"

"Well, I knew when it was being picked up and roughly where it was bound, yes. I passed that information along to my contacts at the Bureau. They had unmarked cars on all the major roads in that vicinity the night of the delivery. Plus they had a description of the truck I had provided."

"Professor Smith, we – Fergal and me – when we read about the arrests in New Jersey, we figured they'd caught Manfred, Jake Muller, and his friend, Hank. We thought Jake and Hank were in on the plot."

The man shook his head. "They were not, miss, not truly. They made the initial pick-up in New Hampshire for Manfred, that much is certain. But so far as the Bureau could tell, those two boys didn't know what they were carrying, nor did they know about either the New Jersey plot or Manfred's scheme. Like I said, no one in Holyoke knew everything, no one except Manfred Becker."

"Well, I must be on my way, but I have a little something for you and Master Dooley. A small token of my appreciation for what you two did." The professor produced a small box from his coat pocket. He handed it to Claire. It was carefully crafted of oak with a hinged lid, and it just fit in Claire's hand. "Go ahead, Miss Bernard, open it."

Claire smiled at the professor, then looked around at the beaming faces of her sister, father, Tom, and Anne. Slowly she lifted the hinged lid. Inside, nestled in shining felt, were two stone spheres no bigger than golf balls, gray and very plain looking. Each had been sliced in two, the halves fitting snuggly together. "Go ahead, miss, open one."

Claire's eyes were wide. As she lifted the top, the interior of the stone revealed itself – hundreds of shining, glimmering crystals with many smooth facets, like diamonds, ranging through a whole spectrum of colors from gleaming white to emerald green to aqua to the deepest, darkest purple. "Oh, my gosh, Professor, It's a geode." Her eyes shone as she gazed on the interior, the light reflected in all directions. "It's – the most beautiful thing I ever saw."

"There's one for you and one for Master Dooley."

"I can't wait to give Fergal his. He will love it, Professor, I know him and I know he will. Where did you get these? Did you buy them?"

"No, indeed, miss. I dug them myself, near Colorado Springs where I was working many years ago."

"Thank you, Professor Smith, for the geode – for everything."

"You are very welcome, Miss Bernard, but it is you, you and Master Dooley, and Thomas here, who deserve to be thanked."

The professor prepared to leave, pulling his coat and scarf on. "Well, I must be going now, if Seaman and Miss Wellington don't mind. My train leaves in just a few hours."

Before he stepped out the front door he turned to Claire one more time. "Thank Master Dooley for me, now, won't you?" She nodded. "And don't forget– "

I know, replied Claire – "*Air – oh – tes – ay pahn – da.*"

~ 42 ~

Claire was up early the following Monday preparing for school. Her father was ready to drive her in the Model-T. Fergal had been out of school the remainder of the previous week. Claire was worried about him and had considered going over to inquire after him, but had not.

At seven a.m. sharp, several raps sounded on the kitchen door. Claire beamed at the sight of Fergal, smiling and looking very much himself. Actually, she thought, he looked different from the skinny creature that accompanied her on the first day of school back in September. He appeared taller, his shoulders wider. Even his expression had changed – somehow he seemed more confident, sure of himself, and genuinely happy to see Claire.

On the short walk along Southampton Road to the car stand, Claire said, "I'm glad you're going back to school, Fergal. I've missed you."

Waiting for the approach of the Holyoke-bound car, Fergal fidgeted as usual. "Three minutes late," he reported, looking at his pocket watch. Then, a minute later, "Four minutes late." Claire smiled. Finally, the car approached and the pair boarded, taking seats together at the rear.

As the car began to move, Claire brought Fergal up to date on school, homework, and the class play. Finally she paused. "Fergal, I hope you don't mind, but I tol' everyone at school what you did, how you rescued me. I told them you were the real hero that day."

He looked at her and smiled briefly, but then shook his head. "I'm sorry you got hurt–"

"It was just a few scrapes and bruises. It looked worse than it was, really." She paused, looking at Fergal, examining his face.

"What?" asked Fergal.

"Fergal, I never knew – you never tol' me – how'd you get in that truck? I – I thought I–"

"I followed you to the quarry. I guess I should have tried to stop you but–"

"I probably wouldn'a listened, right?"

Fergal smiled. "I followed your tracks in the snow. I was hiding behind a rock when they caught you and tied you up. I saw them put you in the back of the ice truck. When they were having trouble starting the motor, I snuck up to the back and climbed in next to you under those tarps. I didn't say anything because I was afraid it would frighten you, and you'd make noise. So I just lay there until the truck started moving." He smiled at Claire. "It was just lucky I had my jackknife in my rucksack."

Claire blushed. "I guess it was lucky, Fergal – very lucky. Listen, Fergal, I – I'm sorry I called you stupid. You are just the opposite of stupid, Fergal. You are – well – a genius, I'd say, like Mr. Edison."

Fergal shrugged. "I never invented anything, not yet, anyway. But I got some ideas."

"Fergal, please forgive me. I been foolish – about a lot of things, but especially about you." He nodded and blushed.

Then she told him about the present from Professor Smith. "There's one for you, too. You won't believe how beautiful it is."

They rode in silence for a few minutes, watching the snowy landscape slip past. Claire had something more to say to Fergal, but she was waiting for the right moment.

She could see Fergal's lips moving. "So, how many are there? Electric poles, I mean."

He looked up. "From Southampton Road to Sargeant Street, two hundred forty-seven." Claire smiled.

Finally, the car turned onto Sargeant Street. It was now or never, thought Claire. "Oh, I almost forgot, this Friday night is the grade eight skating party at Lincoln Park. Everyone is going – it will be great fun, don't you think?" Fergal nodded. "I was wondering, maybe you would have a skate with me?" She looked into his eyes as she spoke.

Fergal looked away for a moment, then turned to Claire. "I don't think I'll be goin'."

"But why, Fergal, I was hopin'–" As she spoke she saw Fergal's expression fall.

"My da–"

~ 43 ~

The Bernard's Model-T chugged along Westfield Road that Friday evening as a silvery sliver of moon was just appearing above the eastern horizon. A few minutes later it pulled up to the curb at Lincoln Park. Jack helped Claire and Julie extricate themselves and their long skirts from the motorcar.

They had arrived early as Jack had volunteered to assist with the lighting of the bonfire, setting up of tables for refreshments, and clearing the ice. Jack went right to work with several teachers and fathers.

Until the bonfire was lit, the only light available was provided by a teacher's motorcar that had been driven down to the pond's edge, its headlamps shining brightly across the ice. Several pupils were already skating despite the snow, their silhouettes visible only when they passed through the two beams. Claire and Julie sat on a bench by the pond, struggling with their skates.

In the next few minutes many more young people arrived. The girls wore long dresses that nearly touched the ice, dark woolen overcoats, and mittens. Some sported colorful bows, scarves, doeskin mittens, or fur mufflers. As to hats, a few were simple, knitted, tight-fitting bonnets that pulled down over the ears, others more elaborate affairs topped with ribbons, silk flowers, even bird feathers. Most of the male skaters displayed less flamboyant finery, woolen or duck trousers, overcoats, mittens, and hats ranging from small, flat golf caps to deerstalkers to fancy bowlers. But for lack of a shaggy beard, one tall boy dressed entirely in black with a tall top hat looked very much like Abraham Lincoln gliding across the ice.

"You don't gotta stay, Jackie," Claire implored when all the preparations were complete. "We'll be fine."

"I just want to see what this shindig is like. I'll just stay around a few moments – I promise not to embarrass you."

"Too late for that," whispered Claire to Julie.

"I'll be back at nine sharp."

"Nine-thirty would be fine."

"Okay, nine-thirty – have a good time – you, too, Julie," replied Jack as the girls sailed off across the pond, firelight glinting off their skates.

By seven the skating party was in full swing. Nearly every young person was on skates, some gliding competently across the ice, others waddling about prepared for a tumble at any moment. The young skaters' faces glowed like beacons when they passed near the bonfire, but faded quickly as they circled away. At the far end of the pond where there was only weak moonlight, they faded to little more than dark silhouettes against the snowy hillside beyond.

One group of nearly a dozen boys had joined hands to form a long chain, and they delighted themselves and onlookers by "cracking the whip." The lead skater would accelerate, then turn abruptly while yanking on his neighbor's arm. The yank then rippled down the chain until it reached the last few skaters who suddenly were propelled through an exhilarating spin that produced shouts and gales of laughter. Inevitably, the whip-cracking ended with several skaters flung wildly across the ice.

Most of the grade eight girls meanwhile were content circling the ice in small groups, inscribing gentle circles with their skates, all the while chatting, laughing, and beaming at teachers and a few parents who looked on from the shore. Two sisters whose family only recently arrived in Holyoke from North Carolina had never skated before and the other girls took pains to assist and encourage them. Claire Bernard, Julie Trottière, Sarah Muller, and Celia Hammond, all capable skaters, formed a tight-knit quartet that moved smoothly and effortlessly around the ice, much to the envy of some of the other girls who were uneasy on skates.

Then, to the surprise of all, the strains of a Strauss waltz floated across the ice. A father, it seemed, had secured a Victrola in the passenger seat of his motorcar parked in the snow near the pond's edge, the instrument's great horn protruding from the window. The sound traveled well through the cold still air, instantly transforming the park into a musical dreamland. Every few minutes when the music began to fade, the operator turned the hand-crank and the musical reverie was restored.

It took a few moments for this innovation to inspire one of the boys, Billy Smith, to separate from the whip-crackers. He approached one of the girls, Yvette Lemieux, smiling, his hand extended. Soon they were skating in tandem, glowing with pride. During one circuit in the firelight, Billy was facing Yvette, both her hands in his, skating backward. They made it look so easy, so natural, so romantic, and their classmates watched in awe and envy. Then slowly, one by one, others extricated themselves from their games to find partners. Within minutes the affair had been transformed from a skating party to a promenade to a dance on ice!

Claire's circle of friends was quickly depleted by importuning young men. Claire was feeling lonely and conspicuous when, out of the darkness, a teetering figure approached, a boy, a fairly tall boy, although she did not at first recognize him so completely was he swaddled in wool. Just as he reached her, his limited balance abandoned him and he fell in a heap at her feet. He groaned, then rolled over and smiled up at Claire. It was Albert Albrecht.

"Miss Bernard," he sputtered, laughing at himself, and lifting one hand pathetically. "May I have this, er, skate?"

Claire was stunned at first. But his smile and comic request amused her and she laughed as well. Then she took his hand and pulled. Gradually, with much flopping and floundering, the young man was back on his skates, although by the look of it his next fall was imminent.

"Albert, are you all right?"

"No serious injury. But – perhaps you could teach me how to skate?"

For the next half-hour Claire and Albert skated, Claire easily and more or less gracefully, Albert awkwardly with ever an eye on his feet that he knew could fly out from beneath him at any moment. They laughed at themselves, knowing they were the very antithesis of grace and style embodied by Billy and Yvette, but neither cared. Claire held Albert's gloved hand to give him some needed support, yet felt no discomfort or embarrassment. As for Albert, he had all he could do to remain upright, so closeness to his partner was never a source of unease.

Finally, Albert was beginning to feel more confident on his skates. "I think I've got it now," he said, drawing just a little closer to Claire and allowing his soft gaze to wash over her. "Thanks to you, Miss Bernard." She smiled and felt suddenly warm. "May I – would you mind if I were to address you as Claire?"

"I suppose you might," she replied with a mock tone of propriety. They laughed together. "But why, Albert, have you insisted on calling me 'Miss Bernard' all this time?"

He looked into her eyes. "My mother told me it's proper when addressing a young lady."

Claire nodded, then blushed. A young lady, she thought. Me?

"Oh, I have something for you," added Albert. He reached into the pocket of his overcoat and produced a bundle of tissue paper which he carefully unfolded, revealing a silk corsage with a pale pink rose.

Claire blushed. "Why, Albert, it's lovely." She pinned it to the collar of her overcoat. "Thank you."

"See, the rose matches your complexion," he observed. Not really, thought Claire, blushing profusely. They made several laps around the pond, Albert holding on to Claire for dear life. Gradually he seemed to gain confidence and attempted a conversation.

"How is your essay coming along?"

"Essay?" replied Claire.

"Yes, you know – animal husbandry."

"Oh, that essay, I changed my topic. I decided to write about Louisa May Alcott – she wrote *Little Women* – it's my favorite book. At least I know a little about her."

"More than about animal husbands?" She and Albert exchanged a glance, then a smile, then a laugh.

Just then Sarah Muller appeared out of the shadows, eyes shining, smiling first at Claire, then at Albert. As always she was immaculately dressed in a blue and white poplin dress with pleats buoyed by several petticoats, a deep blue felt jacket, and a small but delicate hat of black crepe.

"You two seem to be doing well." Suddenly out of the darkness her partner appeared, skidding to a graceful stop at her side. It was Fergal.

"Why Fergal, where did you learn to skate like that?" asked Claire with surprise.

"Last winter, down back by the river, I skated practically every day. I taught myself."

Sarah was beaming. "He's amazing, isn't he?"

"Yes," replied Claire, returning Sarah's smile. "He *is* amazing."

With that Sarah and Fergal were off.

Claire was flummoxed. "That boy," she said, shaking her head.

Albert extended his hand. "Shall we?" And then they too were off.

Marie and her father were seated by the coal stove, Marie reading a novel, Charles engrossed in the *Old Farmer's Almanac*. Soon Jack returned and recounted for his sister and father what the scene was like at the skating party.

"They had a Victrola, Dad, someone set it up in a motorcar on the edge of the ice and it was playin' while the students skated. It was really something – really something. Marie, you wouldn't have believed it. Claire seemed really happy, though seeing me leave was probably the high point of the night for her."

Charles laughed and he and Marie exchanged knowing glances.

"Hey, I saw Fergal Dooley," added Jack. "I don't know how he got there, but there he was just puttin' on his skates as I was leavin'. I thought Claire said his old man wouldn't allow him to go." Charles and Marie again exchanged glances. "What? Did something happen?"

Charles set down the *Almanac* and gazed at his son for a moment. "Had a little chit-chat with Fergal's Aunt Beatrice t'other day."

"Oh?"

"I tol' her how disappointed Claire was that Fergal wouldn't be goin' to the skatin' party, I did."

"Oh, he'll be there, Mr. Bernard, she says, Fergal'll be there."

"Well, ma'am, I'm mighty glad to 'ear it, I said. What changed his mind? I asked. Well that lady, she's a corker. She's little, but has she got some gumption. She says she and her brother-in-law had a little confab t'other night. She told 'im she was thinkin' of goin' back to the Old Sod. Course Eamon got all het up about that. I mean to say, she does all the cookin' and cleanin' round there, and shoppin'. He'd be lost without 'er."

"He gave in, eh, Dad?"

"Yeh, well, weren't that simple. Guess he told her to go back to Ireland – see if he cared. Then she tol' him she might just take Fergal with her, if the boy wanted."

"You can't do that, he tol' her, he's my son and you got no right."

"Yeh, well, maybe so, she says to him, maybe so. But I 'spect if the police knew how you treat that boy, they'd have you in jail pretty quick."

"You shoulda seen 'im, she says, he was boilin' mad. That's when we struck a deal, she says."

"A deal?"

"I'll stay, she says. But the next time you lay a hand on that child, he an' me'll be off to County Donegal, and you'll find yer arse in the hoosegow, understand?"

"Wow, Dad, that's great."

"Yep, and then she made me a cup a tea and give me some of those ginger snaps a hers. Mighty nice lady, Miss Bea."

~ 44 ~

You know, Jack, I remember you telling me about ice fishing way back in grade eight. You talked about it like it was some mystical experience, as if what goes on under the ice is unknown and unknowable. Do you remember?"

Tom and Jack were seated on a log on the margin of Hampton Ponds, a blanket of white laid out before them atop nearly a foot of ice. They had cut holes with Jack's auger and set in place almost two dozen tip-ups, more than an hour's work. Now they were resting, admiring their work, drinking coffee they had heated over a small cooking fire.

Jack wagged his head and smiled. "I don't recall saying things like that, Tommy. But it is relaxing, soothing in a way. "

"You said there are two separate worlds and we can only catch glimpses, shadows, of what lies below. That's what you told me, I swear, Jack."

"I don't know, Tommy, I think you've been reading too many of Annie's books. Like William James, she keeps going on about him. I s'pose I oughtta read one of his books sometime – it's not my kind of reading, though." He turned and looked at Tom.

"Listen, Jack," replied Tom, pointing to the scar on Jack's lip, "I never apologized for – that."

"Forget it."

"No, Jack, I can't forget it. I didn't mean to – honest."

Jack sighed. "It's no big deal, Tommy, really, it's just–" Then he paused, looking out across the ice.

Tom sensed his friend had something more to say. "What?" Jack shook his head. "Go ahead, say it, Jack. Say it."

"It's just that, well, you gotta control your temper, Tommy. That guy in the restaurant that night, it's true, he was a fool. Probably had too much to drink. But you can't–"

Tom's chin was set and his eyes narrowed. "Don't lecture me, Jack – don't try to tell me how to act, huh? I get that enough from my sister."

"I'm not tryin' to tell you–"

"Well, don't. Just drop it, huh?"

With that Tom stood, turned his back to his friend, lit a cigarette, and gazed out across the ice. Just then a flag went up on one of the tip-ups.

"Ah," said Jack as he jumped to his feet and ran off across the ice. Tom did not follow. Jack lifted the tip-up and started to reel in the line, but it wasn't easy – his catch was giving him a good fight. He let out the line a bit, hoping the fish would tire. But suddenly he felt a strong yank on the line, then it went slack. He'd lost it. He shrugged, pulled in the line, rebaited the hook, then reset the tip-up. Finally he walked slowly back to the shore.

"Too bad, that coulda been a good size bass, maybe," he said to Tom without looking at him. Then he stoked the fire.

"I'll get the next one, Jack," answered Tom. Jack nodded but continued to occupy himself with the fire and his tackle box.

Finally, after several uncomfortable minutes had gone by without a word, Tom spoke again. "Listen, Jack, I know you're trying to help – you always are. That's the way you are. But you just don't know, buddy – you just don't understand what it was like."

Jack poured himself more coffee.

"You're right, Tommy, I don't. So why don't you tell me, huh? Make me understand."

"If I tell you, you have to swear not to tell Annie, or Mother and Father. I'll tell them myself, when I'm ready. And when I think they're ready."

Jack nodded. "Swear."

"When we sailed out of New York harbor, they told us we were headed for California. We'd be carrying troops back to the east coast for training, they said. And we'd probably be making lots of trips over the next few months. The guys, they'd all been worried that we were headed to England or France, so when we heard about California everyone relaxed. They worked us hard the next two or three days, morning, noon, and night. But then, maybe early in our third day at sea, we came in sight of land and everyone said we were going into port. It was Hampton, Virginia, a big naval station. We figured we would refuel or take on some supplies, then be headed south to the Panama Canal."

"Middle of the night they mustered everyone and started boarding troops. There must've been a thousand, maybe two thousand. It was a shock, a complete shock, to everyone and rumors started flying around. I guess some of the soldiers let it be known – they were bound for France. We set sail before dawn, headed for Southampton, England – probably trying to keep it all hush-hush. But all that stuff about troops coming from the west coast to the east coast and needing more training was lies. They had orders to get these soldiers to the front – pronto."

"We were in a convoy of nearly fifteen ships, some troop ships, destroyers, destroyer escorts, plus a couple coalers. We were under way for maybe four days when we had our first alert. Everyone went to their assigned stations prepared for hostilities, but nothing happened. I was trying not to think of what was coming, just doing my job. I decided that the radio room would be my world and I'd forget about everything else. That's what I said to myself, and I tried not to think of what an explosion, a well-placed mine or torpedo, would do to the ship, and what it would be like to die in there."

"We finally made it to Southampton and the American soldiers left. God, some of them looked younger than me and so scared. This one really young looking guy I met was talking like he had only days to live. While we were talking he was shaking like a leaf. I don't blame him. I was glad to see those guys leave and thought we'd be heading back home and I'd be able to forget all this."

"But within hours a load of new soldiers started boarding. Most were American infantry and marines, older men than we'd had coming over. There were some English and Scottish soldiers, too, who seemed like they might be specially trained. They could all speak French. What this meant was pretty obvious: we'd be sailing right into the war zone, probably somewhere along the French coast. We set sail really fast and I knew the English Channel wasn't too wide so we could be approaching the coast of Normandy in just a few hours. But I guess we went further south as it turned out."

"It was sometime in the night when the torpedo hit. I don't remember anything, not a thing, but waking up drowning. The water was cold and I felt numb in seconds. And I felt sick. I guess it was the fumes 'cause the water was covered with kerosene. It was dark and I couldn't see a thing in any direction. All I knew was I had to keep moving or I was going down. So I just started swimming. I swam as hard as I could, then I found this piece of lumber floating and I grabbed onto it, then kept kicking. I didn't know where I was heading or why I even bothered – I just kept going. It might have been an hour or two, maybe more, I don't know. I tried to conserve my energy by resting now and then. Besides, I started to think, I could be going away from land, away from help. There was nothing to tell me, no moon, no stars, no lights, no sounds. Once I heard an explosion way off, but other than that it was quiet."

"Then, very, very slowly, the sky got lighter off to my right. So I turned and went in that direction. Eventually the sun rose and I just paddled toward it. I figured I was closer to the coast of France than to England and so going east was my best chance."

"There were banks of fog all around me even as the sun got higher in the sky. Once I thought I saw land but then it just disappeared in the fog. But finally one fog bank got more and more distinct and I started to realize it was land. The cold must have been getting to me because I remember being really confused and thinking I could just drop off to sleep for a while, then wake up and go back to swimming when I was more rested. But in a moment of clear-mindedness I realized I couldn't fall asleep, I had to keep swimming as long as possible. To sleep was to die."

"The sun was pretty well up in the sky so maybe it was mid-morning or so when I heard a boat. It sounded like a small boat but my first thought was maybe it was someone coming to rescue me. I turned and started swimming toward the sound. Finally, it came into sight and I realized it was a German patrol boat. At first it seemed to be going past me when someone aboard spotted me and it turned and came my way. I was ready to die, Jack, I swear I was, right there and then. But then they cut the engine and came along side me. These three German sailors pulled me over the gunnels. I must've passed out because I don't remember anything until we approached this big port – I think it was Ostend."

"They marched me and maybe a dozen other sailors and soldiers – I think they were English – along the dock to a train. They pushed us into this empty boxcar and closed and locked the door. It was pitch black and freezing cold. We were in there until early the next morning, no food, no water, when the train started moving. The Englishmen talked on and on about escaping, but I couldn't even think I was so tired and confused. The train stopped once and we could hear lots of German soldiers' voices. We thought we'd arrived at some prison. Then the train started moving again."

"Five, maybe ten minutes later we heard this screeching sound up ahead and the whole train lurched to one side, then turned right over. We were thrown against the floor. I could feel my left arm shattering, Jack. And then I don't remember anything until we were out on the tracks. We heard later that some Belgians had sabotaged the tracks – it was happening almost every night, they said. Anyway, one of the big doors on the car had sheared off and there was a gap just big enough for us to get out. Some of the English soldiers helped me out. I remember they asked me my name. They could have left me there, Jack, they didn't have to help me, but they did."

"Next thing I remember is trying to run through woods, pitch dark, no moon or any light anywhere, me and two of the English soldiers. I remember the smell of fallen leaves, of autumn, and smoke, maybe the train was on fire behind us. Anyway, we kept going as fast as we could. One of the Englishmen was sure we were going south, toward France, but I don't know how he knew. Maybe from the direction the train had been traveling. At one point we came in sight of this road and there was a convoy of German trucks on it, so we waited, seemed like an hour, 'til all the trucks had passed, then we crossed the road and continued in the same direction."

"The sky was starting to get light to our left – that helped reassure us we were headed south toward Allied territory. I could barely keep walking I was so weak with the pain. I was about to ask the guys if we could rest a while when we came to this village. One of the Englishmen, John, went ahead to scout it out. The other, Mark, stayed with me and I think I fell asleep or passed out because the next thing I remember is waking up in this room, this dark room, with stone walls. It was round and I thought: Am I in some castle? I was weak and my arm hurt so I just lay on this small bed. This old man and woman kept coming to look in on me; I could hear them climbing the stairs

267

to my room so I knew I was up on the second floor, maybe the third. They brought me hot tea and some kind of bread and they built a small fire in a tiny stove that made the room very warm. They called it *le pigeonnerie* – I guess it used to be where they kept pigeons. But it was like a castle to me, Jack."

"I don't know how long I was there, just lying in bed, sleeping, eating hot food every few hours, then sleeping some more. Eventually a doctor came and examined me. He came at night and he seemed to be scolding the man and woman. He called them by name: Eloise and Guillaume. I think he was telling them they shouldn't be doing this, taking in an American. He spoke a little English and he told me my arm was healing but it might need surgery in time. He said, 'You must leave,' several times under his breath to me. Once he said, 'They are in danger, *monsieur et madame*.' I didn't say anything but I started to think I shouldn't stay with them a day longer than necessary, for their safety."

"A few days later Guillaume brought me tea. As he climbed the stairs I could hear footsteps behind his and a voice speaking French but with a little English added. I couldn't believe my eyes when he appeared, an American. It was such a relief to hear someone speaking English, especially an American. But then I found out that this guy had also been injured in battle and taken in by neighbors of Eloise and Guillaume. His name was Jim, Lieutenant Jim Markham of the Third Infantry. His unit had seen action near Nantes and he had been injured, then like me rescued by locals. As soon as he was well enough they'd taken risks to bring him to see me. "

"'ere's the plan, Commodore,' he said – that's what he called me, The Commodore. The plan was for him and me and one other American to leave together, soon. He explained that we were in southern Belgium, an area occupied by the Germans, but their forces were stretched thin. The plan was for us to leave within a few days, to travel on foot during the nighttime only and to hide during the daytime. The nearest

Allied forces were about twenty kilometers south and east, near Amiens. It was risky, he admitted, but we had to get to safety. I was thinking more of Eloise and Guillaume, that we had to leave them before the Germans found us and they faced imprisonment for harboring enemy soldiers."

"The last evening before we left there was this commotion in the house. I could hear voices, grownups and children, and then Guillaume came to see me. 'We wish you meet our family, Thomas,' he said in carefully rehearsed English. In the house were their two sons, their wives, and five grandchildren. The children treated me like I was royalty. The little ones each sat in my lap. Each one had a little gift for me, a shiny pebble, a Belgian coin. The littlest girl gave me a bird's feather that was very pretty and delicate. They served me cider – not like American cider at all – and we had this wonderful meal with so many foods I couldn't begin to describe."

"Finally it was time for them to go and each of the children hugged me and kissed me." He paused. "They thanked me, Jack. *They* thanked *me*." Tom paused and looked away at the distant hills, trying to bring his emotions at the memories under control. Finally he continued.

"Jack, I couldn't imagine why they were thanking me, all I'd done was put them all in danger. That night I couldn't sleep, partly knowing what was ahead. But also I felt I wanted to stay among these people, war or no war. It felt like home."

Remembering those feelings, Tom's face glowed. He smiled, briefly. It seemed like the first time Jack had seen Tom truly smile since he got home. But as he looked at Tom's smiling face, right before his eyes he observed a pall, a shadow, fall over it.

"The next night we were preparing to leave." Tom's voice became shaky and he began to struggle to keep his composure. "We each had a small rucksack and were filling them with as much food and clothing as possible. I was just about to finish my packing when we heard a truck approaching, then two, maybe three. Jim looked out through one of the narrow windows in the *pigeonnerie*."

"Krauts. Let's get out of here," he whispered. "And we both grabbed our rucksacks, descended the stairs silently, and ran behind several sheds into the woods. We paused, hoping the Germans would leave again and we could gather the rest of our belongings. But they didn't leave."

Suddenly Tom was silent, his skin a ghastly gray. He turned away from Jack just as tears began to well up in his eyes.

"What is it, Tom? What happened? Did they chase you?" Tom stood with his back to Jack, shaking his head. "Did they arrest them? Eloise and Guillaume?"

Tom stood motionless. Nearly a minute went by. Then the words came out like the croaking of a frog.

"They shot him, Jack. They shot Guillaume – we saw him fall."

"Tommy, maybe –"

"I heard Eloise crying and screaming, Ghee – Ghee. I can still hear her crying. There was this – quiet – this moment – when all I could hear was Eloise – crying. Then another shot was fired and the crying stopped. They killed her, too, Jack, shot her, just like that."

Jack stood helpless as Tom bent over in pain, half crying, trying to catch his breath.

"They must have found some gear we left behind in the *pigeonnerie*."

Jack patted his friend on the back.

"They were the brave ones, Jack – *they* were the heroes, don't you see? I'm no hero. They were." Tom managed to get his emotions under control, just barely, and he sat down, his head bent, his forehead pressed against his knees.

Jack's first impulse was to argue that point, to try to reassure his friend that he too was a hero. But he thought better of it. "What happened then? Did they come after you guys?"

"We took off as fast as we could without looking back. There were these wide fields divided by ditches and we got down in the ditches so we couldn't be seen. The going was slow – pools of mud in places, thick brambles – but we just kept heading south. We had to cross a lot of roads, mostly just narrow tracks, but a couple were big, wide roads with military trucks, horse-drawn wagons, and men – all Krauts – Bosch, Jim called them. So we waited for a break in the traffic, then crossed. We avoided towns, farmhouses – we had no way to know who was cooperating with the Krauts and who was a resister. And neither of us spoke much French so we weren't sure we could explain who we were to farmers and townspeople. So we just kept walking, night and day."

"We hadn't had any food in over twenty-four hours and we were hungry as hell so we finally took a chance and snuck up to this bakery in a little village early the next morning. The guy saw us and came out the door with a long knife in his hand – he thought we were thieves – well, I guess we were, come to think of it. Anyway, Jim tried to say a few words in French. The man said something neither of us could understand and we couldn't tell what he was thinking. But he went back inside and came out with a loaf of bread and a big round of cheese for us – and he smiled. Then he brought us some coffee."

"It was the biggest banquet I'd ever had, Jack, or that's how it seemed. I just couldn't stop eating. Finally, the Frenchman tried to explain to Jim where we should go. He said there was a big British installation. He would have taken us there but the Jerries had stolen his horses and wagon. We thanked him and that evening, after dark, we started down this narrow farm road he showed us. We must've walked most of the night but just before dawn we came over this rise and there it was, the British Field Headquarters."

"A couple of medics took us away to the field hospital and I swear I slept for a week. They kept tellin' me that I would need an operation on my arm but, hell, there were lots of soldiers in

271

much worse shape there so I knew I was low on the list. As it turned out the surgery didn't get done until I was back in England, some big hospital out in the countryside. That's where I got those letters from Mother and Father and Annie – and you, Jack."

It was Jack who was speechless this time, overcome with emotion.

"*They* were the brave ones, Jack – *they* were the heroes, don't you see? Guillaume and Eloise, and all those folks who helped us. I'm no hero. *They* were. "

The two sat in silence for several minutes.

"Can you see now, Jack, why I don't want to tell Mother, Father, Annie. It's *my* nightmare, Jack. I don't want it to be theirs, too. Can't you see that?"

Jack nodded.

Tom looked out across the ice and noticed several flags aloft. "Hey, looks like we got some work to do." And they took off in a lope across the ice.

Sometime later, when they had reeled in three good-sized bass and a pickerel, they stood admiring their catch.

"So Newport, eh?" said Jack.

"Yeh. I gotta do something, you know? The worst thing for me is being home without a job. Too much time for sitting, thinking, drinking. I won't be on the front line, but at least I'll have the satisfaction of knowing I'm helping the cause."

"Yeh, I can understand, Tommy. Listen, as long as we're telling all. I went to see Doc Gibson yesterday. He said I'm fine. And, if I want him to, he'll put in a special request to the Westfield Draft Board and the War Department."

"Request?"

"Yup. He says if I go another six months without a seizure, he can see if they'll let me enlist. He said they probably wouldn't allow me to be in the infantry, you know, but maybe the Corps of Engineers. Building bridges, roads, docks, that kind of thing. I'd learn a lot, Tommy, I'm sure of it. And, like you said, I'd be helping the cause."

"Wow, Jack, that's great. So, maybe May or June?"

"Yeh, give me a chance to finish my freshman year, right? But, Tommy, you can't tell Anne. I figure no need to upset her until it's for sure."

The pair stood there in the late afternoon sun, eyes on their tip-ups, waiting for some action.

~ 45 ~

Thank you so much, Mr. Bernard, for inviting me to join your family on Christmas Eve," said Anne as Jack took her coat, scarf, and hat in the Bernards' kitchen. The ride from Holyoke in the Model-T had been slow going – nearly a foot of new snow had fallen overnight. Candles twinkled in the windows of the farmhouse as the motorcar pulled into the yard.

"Very 'appy to have you, miss, very 'appy," replied Charles. "We just finished our devotions," he added, referring to the one hundred Hail Marys each family member said on this special day. "In Québec when I was a boy, we could earn a treat if we said the Hail Mary a thousand times on Christmas Eve."

"Oh, my goodness. How long did that take?" asked Anne aghast.

"I couldn't say, miss, never really finished it myself." Charles grinned impishly. "My sister Thérèse would do it, take 'er all afternoon. Me and my brothers'd cheat a bit, ya know? A course, then we'd have to own up to it come next confession." Charles' eyes lit up and he wagged his head and laughed at the memory.

"Tom asked me to extend Christmas greetings to all. He is preparing to leave for Newport tomorrow afternoon."

"On Christmas Day? My, that fella must be in a awful 'urry to be back in the Navy."

"I believe he is, sir. Yes, very excited."

Jack excused himself to bring in wood from the barn just as Marie and Claire appeared and greeted Anne. Claire immediately reached for Anne's valise. "I'll take that for you, Anne. You'll be staying in my room. Won't that be swell?"

As soon as Claire was out of earshot Marie added, "She insisted, Anne. She even went so far as to tidy up her room in your honor. That shows how delighted she is that you are staying with her. But I must warn you, my sister is a noisy sleeper."

Anne smiled. "Marie, what is that heavenly aroma?"

"Oh, that's the *tourtière*, Anne," replied Marie, referring to the spiced meat pie baking in the oven. It had been Evelyne Bernard's specialty and now, everyone agreed, Marie had mastered it as well. The Christmas Eve meal was second in importance only to Thanksgiving dinner in the Bernard household. Besides the *tourtière* the menu included roasted turnips, Brussels sprouts, potatoes, and baked apples, followed by generous slices of mincemeat and pumpkin pie.

"Heavens, Marie, let me help," replied Anne, rolling up her sleeves. A few minutes later, as Anne was trimming and cutting the Brussels sprouts, she and Marie had a chance to talk.

"Jack drove me into Westfield the other day to purchase provisions," explained Marie enthusiastically. "He had an appointment with Doctor Gibson so he let me off at Park Square. I went to the grocery market, picked up the pork at the butcher's, and managed to make a few last-minute gift purchases. I so rarely get to shop these days, Anne, it was a real treat."

"Richly deserved, Marie, I am sure," commented Anne as she cautiously wielded a paring knife on the sprouts. "Did you say Jack had a doctor's appointment? Has he been ill?"

"Oh, no, I don't believe so. He visits the doctor every few months, just routine I suppose."

Just then Claire returned. "Come to my room, Anne, please? I've made it just perfect. We're going to be wonderful roommates, don't you think?" With that she tugged on Anne's arm and the two disappeared down the back hallway to Claire's room. Anne was impressed with the general tidiness as well as many decorative touches that Claire had added. All was in order, crisp linens on the bed, one of Claire's mother's own quilts on top, lacy pillows, even a dainty potpourri ball hanging from the bedpost.

"My, Claire, this is lovely. I feel badly, dear, that you have to be inconvenienced."

"Not at all, Anne. Not at all. There's an old divan mattress in the hall closet that I will bring in for myself. I'll be over here, in the corner under the window – quiet as a mouse, I promise."

Anne was gazing at the objects on Claire's dresser, the framed portrait of her mother, a silver comb and hairbrush, and a silk flower arrangement.

"My, what a lovely corsage. Was it a gift?"

Claire shrugged. "Sort of, I suppose."

Claire's vague response served only to stimulate Anne's curiosity. "Sort of a gift? What does that mean?" Claire was standing in front of the dresser, brushing her hair. Anne gazed at her face in the mirror and could see her color rise. "You are being very mysterious, Claire."

"Well, that's the new me, Anne. Claire Bernard, woman of mystery." They both laughed.

Then Anne sat on the bed and patted the coverlet next to her. "Come, please, sit down." Claire sighed, then set the brush on the washstand and sat beside Anne. "Now, tell all. Do you have a secret admirer?"

Again Claire sighed. "Well, I wouldn't say secret."

"But an admirer?"

Claire smiled shyly. "I suppose you could call him that."

"And who might this thoughtful young man be who gave you such a lovely gift?"

"Albert – Albert Albrecht. He's in Mr. Harmon's class."

"Ah. Let me guess, you met at lunchtime – or in the schoolyard?"

Claire nodded. "The first time I met him was when those foolish boys splattered paint on him and Sarah Muller, just because they were German."

"Oh, dear. How could they be so cruel?" Anne paused. "Well, tell me about your – Albert."

Claire shrugged. "He's in grade eight."

"I see," replied Anne. "And does Albert have any particular features of note?" Claire did not respond. "Hair, for example. Does the young man have hair? And eyes? I'll bet he has eyes." Claire nodded but still had nothing to say. "Oh, come now, Claire Bernard. I know we're not sisters, but we are bosom friends, are we not? Could you give me just a few details?"

Finally Claire laughed. "Well, he has brown hair, I guess you might call it chestnut brown. And I think his eyes are green – or maybe hazel. He has very long eyelashes, longer than most boys."

"Ahh. And what else?"

"He's tall."

"He sounds very handsome, Claire. And I imagine he is positively besotted with you?"

"Oh, I wouldn't say that."

"Well, he gave you a lovely silk corsage."

"At the skating party last week. It's just a silly thing."

"Claire," replied Anne softly, a slight lilt in her voice. She waited for Claire to look up. "Do you – are you – enamored of young Mister Albrecht?"

Suddenly Claire's face was florid. She looked away from Anne. Then she turned back to her. "Oh, I don't know, Anne. I'm not certain. Maybe I am, maybe I'm not."

"Your words equivocate, young lady, but your face is crystal clear."

Finally Claire laughed. "He's very handsome, Anne, and very smart. He's writing an essay about Mark Twain and how his boyhood experiences led him to write those books – you know – Tom Sawyer – and Huck Finn."

"Sounds like young Albert has many admirable traits, Claire. Tell me, then, has he any faults?"

Claire nodded, then chuckled. "He is a *terrible* skater, Anne." Her eyes lit up at the thought.

"Oh?" replied Anne.

"Yes, he was forever slipping and falling on the ice. He had to hang onto my hand every minute."

"Oh, Claire," teased Anne, her brow knitted and head shaking, "that must have been so *very* annoying."

They laughed together. Then Anne spotted the carved oak box from Professor Smith on Claire's bedside table. "I never had a chance to take a good look at this, Claire, the day the professor presented it to you. May I?"

Claire nodded. Anne picked up the oak box, opened it, and examined the crystalline wonder within.

"My goodness, it is the most beautiful thing in the world, is it not?" said Anne. Claire nodded. "Look at all those facets, how they glitter and shine. And the colors are just magnificent." When Claire didn't reply, Anne looked up at her and sensed unease. "Claire, what is wrong?"

"I feel as though I don't really deserve such a wonderful gift from the professor. I – I misjudged him, Anne. I was convinced he was working with those dreadful German saberaters."

"Saboteurs? Well, yes – but we were all fooled. Tommy and he practically came to fisticuffs."

"And Fergal. I been so mean to that boy. And look what he did for me."

"Well, Claire, as you are now a young lady, you are sufficiently mature to realize that things are not always as they appear. Remember how people thought those tracks we saw at Smith's Ferry were made by a giant bird? *Noah's raven,* I believe they called it. But paleontologists studied them exhaustively, over many years, and eventually learned their true nature."

Claire nodded.

"The same could be said about people, especially folks we do not know. It is so very easy to misjudge others, to reach conclusions about them based upon superficial or incomplete knowledge. We must always keep an open mind, Claire, about the world, and about others, wouldn't you agree?"

Claire nodded. *"Air – oh – tes – ay pahn – da?"*

"Exactly. They say a little knowledge is a dangerous thing. We must always strive to learn more, to be better informed."

"Okay, boys – easy, boys – easy nah," spoke Émile softly to his team as they stood in the moonlight, stomping the snow underfoot, ready and eager to get to work. The young man had a way with horses, no doubt about that. He could calm a frightened mare, reign in a feisty stallion, even bring a mischievous colt to bay with his subtle ministrations – a look, a soft word, a stroke along the animal's flank or mane. His horse-gentling skills were in part a result of years of practice, particularly with Thor, a Percheron that had been part of the Bousquet family almost as long as Émile. But there was a special bond between this young man and his equine friends, ever since he had contracted German measles at age two and lost his hearing. While Émile's ability to communicate with humans may have been affected, somehow his connection to horses seemed all the stronger for his deafness.

The sleigh ride to midnight Mass at St. Agnes Church, just a mile and a half down Southampton Road, had become a longstanding tradition for the Bernards and Bousquets. For the elders it was a welcome link to the not-too-distant past, for the young it was a thrill, even if the cold winter air was bracing, sometimes literally breath-taking. The heavy, flatbed sleigh of oak and chestnut, crafted by Felix and Charles shortly after they moved to Westfield, was designed to haul maple sap and it served that purpose perfectly for many years during the sugaring season, *le temps des sucres*, in late winter. Nothing fancy about this sleigh, simply a low, heavy bed perched on iron runners, with an elevated driver's seat and a doubletree that accommodated a team of horses. A little hay for cushioning and insulation, a few heavy blankets and comforters, and a half-hour ride on a December night was tolerable, for some even refreshing to the soul.

Charles was seated in the hay just behind the driver's bench, next to Felix and Madeleine Bousquet, Jack and Anne were in the middle, while Claire and Elaine sat together at the rear, their legs dangling over the back end of the sleigh.

"Ah, here's Bea and Fergal," said Charles brightly as the two neighbors appeared trudging through the knee-deep snow. Charles rose, stepped down to the ground, and tipped his hat. "We were 'bout to get worried." He took Beatrice's hand and helped her up. Fergal jumped onto the sleigh and settled himself into the hay next to his aunt. Eamon Dooley had been invited as well, but his absence did not surprise Charles. He had never seen the man at Mass nor, for that matter, at any social occasion.

Charles turned and waved to Émile. "Okay, son, let 'er rip." Émile gave one reassuring word to each member of his team, seized the reins, and climbed into the seat. He smiled at Marie, seated next to him, turned to look over his passengers, then turned again to his team.

"Walk on Thor, Bonnie – walk on now." He gave the reins a shake and, with only the slightest jerk as the runners broke free, they were off.

The moon was in its second quarter, its light shimmering in the chill night air. Thankfully hardly a breath of wind could be felt, but the movement of the sleigh alone allowed the cold to insinuate itself into every opening in one's clothing. Jack pulled a heavy blanket over Anne and himself, nearly covering their faces.

"Well, isn't this cozy, Jackie?" said Anne, snuggling up close to him and nuzzling his ear.

"Are you happy?" he asked.

"Yes, Jackie, very happy. Thank you for inviting me to Christmas with your family. It is lovely." She drew in closer and spoke softly into his ear. "And thank you for getting through to Tommy."

"What do you mean?"

"He told us, last night, about his – ordeal. His ship, the rescue, the train derailment, that couple who took him in – Guillaume and Eloise – everything. He said he told you yesterday while you were ice-fishing, and you convinced him he should tell us."

"Well, yeh, I tried. But I really didn't expect him to do it. I suppose that's good, eh?"

"Of course, Jackie. Now we understand what he is coping with. And who knows, perhaps – perhaps talking it through will be good for him."

Jack nodded. "Maybe."

"I had an idea, Jackie, that I talked to Tommy about afterwards. Perhaps, once the war is over, he can go back to Belgium, you know?" Again Jack looked at her curiously. "Maybe he can help them."

"Help who?"

"Guillaume and Eloise. I mean, it sounds like their farm was in a bad state. Maybe he can help them with repairs and get them a new herd of dairy cows."

Just then the sleigh crossed Southampton Road, the horses hooves clopping loudly against the hard surface. Then they entered the tobacco fields on the east side of the road.

Jack was mystified. "But – so, what did Tommy say about them – Guillaume and Eloise?"

"Just that they would need a lot of help once the fighting was over. I think that would be wonderful for him, a way to return their kindnesses, and good for them, their children, their grandchildren. And I know he'd love to see them again. Don't you see?"

"Yes, Annie, that would be wonderful. How did Tommy react to your idea?"

"Oh, he said he would think about it." Jack nodded. Anne leaned close. "Right now I believe my brother has just one thing in his head, getting back into the Navy, even if it is just a desk job. Oh, and he told me about this friend he made in Newport – Ellie."

"What? Who's Ellie?"

"Eleanor – Eleanor Russell, I believe. Oh, I am surprised that he didn't tell you about her. He met her in Newport in September, during training. She's a yeomanette." Their eyes met. "I know, he was engaged to Carolyn at the time. Some men are just like that, I suppose."

Jack was astonished.

"But not all men, Jackie. Right? You're not that kind of man, are you? You know, the kind who has a girl in every port?"

Jack shook his head and smiled. "Only one port for this sailor, and only one girl." He kissed her lightly on her forehead. Her face was warm despite the cold. "You seem happy, Annie."

"I am, Jackie, I really am. Oh, I'm worried about Tommy, naturally, but, everything else – very, very happy." She looked into Jack's eyes. "Jack," said Anne, an anxious look in her eyes. "Marie said you went to the doctor yesterday. Is everything okay?"

"Oh, that – oh, sure. Just a check-up. I see him every few months, you know, just a precaution is all."

"Are you sure, Jackie? You're not keeping anything from me?"

"I'm in perfectly good health, Annie, I swear."

"And you, Jack, are you content?"

Jack nodded. "These last few months – you know, with school, then Tommy, then Claire and Fergal's adventures – it seemed like one crisis after another, one change after another. Now, at least, I'm feelin' more settled. Enough changes for a while."

"I know what you mean. But Jackie–" She paused, then continued. "Let's face it, things in your life are not likely to be settled soon. You know what I mean, don't you?"

Suddenly Jack was wondering if Tom had divulged his secret to Anne. He shook his head.

She nodded toward Claire. "Well, for one thing, your little sister is now a young lady – even she owns to that. And did you know, she has a new beau?"

"A beau? Claire? Who d'you mean – Fergal?" whispered Jack, shaking his head. "I kind of doubt that, Anne."

"So you *don't* know."

"I don't know what?"

"About Albert."

"Who's Albert?"

"Your little sister's new beau."

"And how do you know this?"

"She told me all about him, just this afternoon. You really are in a cloud, Jackie. His name is Albert Albrecht, he's very handsome, very smart, and – according to Claire – he treats her like a young lady."

"Wow, I guess I *am* in a cloud, Annie."

"And Jackie, there's one more thing of which you might not be aware."

Again Jack felt uneasy. Anne reached out and nudged his chin toward the rear of the sleigh. "Look."

As Jack turned he saw his father. He was laughing and smiling at Beatrice who was seated very close to him and was also laughing and smiling back at Charles.

"See what I mean, Jackie? You never know what's coming around the bend."

"Yep, you're right there, Annie, you just never know."

As the sleigh glided down a narrow farm road, the steeple of St. Agnes came into view, shining in the moonlight. Claire turned and looked back at Fergal, seated next to his aunt, and gestured to him. At first he didn't understand, but finally he slid through the hay, then sidled in next to Claire and Julie. She smiled at him but he wouldn't look up.

"Are you mad at me, Fergal?"

He looked at her briefly, as if considering his reply. Then he shook his head.

"Good, I thought maybe you – maybe I–" She paused. "So, d'you an' Sarah have a nice time at the skating party?"

Fergal nodded, then smiled. "Yeh. She didn't fall once. She's pretty good – on skates."

"So are you, Fergal, you're a very good skater. I never knew."

"Sorry we didn't get to have a skate. But I guess Albert kept you pretty busy?"

Claire shrugged, then chuckled. "That boy is hopeless on skates. I tried to show him how. But he's still hopeless." She paused, blinking as the cold air froze on contact with her eyelashes. "Say, Fergal, I hope – you know – that we can still be friends now."

Fergal nodded. "Sure, why wouldn't we?" He suddenly sounded very serious. "Just one condition."

"What?" asked Claire.

He looked directly into her eyes. "No more investigating." Then he smiled.

Claire blushed, then chuckled. "Okay, Fergal, no more investigating."

"Do you swear?" he asked.

"Yes, Fergal, yes," she replied with a twinkle in her eye and a wry smile, "I swear on a stack of bibles."

THE END

BIBLIOGRAPHY

Blum, Howard. 2014. *Dark Invasion*. Harper Collins, New York, NY USA.

Brault, Gerard J. 1986. *The French-Canadian Heritage in New England*. University Press of New England, Hanover, NH USA.

Hitchcock, Edward. 1858. *Ichnology of New England. A Report on the sandstone of the Connecticut Valley, especially its fossil footmarks, made to the government of the Commonwealth of Massachusetts*. William White Printer, Boston, MA USA.

Jenkins, Philip. 1996. Spy Mad? Investigating Subversion in Pennsylvania, 1917-1918. *Pennsylvania History: A Journal of Mid-Atlantic Studies*, Volume 63, No. 2, pp. 204-231.

Lull, Richard S. 1915. *Triassic Life of the Connecticut Valley*. Bulletin of the State Geological and Natural History Survey of Connecticut, Hartford, CT USA.

Patrick, Jeffrey L. [ed.]. 1993. On Convoy Duty in World War I: The Diary of Hoosier Guy Connor. *Indiana Magazine of History*, Volume 89, No. 4, pp. 335-352.

Richards Standard Atlas of the City of Holyoke, Massachusetts. 1911. Richards Map Company, Springfield, MA USA.

Strachan, Hew. 2005. *The First World War*. Penguin Books, New York, NY USA.

Zack, Charles S. 1919. *Holyoke in the Great War*. Transcript Publishing Company, Holyoke, MA USA.

ILLUSTRATIONS

ACKNOWLEDGMENTS

While the characters and plot of *Noah's Raven* are fictitious, they were inspired by real people and real events. The character Jack Bernard is based on my father, Robert W. McMaster, an earnest, hard-working young man who attended Worcester Polytechnic Institute and did in fact own a Near-a-car motorcycle. Years later my mother, Ellen Stowers McMaster, would regale my sisters and me with accounts of riding that noisy, smoke-spewing machine. It sat in a dusty corner of our basement throughout my childhood. Unfortunately, it was sold while I was away at college – otherwise I might be riding it to this day!

Many details of daily life in Holyoke in 1917 were derived from reading the *Holyoke Daily Transcript* courtesy of the Holyoke History Room at the Holyoke Public Library. The Richards 1911 maps of Holyoke were used to identify locations in and around the city. Many of Holyoke's dinosaur footprints are preserved on a site now owned by the Trustees of Reservations. Descriptions of the tracks are based largely on the writing of Dr. Richard Swann Lull, paleontologist at Yale University during that period. A collection of some 200 McMaster family letters, many dating from 1850 to 1920, provided additional insight into the language of that era.

America was deeply divided over the nation's entry into the war in Europe. Once the Declaration of War was passed by Congress in April, 1917, however, patriotic fervor prevailed, accompanied by strong anti-immigrant sentiments and xenophobia. Incidents like the one described in the schoolyard of Forestdale Grammar School and editorials such as the one described in the Holyoke newspaper were all too common.

The story of German sabotage plots in America during World War I is a well-documented episode in American history. Nearly one hundred bombings have been attributed to German spies in the United States between 1914 and 1917. Cigar bombs were the device of choice. While German sabotage efforts may have ended with the Declaration of War, it seems plausible that a plot like the one in *Noah's Raven* might have been undertaken after America's entry into the war. Many mills and factories in and around Holyoke had military contracts and it is not difficult to imagine those businesses as targets of German saboteurs. The Springfield Arsenal had in fact been placed under high security during that time.

The Holyoke Women's Home is based on the Skinner Coffee House in Holyoke and similar settlement houses established in many American cities in that era. Descriptions of the Wellington home are based on the remarkable Wistariahurst mansion in Holyoke.

The *USS York* never existed. However, the story of that ship's demise is based on a real American naval vessel, the destroyer *USS Jacob Jones*, that was sunk by a German U-boat in November, 1917.

As always I am indebted to my wife, Susan D. Milsom, for her careful editing of draft versions of the book.

ABOUT THE AUTHOR

Robert T. McMaster grew up in Southbridge, Massachusetts, a New England mill town. He holds a B.A. from Clark University and graduate degrees from Boston College, Smith College, and the University of Massachusetts. He taught biology at Holyoke Community College in Massachusetts from 1994 to 2014. His parents' reminiscences of growing up in early 20th century America were the inspiration for his three novels, *Trolley Days* (2012), *The Dyeing Room* (2014), and *Noah's Raven* (2017).

THE TROLLEY DAYS BOOK SERIES
Novels of early 20th century America

Book 1   Book 2   Book 3   Book 4

The nineteen-teens was a tumultuous era in American history. The pace of social change was dizzying: the rising tide of worker unrest, the battle for women's suffrage, the scourge of discrimination against minorities. New technologies – electricity, the telephone, the automobile – were transforming life. Meanwhile the war raging in Europe was drawing America inexorably into its vortex.

Author Robert T. McMaster transports his readers back in time to early 20th century America in the Trolley Days Series of historical novels. Set in a bustling New England industrial city, these books follow the lives of teenagers Jack Bernard and Tom Wellington through good times and bad, hope and despair, love and loss. Readers young and old will be captivated by the world of their grandparents and great-grandparents, an era seemingly remote that nonetheless speaks to us across the generations.

Trolley Days, The Dyeing Room, Noah's Raven, and *Darkest Before Dawn* are currently available in paperback and in several eBook formats.

For additional information visit
www.TrolleyDays.net